SLICE

An addictive crime thriller full of twists

DAVID HODGES

JOFFE BOOKS

Revised edition 2019
Joffe Books, London
www.joffebooks.com

First published in Great Britain 2010

We hate typos too but sometimes they slip through.
Please send any errors you find to
corrections@joffebooks.com
We'll get them fixed ASAP. We're very grateful to eagle-eyed readers who take the time to contact us.

Please join our mailing list for free Kindle crime thriller, detective, mystery books and new releases.
http://www.joffebooks.com/contact/

ISBN: 978-1-78931-181-5

DEDICATION

This book is dedicated to my wife, Elizabeth, for all her love, patience and support over so many wonderful years

BEFORE THE FACT

HE FOUND THE lump on his left testicle while he was taking a bath. There was no pain when he examined himself, no sense of discomfort. It was just a lump, hard and irregular, and it scared the hell out of him. He didn't get out of the bath immediately. What was the point? The lump would still be there, wouldn't it? Furthermore, after the surgical removal of his right testicle three years ago, he had no illusions as to the likely outcome this time. So he lay there in the heat and the suds and reflected on his life and all that he had not achieved, instinctively knowing that what remained of it could now be measured in months at most.

He was a bit of a non-person really. No striking qualities to make people sit up and take notice. Not a man to stand out in a crowd. Just an anybody. The world was full of people like him. Ordinary, feature less, characterless. When the cancer finally spread to his liver and the rest, as he knew it must, there would only be the nurses at the hospice to briefly mourn his passing. Few others knew him that well and those who did would hardly care anyway. He hadn't made an impact on anything, that was the trouble, so there was nothing to distinguish him from millions of others. He was Mister Nobody.

He cried at first, there among the suds, cried for himself and the awful fate that awaited him; cried at the prospect of his life being snatched away before he had managed to do anything with it. Then the bitterness took him, years of it silently eating away at him like another form of cancer, and now surfacing in a cold all-consuming rage.

OK, so he was not entirely the poor, hard-done-by innocent. There were things he had done in his life that he could never be proud of and one terrible transgression in particular had haunted him for more years than he could remember. In fact, he was probably being punished for it right now. But why should he be the only one singled out for retribution? What about the others who had been involved? Those arrogant self-seeking arseholes who were even more to blame for what had happened than he was. Why should they go on living their lives of deceit and lies, enjoying a success, status and wealth they were not entitled to, while he had nothing to look forward to but an early grave? It just wasn't fair.

He had thought about punishing them before, of course – oh yes, it had been one of his fantasies day in, day out for years, but the risk of being caught had always seemed too great. Now though, what did it matter? He was likely to be dead in a matter of months (maybe even weeks) anyway.

He clenched his fists so tightly beneath the water that he almost locked the muscles in one arm. Yes, the time had come for a reckoning; for wrongs to be redressed and the arrogant humbled. And he would be the instrument for that; a sort of Nemesis, who would impose his own brand of justice on those who needed to be punished, one by one, which was good, because then he would become known at last, notorious perhaps, but at least a *somebody*.

As he dried himself and emptied the bath, he studied the face staring at him from the clouded mirror. Strange how a terminal illness could concentrate the mind and make a person see things so much more clearly. It was just like a revelation, as if something that had lain dormant for so long in his subconscious had suddenly blasted to the surface – ignited like a fuse by the shock of his own terrible discovery. And its impact on his senses was almost orgasmic. Every part of him tingled with excitement, an acute sensitivity that cried out to be satisfied, and it was all he could do to hold himself in check. But he knew he had to be strong. It was no good rushing into things before he was ready. Good planning and proper preparation were both essential. He could not afford to be sloppy or he would ruin everything. And the first thing he had to do was to confirm his own diagnosis.

The lady doctor saw him straight away and subjected him to a detailed examination. She was moderately pretty and if the circumstances had been different he would have enjoyed the experience, but not now: there was too much at stake. The usual tests and the trip to the oncology unit at the local hospital followed, and the results came back within seven days. Big C. 'Quite advanced, we think,' the lady doctor said. 'Frankly, it could have spread to other organs. We'll need to investigate more fully.' He nodded, pleased in a rather ironic way that his own diagnosis had actually proved to be right. No, he wouldn't have any more investigations or the humiliating amputation and chemo that he knew from past experience would automatically follow. Being a non-person was bad enough, but there was no way he could face the indignity of total emasculation. Better to be dead! Before that awful day, though, there was a lot of work to be done and he was determined to start right away; not tomorrow or the next day, but that very afternoon.

As he left the surgery the image of an old barn from his childhood flashed through his mind. The fading light and strange smell of the place stimulated the excitement of the hide-and-seek game. Then there were the words, racing down the years, echoing through the spooky gloom: 'Coming, ready or not.' Making his way to the medical centre's hilltop car park, he stopped to look at the small town spread out below him. 'Coming, ready or not,' he murmured and he laughed out loud as he climbed into his car and drove away.

Fulton grunted. 'Well, someone wasn't very appreciative by the look of things,' he observed. 'Any ideas on the murder weapon?'

Abbey straightened up. 'Something like a cut-throat razor might be a good place to start,' she said.

Fulton turned back to Morrison. 'But nothing found?'

The DI shook his head. 'Not yet, but I've arranged search of rec by ops team soon as it's light.'

'So who discovered the body?'

'Local plod – John Derringer – 01.15 hours. Lot of nicked cars get dumped here and he was checking place out.'

Fulton gave a disparaging snort. 'That makes a change,' he retorted. 'I didn't think the plods went out after dark anymore.'

The DI coughed loudly to conceal the beginnings of a chortle. 'Yes, guv. Anyway, he's now back at Saddler Street nick. I said you'd want a word with him before he went off duty.'

Fulton glanced around him. 'Damned right I will – but more important than that, where's my forensic team? They should be here by now.'

Morrison looked even more uncomfortable. 'On their way, guv. SOCO had manpower problems. Traffic loaned us floodlights until they could get here and—'

'Until they could get here?' Fulton blazed, rounding on him. 'What do they think this is – a bloody neighbourhood watch meeting? They should have been on site *before* the pathologist, not after, and this scene needs to be protected or we could lose every scrap of evidence there is. Get on to control and tell them I want SOCO here *now*!'

'You really have got out of bed on the wrong side this morning, haven't you?' Abbey observed as the DI moved away, speaking rapidly into his personal radio.

Fulton grunted. 'And you must have been up all night to have got here so damned quick,' he snapped back. 'You suffering from insomnia or something?'

Abbey gestured to another plainclothes officer that she had finished her preliminary examination. '*Actually* I haven't been to bed yet,' she said. 'I had just attended another job at Duttoncote when the call came through and as your little murder here at Maddington was only a few miles away, I said I'd deal with it. Now, is that OK with you?'

Fulton ignored her sarcasm. 'So why would our killer want to mutilate his victim and stick him on a kiddie's swing?' he growled, following her slim athletic figure as she ducked under the security tape and headed towards the lane, exchanging the floodlights for the pale opalescence of the moon.

'You're the detective, Jack,' she parried, dropping the professional formalities. 'Maybe it was a disgruntled lover, though that seems a bit unlikely as he must be well into his seventies.'

'A woman scorned, you mean?'

Abbey shrugged. 'Or man,' she suggested. 'We live in enlightened times.'

Fulton frowned, his gaze roving round the moonlit recreation ground and fastening briefly on a small copse near the entrance. 'So why dump him here stark naked like some bloody exhibit?'

'I'm a pathologist, not a forensic psychologist. Maybe he was meant to be an exhibit. It could have been a sort of humiliation thing.'

'And was the job done here, do you think?'

Abbey turned to face him. 'Going by the condition of the corpse – blood loss and so forth – my guess is not. But your forensics team should be able to help you a lot more in that respect once they've had a chance to look around in daylight.'

'And the time of death?'

Abbey pursed her lips. 'I'd say he's been dead about four hours.'

Fulton consulted the luminous dial of his wristwatch. 'So, around 23.00 hours last night?'

'Perhaps, yes.'

Abbey had stopped in the lane by her silver Honda four-by-four and now leaned on the rear bumper to pull off the plastic booties she had been wearing at the scene. She opened the boot door wide, deposited them inside, then began shrugging herself out of her protective one-piece nylon suit.

'So, where's your faithful sidekick this morning?'

Fulton produced a filter-tip cigarette from somewhere and lit up, but her question failed to register with him for a second or two.

It was her turn to frown and she paused in the act of kicking herself free of the nylon suit. 'Hello?' she said. 'Anyone in there?'

He started and surfaced from wherever it was he had disappeared to. 'Sorry, Ab, miles away. What did you say?'

'Phil Gilham – your detective chief inspector. Remember him?'

He gave her an old-fashioned look, which was wasted in the moonlit shadows. 'Due back from leave tomorrow … ' He consulted his watch again. 'I mean today. DI Morrison's been doing an unofficial acting job while he was away sunning himself.'

She tossed the nylon suit into the car after the booties and slammed the door shut. 'You look awful – even in the dark,' she observed. 'It's about time you gave up that damned weed, I keep telling you.'

'People keep telling me a lot of things, Ab: stop smoking, lose weight, get more exercise. It's the same long-playing record.'

'You should start listening to it then.'

He took a long pull on his cigarette, his breathing like a leaking steam valve. 'If I did that, I might as well be in a nursing home.'

Her mouth tightened in the darkness. 'You're likely to be in an early grave if you don't – especially as you seem to think you have to be at work every damned hour God made.'

He peered at her strangely. 'What's brought all this on, Ab? Starting to fancy me at last?'

She gave a short humourless laugh. 'You have to be joking. In your condition? If you even thought about sex, you'd probably have an aneurism.'

A responding chuckle in the gloom. 'I'm prepared to take the risk if you are.'

She was grateful for the shadows that concealed the flush spreading over her face. 'Why don't you get Phil to take some of the load off, eh?' she went on, changing the subject. 'You need a holiday.'

He snorted. 'A holiday? Wouldn't know what to do with myself on one of those anymore.'

She hesitated. 'I can understand why,' she said quietly, 'and I *am* very sorry to hear about Janet.'

He muttered something under his breath. 'So you know about that already, do you?' he retorted. 'News certainly travels fast in this bloody force.'

She leaned back against the car, studying him in the moonlight. 'Any idea where she is now?'

He took another pull on his cigarette. 'Nope and I really don't care. She walked out on me and, as far as I'm concerned, she can stay out.'

'Must have had a reason though.'

He threw her a keen glance. 'My business, Ab,' he censured. 'So leave it there, will you?'

'Word is you were knocking her about.'

'*I* was knocking *her* about? More likely the other way round. She's psychotic.'

'Your drink problem all over then, is it?'

He glared at her. 'What is this? Some kind of interrogation?'

She shrugged. 'Just curious, that's all.'

'Well, don't be. Just stick to your pathology bit, OK? Leave the marriage counselling to social services.'

She tossed her head, the black shoulder-length hair gleaming in the moonlight. 'Suit yourself.'

'I always do.'

She jerked open the driver's door of the car and climbed behind the wheel. 'You are such an arsehole.'

Another laugh. 'Thanks for the compliment, Ab.' He slammed the door shut. 'At least they're useful.'

CHAPTER 2

THE INCIDENT ROOM team was setting up its equipment in the mothballed police club at Maddington's Saddler Street police station when Jack Fulton lumbered into the room shortly after dawn. In the confusion of bodies moving desks, screens and electronic kit in all directions he almost collided with a computer monitor as the IT technician carrying it stepped in front of him – only to receive the rough side of Fulton's tongue when the big man tripped over the trailing plug lead.

Detective Chief Inspector Phil Gilham was waiting for him in what had once been the club's TV lounge at the far end of the vast room, immaculate in his pinstripe grey suit and matching silk tie, but grim-faced, his arctic blue eyes as watchful as ever.

''Morning, Jack,' Gilham said. 'Seems we've got a bad one this time.'

Fulton nodded, eyeing his dapper number two with undisguised envy. Why did Gilham always have to look as if he'd stepped out of a Savile Row shop window, while he could never make his cumbersome bulk (enhanced by years of best bitter and Chinese takeaways) look anything other than what his wife had once described as 'shit off a shovel'?

With his curly fair hair cut neatly to just below his ears, tanned athletic appearance and designer clothes, Gilham had the sort of celebrity image that guaranteed a speedy route to the top echelons of the service, especially as he had a first-class honours degree in criminal law and the sort of charismatic articulate persona (never one to resort to abuse, even under pressure) that could not but fail to impress even the most critical interview panel. Just thirty years old, already through his superintendent's board and waiting for a vacancy, he had everything going for him and CID was simply a brief stepping-stone to more sophisticated environments.

Fulton shook his head, thinking that it had taken him twenty-three years to get his crown after five years in uniform and eighteen as a career detective. There was no real bitterness there – after all, it was a sign of the times – just a sense of cynical amusement at the way the service was going.

'Good holiday, Phil?' he queried, dropping heavily into a swivel-chair someone had wheeled into the makeshift office for him and shaking a cigarette out of the battered packet he had pulled from his coat pocket.

Gilham shrugged. 'Good enough,' he replied, studying his boss intently. 'Sorry to hear about Janet.'

Fulton's slab-like face froze into a rock wall. 'So is half the bloody force, it seems,' he rasped, lighting up. 'Well, forget her and concentrate instead on Mr Justice Lyall, will you? Someone seems to have cut his throat and chopped off his balls – and not necessarily in that order – which is a tad more important!'

Gilham nodded. 'So I gather,' he murmured and thrust a plastic cup into Fulton's meat hook of a hand. 'Got some Irish in it,' he said, pouring strong coffee into the cup from a flask he had lifted off the windowsill.

The big man took a sip and grunted his approval. 'I need you to get up to speed on this thing as quickly as possible,' he snapped.

Gilham pursed his lips. 'I *will* do once I've visited the scene and got myself properly orientated. Don't forget, I was still on my way back from the airport two hours ago.'

Fulton nodded. 'Nice to see Jamaica hasn't dented your enthusiasm for the job,' he said drily.

Gilham chuckled. 'How could I resist the compelling invitation you left on my mobile? What was it you said? Something about getting my tanned arse back in gear?'

Fulton smiled faintly, remembering his frame of mind after being called out to the murder scene from a nice warm bed. 'So let's see you do just that,' he said.

He hauled himself to his feet and drained his cup before crushing the thin plastic in one hand and tossing it into the corner of the room. 'And you can start by sorting out this bloody incident room before I blow a gasket.'

The young detective sergeant gave a good-natured grin as Fulton's shed-like bulk stormed from the room, trailing smoke from the cigarette jammed in the corner of his mouth. 'The Grunt didn't look too happy, guv,' he called across to Gilham.

'Shut it, Bryant,' the other threw back with a tight smile, 'or I'll get him to sit on your head!'

Herbert Lyall owned a big Georgian house with extensive wooded grounds, enclosed by a seven-foot-high wall, just outside the town. Fulton was pleased to see the uniformed constable manning what appeared to be electronically operated entrance gates at the front entrance and he was only admitted after the lad had radioed to the house. The early-turn inspector had obviously followed his instructions to the letter by making sure the place was properly secured.

He already knew that Lyall was a widower, but was surprised to discover just how much of a recluse he was.

'Couple of cleaning ladies came in each day apparently,' the hard-bitten detective sergeant told him after ushering him into the hall. 'One of them turned up here this morning after we had arrived – a Mrs Doreen Mason. Otherwise, the old boy seems to have kept pretty much to himself.'

Fulton studied his sergeant's sallow pockmarked face, noting with undisguised distaste the greasy black shoulder-length hair and half-buried earring, which might have suited a twenty-something pop star guitarist, but was hardly appropriate for an ageing detective sergeant with a wife and three children. Dick Prentice was a rather grubby and not very personable man and he had few friends to speak of, but he had been around like forever and was well known for his attention to detail. Little escaped the notice of the lean taciturn detective and that made him a particularly useful member of the investigation team.

'Not married then?' Fulton tested.

Prentice nodded. 'Was. Wife died four or five years ago and his only relative is a recently married daughter, Emily Ford, who lives in Hampshire. We've asked the local Bill to get hold of her for ID purposes.'

'No dogs or anything?'

The DS shook his head. 'Only a couple of cats.'

'So someone could easily have broken in here?'

'No sign of a break-in, guv – except by us when we forced the front door – and it wouldn't have been an easy job anyway. Perimeter wall has razor wire on top and a camera covers the electric gates at the front. Old boy controlled them from his study. Also the place is immaculate. Bed looks as though it hasn't been slept in and the burglar alarm was set.'

'Burglar alarm?'

'Yeah, we triggered it when we went in. Mrs Mason has only just turned the damned thing off.'

'But how did you get through the front gates if they are operated from inside the house?'

The sergeant frowned. 'That's the funny thing, guv. The gates were wide open when we turned up here, even though the burglar alarm was set. Maybe Lyall forgot to close them when he left.'

Fulton ran a hand across the stubble on his chin. 'So it looks as though he left the house of his own accord?'

'Yes, but not in his own car.'

'Why do you say that?'

'According to Mrs Mason, he owned two cars – an old Morgan and a 4.2 Jag. They're both still in the garage. We checked.'

'Tyre tracks?'

For the first time the DS looked uncomfortable. 'Plenty, guv. Three police vehicles turned up here.'

'So if there was anything worth looking at, the plods have destroyed it?'

There was no answer at first, then the other added helpfully: 'Lyall could have used a taxi. We're checking round the local firms now.'

Fulton grunted. 'And if he didn't, then our killer must be someone he knew and trusted enough to let in. Now there's a whole can of worms.'

Fulton got home around ten o'clock that morning, tired, even more irritable than usual and very hungry. But he found the small detached bungalow on the outskirts of Hodham village where he had lived with Janet for close on twenty years far from welcoming without the woman's touch he had come to expect for so long.

The smell of the takeaway he had bolted down the previous evening still lingered, the kitchen sink was overflowing with unwashed crockery and the crammed waste-bin had started disgorging its sticky contents all over the floor. The place was a tip and, to make matters worse, the cafetière needed thoroughly cleaning out before it could be used again, the stale coffee gunge at the bottom smelling like a week old ashtray.

Slumping into an armchair in the lounge, he settled for a whisky and another cigarette instead of breakfast. The day had started badly and with the corpse of a murdered judge now lying in the mortuary, it could only get worse. A juicy story like this was almost certain to have been passed to the press by now – maybe filed by a local stringer or even leaked by one of his own officers for a bit of back-pocket money – and he knew from bitter experience that the newshounds and 'houndesses' would soon be all over him like a rash. Time to reflect for a few moments in the sanctity of 6 Colmore Gardens before the whatnot hit the fan in tsunami-like quantities. Not that he had much to reflect *on* as yet. His visit to Lyall's house had raised more questions than it had answered and his interview with the bobby who had found his body had produced nothing of significance – except managing to raise his blood pressure.

Fulton had never liked sycophants – they turned his stomach – which was probably why he had taken such an instant dislike to PC John Derringer.

Thin and weasel-like, with restless dark eyes and an inbuilt obsequious manner, there was nevertheless a hint of contempt in the set of the slightly crooked mouth, suggesting that, deep down, Derringer saw himself as a cut above the rest. Not a young man (he had to be in his late thirties) Derringer was an experienced mid-service bobby who knew most of the wrinkles associated with the job and, according to the shift inspector Fulton had chatted to on his way to see him, not averse to taking liberties if he thought he could get away with it. But he was also one of those lucky officers who always seemed to be in the right place at the right time and although not promotion material, having failed the selection board for sergeant regularly over the past ten years, he had been commended for good police work on five separate occasions.

His discovery of Lyall's body was another of his successes and though Fulton did not like the man, he was forced to acknowledge in a grudging way that Derringer had produced a good result and therefore had every reason to be pleased about it. But that was about as far as things went. The patrolman hadn't noticed anyone at the scene or any cars parked in the lane next door. In fact, other than being able to confirm his discovery of the body at a quarter past one precisely, he had had nothing really useful to offer the investigation – apart from himself, of course, and he made absolutely certain Fulton was aware of his interest in joining the inquiry team.

'Prick!' Fulton muttered, drawing the smoke from his cigarette deep into his lungs and leaning back in the chair to stare at the discoloured ceiling. Where the hell did the force get arseholes like Derringer?

But he didn't get the chance to ponder that particular point any further, for the telephone by his elbow shrilled.

'Yeah?' he barked into the receiver.

'Hello, Jack.'

He recognized the seductive voice at once. 'Hello, Janet,' he said quietly, straightening in the armchair.

There was a chuckle at the other end of the line. 'Missing me?'

He took a deep breath. 'Where are you, Janet?'

'Wouldn't you like to know?'

He stubbed out his cigarette in the dried-out earth of a dying potted plant. 'I'm too busy to play games, Janet.'

'Ah, busy again are we, Jack? The famous detective superintendent has another case to solve, has he?'

'Come on, Janet. This is stupid. Tell me where you are.'

'You're the detective, Jack. Why don't you find out?'

Before he could say anything else the telephone went dead.

Cursing, he checked the answerphone – only to be rewarded by the automated voice telling him the caller had withheld their number. Slamming the receiver back on its rest, he reached for his whisky glass and drained it. Brilliant! Now, as well as a high-profile murder inquiry, which looked to be heading straight into a cul-de-sac, he had a psychotic wife who was intent on playing some kind of off-the-wall game of hide-and-seek with him.

He lurched to his feet. Well, she could play the game on her own. He had more important things to do – like taking a shower, for instance – and the phone could ring as much as it liked for the next half-hour.

In fact, it rang again within ten minutes, choosing the worst possible moment just after he had settled himself on the toilet seat with the morning newspaper. Sticking to his decision, he ignored it completely, but that was a mistake, for the next moment the mobile chirped in the pocket of his trousers.

'What now?' he rapped, clutching the phone to his ear and waiting for Janet's soft voice to start mocking him again.

'What now indeed?' a familiar male voice commented.

He grinned, recognizing the speaker as Detective Chief Superintendent Andy Stoller, the head of force CID. ''Morning, Andy,' he said. 'I thought you were someone else.'

There was an unimpressed grunt. 'Where are you, Jack?'

Fulton grinned. 'On the bog at the moment,' he replied.

'Oh … nice. Well, when you're *off* it, perhaps you'll come and see me – and make it like yesterday, will you?'

Fulton had never attached much importance to the police hierarchy's obsession with urgency, aware from past experience that in the final analysis it was seldom justified, and as he knew that the journey to headquarters only took about half an hour anyway, he insisted on having a quick shower before going to see his chief. But that turned out to be a mistake, for when he eventually left the house twenty-five minutes later and went to his car parked in the driveway, he found he was facing a substantial handicap: the two nearside tyres of the Volvo were completely flat.

For a moment he just stood there, studying the buckled rubber with a mixture of anger and disbelief. There was no way he could have incurred a double puncture accidentally – that was stretching coincidence much too far – which meant that some little toe-rag must have actually sneaked up his driveway and slashed the tyres while he was in the shower. The bloody cheek of it!

With fists tightly clenched and head thrust forward belligerently, he headed for the gateway in a futile attempt to spot any likely offender lurking in the vicinity, but the street was empty and he was on the point of turning back to re-examine the damage, when for some reason his attention was drawn to a red MG sports car pulling out of a lay-by a couple of hundred yards to his right. The car, which had its hood down, slowed as it drew level with the driveway, suggesting it was about to stop, but when he stepped to the edge of the pavement, it suddenly revved up and accelerated away with squealing tyres. He glimpsed a thin-faced man in the driving seat and a blonde-haired woman sitting beside him, who waved extravagantly in his direction as they drove off, then the car was gone, careering round a bend in the road, its horn blasting as it went.

Realization dawned immediately and his face was grim as he jerked his police notebook from his pocket. 'Janet,' he grated, quickly jotting down the registration number of the car on the back cover. 'Well, I'll soon find you now, my lovely, you can bet on it!'

Then he slipped the notebook back into his pocket and telephoned for the emergency breakdown.

Janet Fulton was on a high as the red MG left the outskirts of the town behind and headed into the wooded countryside beyond. She had enjoyed slashing the tyres on her husband's car almost as much as seeing the look on his face when he had lumbered out of the driveway. Maybe now Jack would give her the attention she deserved after years of having to play second fiddle to his wonderful job. She knew her affair wouldn't last long; they rarely did. She also knew Jack would take her back afterwards; he was daft that way. But until it all came to an end, she was determined to make the most of her new-found freedom and the opportunity it gave her to remind *Mr Superintendent Fulton* on which side his bread was buttered.

She glanced slyly at the thin unshaven man beside her, appraising the dark curly hair and aesthetic features and inwardly congratulating herself on her catch.

She had first met Doyle at art school. He was half her age, good-looking, athletic and naked. Modelling for art classes, he explained later, was just a beer-money job; his main interest in life was contemporary writing. As far as she was aware, he was not actually published, but he was always talking about his ideas for a real blockbuster and his rented cottage was coming down with books on the craft of writing and piles of unfinished manuscripts. Deep down, she knew he was a fraud, with the modelling jobs just a means of supplementing his income from social security handouts and the money he managed to milk from frustrated middle-aged women like herself to keep his rented cottage going and his car on the road. But she didn't care, for he was also suave, gentle and considerate – all the things Jack had never been – and he made her feel alive again. Even more important, he liked to have sex with older women and she had discovered that particular fact just two hours into their first clandestine date.

She had never had any illusions about herself. Forty plus, plump with thinning blonde hair and a nice long scar down her abdomen where they had wrenched her stillborn baby from her two years ago, she was hardly the most desirable conquest. Yet Doyle had treated her like some ravishing twenty-year-old and she was determined to keep that part of the fantasy going for as long as possible.

'Satisfied now?' he said, breaking in on her reverie.

She grinned. 'Oh, very. I reckon I ought to have been a criminal myself, you know.'

He made a face. 'You can say that again.'

'Ringing him to make sure he was at home before we went over was a brilliant ploy.'

He frowned. 'I just hope your hubby didn't clock our number when you thumped the horn as we drove away. Stupid that was.'

She shrugged. 'What if he did clock it? He can't prove I was the one who slashed his tyres.'

'No, but he could come looking for us and he's a big guy.'

'He's also a senior policeman and he wouldn't wreck his beloved career in that way.' She stared at him keenly now, a flicker of disappointment in her blue eyes. 'Not scared, are you?'

He ignored the question. 'I just don't know why you keep trying to antagonize him,' he said. 'You should be concentrating on us, not playing silly games with your ex.'

She lit a cigarette. 'Oh I am, believe me, I am – and, on that subject, my stomach feels as though my throat's been cut. We need to find somewhere to eat.'

He made a face. 'Ah, yes. Well, the trouble is I'm – er – a bit short at the moment and—'

She produced a credit card from her handbag as he was speaking. 'No problem, we'll use my plastic.'

He brightened. 'That's very generous of you. There's a nice pub half a mile from my cottage.' He cast her a sidelong glance. 'Look, I know you keep paying for things and I will make it up to you when I can, you know that, don't you?'

She ran a hand down his thigh and grinned. 'Oh you'll make it up to me all right, Doyle,' she promised, 'you'll make it up to me big time.'

CHAPTER 3

'YOU'RE LATE!' Detective Chief Superintendent Stoller commented from behind his newspaper as Fulton was ushered into his office on the middle floor of police headquarters.

'Tell me about it,' the big man retorted, a sour expression on his face as he dropped into a chair in front of the worn oak desk without offering any explanation.

Stoller threw him a quick glance before returning to his newspaper. 'I hope you washed your hands properly,' he said.

Fulton's mouth registered a faint smile. He and Stoller went back a long way. In fact, they had gone through initial recruit training together twenty-seven years before and the balding ex-Royal Navy intelligence officer had spent even longer on CID than Fulton himself. Promoted to chief super from the National Crime Squad, Stoller had a shrewd analytical brain and was rated highly by the top team, having already been earmarked for assistant chief constable rank when a suitable vacancy was advertised.

It was no secret that Fulton saw himself slipping into Stoller's shoes the day his boss moved on, but jobs didn't come with any guarantees in the police service and he knew there were those at chief officer level who would prefer to see him buried rather than promoted.

'Not a very good photograph fortunately,' Stoller said, folding the newspaper and tossing it across the desk. 'But there's as much info in the article as the detailed incident report your DI sent up here this morning.'

Fulton's face darkened when he opened the newspaper at arm's length. The headline screamed at him: JUDGE'S LAST SITTING. Below was a fuzzy photograph of Lyall's naked corpse slumped forward over the rope that tied him to the swing. 'How the hell...?' he began, his voice trailing off as he read on.

'Easy enough with a telephoto lens,' Stoller replied, 'but I have to say it's a rather unsavoury pic, even though it's too dark to actually identify our man.'

Fulton stopped reading for a second to throw him a baleful glance. 'And what about this bloody headline?' he blazed, stabbing the newspaper with a large finger. 'It's diabolical.'

Stoller nodded. 'Way out of line in my opinion, especially as there hasn't yet been any formal identification or opening inquest by the coroner. As for the piece itself, while it doesn't actually come up with a name, it doesn't leave much to the imagination. Clear breach of the rules, I'd say. The chief constable is not at all amused and the force press officer is on her way to see the editor even as we speak.'

'But how did they manage to get to the scene so soon after Lyall was found? Body went to the morgue just before I left and there was no sign of any press while I was there.'

Stoller shrugged. 'Probably a stringer living nearby – maybe did the job before you even arrived.'

'Or one of our own after a quick buck.'

Stoller winced. 'That's a bit harsh, even for you, Jack.'

Fulton didn't acknowledge the criticism, but finished speed-reading the article before tossing the newspaper back across the desk in disgust. 'The whole lot's in there,' he said. 'Every bloody detail.' He made an angry gesture with one hand. 'Now we've got sod all to keep back for interview if and when we pull anyone in. We're totally stuffed.'

'Maybe the post-mortem will turn up something?'

'Yeah, maybe, but I wouldn't want to hold my breath on that.'

'When is it scheduled for?'

'Probably tomorrow, once we've sorted out formal ID.'

'And you'll be there, I presume?'

Fulton threw him an old-fashioned look. 'No, I'll be playing golf, what do *you* think?'

Stoller gave a faint smile. He was well used to his old friend's sarcasm and his almost legendary irreverence towards rank. 'So what about the inquiry itself? Anything you need?'

Fulton shook his head, still preoccupied with his thoughts. 'Incident room should be up and running by the time I get back and arrangements have already been made for uniform to carry out a fingertip search of the rec and start local house-to-house enquiries this morning. As for publicity, it seems we've already got that in abundance.'

'And the opening inquest?'

'Coroner's officer already has that in hand. Few days yet, I gather.'

'And what about a press conference?'

'You ask a lot of bloody questions.'

Another smile. 'Just trying to be helpful, Jack. HQ press office can field things for a while, but the media will be on your back with a vengeance from now on.'

Fulton grimaced. 'Don't I know it! I'll get the press office to put out a prepared statement. That will have to hold them until we've got something relevant to say.'

'And you'll keep me informed of any developments?'

Fulton's eyes narrowed. 'As senior investigating officer,' he said with emphasis, 'I'll tell you everything I think you need to know, OK?'

Stoller nodded again, digesting the rebuke. 'SIO or not, Jack, you've got a scorpion by the tail on this one,' he said. 'Lyall was very well connected. Personal friend of the Lord Lieutenant and the Lord Chief Justice. The inquiry will require sensitive handling.'

'So?'

Stoller hesitated, then fixed him with a hard stare. 'In the strictest confidence, Jack, I have to tell you that our assistant chief constable operations has questioned whether you're the right man for the job. He feels you lack the necessary tact and diplomacy.'

'Bollocks!'

'Which is exactly the sort of response he's talking about.'

'And what do *you* think?'

'Depends on whether you've kicked the booze and can keep a lid on your domestic problems – which, to be brutal, is unlikely now that Janet seems to have done a bunk.'

'My private life is *my* business.'

There was a flicker of anger in Stoller's grey eyes now.

'Not when it interferes with your job performance it isn't.'

Fulton leaned forward in his chair, his expression a mixture of hurt and anger. 'My performance, as you put it, has never been in doubt and my detection record is the best in the force, even though I do say so myself.'

Stoller sat back in his chair. 'You wouldn't have survived if it weren't,' he said bluntly. 'But it isn't just about detections any more, Jack. Things have moved on and you've got to learn to move with them. Bulldozing your way through the rules and kicking arse to get a result is no longer acceptable.'

'So who has ACC operations "I have a degree" Skellet got in mind as my replacement?'

'No one is going to replace you, Jack. He's just expressed the view that maybe this type of inquiry should be handled by someone a little less – er – direct.'

Fulton wasn't about to give up. 'Like who, for instance?'

Stoller fidgeted uncomfortably and fiddled with a paper-clip tray on his desk. 'Phil Gilham's name has been mentioned—'

Fulton virtually erupted from his chair. 'Phil Gilham!'

'Well, he *is* a superintendent in waiting.'

'Replaced by my own DCI?' Fulton blazed, his hands clenching and unclenching in indignant fury. 'Why doesn't

Skellet just chop *my* balls off and stick me on a swing like Lyall? At least then everyone gets a laugh at my expense!'

'I've just told you, no one is going to replace you. I'm simply giving you a bit of friendly advice, that's all. Don't make any unnecessary waves, OK?'

On his way to the door, Fulton half-turned. 'And watch my back, eh?'

Another fleeting smile from Stoller. 'That goes with the territory, doesn't it, Jack?'

'Well, has he gone?' Assistant Chief Constable Norman Skellet closed Stoller's door behind him and stood there for a moment, the sharp penetrating eyes giving an unexpected vitality to the pale cadaverous features as they fastened on Stoller like those of a cobra.

Stoller nodded and Skellet crossed to the window to settle his virtually non-existent rump on the edge of the windowsill. 'Did you tell him of my misgivings?'

'I did.'

'How did he take it?'

'Predictably.'

'Aha.' Skellet opened a tin of throat lozenges and slipped one into his mouth. 'And you still think he's the man for the job?'

'He's the only one we have at present. All our other area detective superintendents are either on leave or tied up on existing enquiries.'

'Hobson's choice then?'

Stoller winced. 'I didn't mean it like that – Look, sir, I know he doesn't come across as such, but he's one of the most experienced detective superintendents in the force, with a first-class track record.'

'Just an image problem then, is it?'

Stoller shook his head. 'I didn't say that. At times he can be a bit of a bull in a china shop, but he has a very sharp mind and the sort of tenacity that this case requires.'

'But minus any semblance of the tact and diplomacy that is so essential here?'

'He *is* a John Blunt, I agree, but solving Lyall's murder is a tad more important than having the right social skills.'

'Even if our sharp tenacious SIO looks like a slob, drinks too much and knocks his wife about?'

'That's a bit unkind, sir. I've known him for years and underneath that rough exterior he's quite a sensitive, caring man. I certainly don't see him as a wife beater and I know his other half has always been a bit of a problem. As for the drink' – he shrugged – 'he's from an era when that was all part of the CID culture.'

'Not any more, it isn't.'

'OK, so the world has moved on and he hasn't, but that doesn't mean he can't do the job anymore and he has a lot of street cred among his troops. They think the world of him. He may shout and swear at everyone in sight, but he's fiercely protective of his own and he has stood up for members of his team on more than one occasion in the past.'

Skellet frowned. 'I've never understood that stupid clan thing. The job comes first, not the individuals in it.'

Stoller sat back in his chair, twiddling a pen between his fingers. 'Loyalty is important, sir,' he murmured, 'and it works both ways.'

Skellet's eyes narrowed as the reproof slammed home, but he chose not to respond to it and instead snapped to his feet and turned towards the door. 'On your head be it then, Andrew,' he threw back. 'But remember, this is a very sensitive case and the chief needs a result like yesterday. You'd better make sure your *star* superintendent delivers the goods!'

Fulton stopped by a burger bar to refuel on his way back to Saddler Street police station. The hollow pain in his stomach only subsided after he had demolished a double cheeseburger and chips.

He was both angry and upset by Andy Stoller's pep talk and although he would not have admitted it to anyone else, he felt strangely vulnerable now that he knew the knives were out for him. He had never fitted in with the new modernizing regime: the legion of bright young things who were flooding into the police service from university with their liberalist theories and obsession with rehabilitation, so-called restorative justice and political correctness. Like Stoller, he was an old-school copper, brought up with the rough 'nick your own granny' hard-liners who had once formed the backbone of the police service but, unlike Stoller, he had been unable to adapt to the rapidly changing environment around him and that had immediately typecast him in the eyes of his peers as a dinosaur.

Maybe they were right too, he thought bitterly, feeding off his own sour mood and corrosive negativity, maybe he *was* a dinosaur – the sort of washed-up has-been who should have been got rid of years ago. Could be he was past his sell-by date in other aspects of his life too. That would explain why Janet had run out on him; no doubt seeing the man she had married as an overweight, sexually inept slob, joined at the hip to the job and the whisky bottle in equal measures and destined for the scrapheap. In fact, looking at his life, he didn't seem to have made much of it overall, apart from putting villains behind bars.

He had certainly been a great disappointment to his late parents and his older brother, Charlie. After a strict Christian upbringing, demanding total commitment to the local church and membership of both the choir and what he had privately referred to as its 'coven of bell-ringers', it had naturally been assumed by his father – the rural dean – that he would one day enter the ministry too, just like his old man and good old Charlie. Instead, he had thrown in his lot with the police force and as a result, after a monumental row in the vicarage, had suffered the pain of being 'excommunicated' by the family and shunned by his friends.

He had tried desperately in those early years to come to terms with the hurt that had followed his rejection, but stubborn pride had prevented him from making the first moves to try to repair the damage and then, two years later, he was denied the opportunity when both his parents were killed in a boating accident while on holiday in Crete. As for Charlie, he graduated to archdeacon status and in the proper Christian tradition of forgiveness and reconciliation, wrote his errant brother off for good.

He had never forgiven himself for failing to make his peace with his mother and father while he had had the chance and in an attempt to bury his feelings of guilt, had thrown himself into his career completely, excluding everything else and working horrendous hours that, perhaps inevitably, had culminated in an internal haemorrhage. He had met Janet then – a staff nurse, working in the local hospital's casualty unit – and embarked on a torrid love affair with her. But he sorely underestimated the pretty girl from Basingstoke, and when she said she was pregnant he believed her and did the so-called decent thing of his generation. By the time he found out that she had deceived him, it was too late to do anything, but the ironic thing was that when, just two years ago, she finally decided to give up her nursing career to start a family and *genuinely* became pregnant she lost the baby.

Ever since then his domestic life had become a living hell, with Janet blaming him and his preoccupation with his job for the tragedy, and turning to alcohol and other men for release. And now, despite all that he had on his plate, it looked like the very force he had sacrificed everything for was seeking to reward his dedication by plunging a knife in his back – with the one man he had always thought he could trust quietly taking on the role of Brutus. What a bloody awful mess!

The bitterness and frustration welled up inside him as he sat at the little table and unconsciously he tightened his grip on the plastic cup he was holding, crushing it in seconds and spilling hot coffee over his hand and most of the table. As he tried to clean up the mess with a wad of paper napkins, cursing under his breath at the smarting pain in his hand, his mobile rang.

'Hello, Jack.'

He wiped his stinging hand with the last dry napkin as he held the mobile between his ear and one hunched shoulder. 'What do you want now, Janet?'

A throaty chuckle. 'Murder inquiry going well, is it? It's in all the newspapers.'

He dropped the napkin in the middle of the coffee lake with the rest and eased back in his chair as an elderly woman in uniform bent over the table to wipe up the spillage with a dishcloth, shaking her head and muttering her disapproval.

'Why are you doing this, Janet?'

'Doing what, Jack? Don't you want to talk to me?'

'Of course I do, so where can we meet? We need to sort out this silly business.'

'All in good time, Jack, all in good time. The game's just beginning.'

The telephone went dead again.

'You are a messy pup!' the elderly woman snapped as she bustled away.

He ignored her, instead quickly interrogating his telephone. Janet's call came up as 'Unknown application'.

'Bugger it!' he snarled, slamming the phone on the table and attracting curious glances from the other diners.

'Bad news, Mr Fulton?'

He looked up quickly and scowled at the thin bearded man in the faded blue anorak who was standing there. 'What do you want, McGuigan?' he said. 'Come to gloat, have you?'

The other laughed and pulled out a chair. 'That's not very nice, Mr Fulton. Mind if I join you?'

'Yes, I do, so sod off!'

McGuigan sat down anyway. 'How's the old murder inquiry going?'

'Why don't you read the bloody newspapers? They must all have the story by now.'

'No point really, since I wrote it.'

Fulton glared at him. 'Didn't you just, and a heap of the smelly stuff is soon going to drop on you from a great height.'

McGuigan's grin faded. 'I simply report the news as it happens, Mr Fulton.'

'Yeah, and foul up a police murder inquiry in the process.'

'The public have a right to be told about violent crime.'

Fulton leaned forward, studying him with absolute contempt. 'Listen, McGuigan, I've known you too long to expect anything decent from you, but what kind of scumbag actually photographs a victim at a murder scene, then sells the pic to a national newspaper? You have to be sick.'

The journalist flinched. 'Selling stories is what I do as a freelance news agency, Mr Fulton,' he snapped. 'But it so happens that I didn't take the picture this time. It was sent to me.'

'Sent to you? How could that be? Damned body was only found a few hours ago.'

McGuigan shrugged. 'I don't know about that, but the photo was pushed through my letterbox last night in a sealed envelope, accompanied by a sheet of A4, giving full details of the incident and its location. Then someone rang my doorbell repeatedly to make sure I got out of bed and found it.'

'I don't believe you – you're spinning me a line.'

'And what would be the point in my doing that? According to you, I'm in the mire for filing the story anyway, so why would I bother to make all this up?'

'To protect a source maybe?'

McGuigan shook his head firmly. 'You're way off beam this time.'

'And I bet you didn't get a look at your nocturnal postman?'

'Unfortunately, no. By the time I got to the front door he or she had gone.'

'Convenient. Didn't you think of looking out of the window before going to the front door?'

'Why would I?'

'So you just went downstairs to answer the door in the middle of the night, not knowing who was on your doorstep? You were either very brave or plain stupid.'

'Maybe I was stupid then, but that's what I did, and when I opened the door there was no one there, just the envelope on the mat and an empty street – well, almost empty.'

'What do you mean, almost?'

McGuigan shrugged again. 'There was a police patrol car cruising past. I waved to him actually and he waved back.' He grunted. 'Maybe you should have a word with the copper who was covering my area. You know where I live.'

'I'll do just that; you can count on it. I might even get your letterbox printed to see what else we can find.'

'Be my guest, though I think that that would be a bit of a long shot. There must be any number of different fingerprints on it from a whole variety of callers.'

Fulton grunted. 'So, what time did your postman call?'

'About twelve-forty-five.'

For a moment the detective's brain froze as the full implication of what McGuigan had just said dawned on him. 'Twelve-forty-five? You sure about that?'

'Give or take five minutes, yes. I'd only just gone to bed as a matter of fact. Watched some stupid TV documentary about the Iraq war. Why, is it important?'

Fulton's heart was racing. Damned right it was. If McGuigan had received the envelope then, it meant that Lyall's body must have been left tied to the swing at least half an hour before it was found by police. He was conscious of McGuigan staring at him intently and tried to conceal his excitement, but it was too late.

'You think that envelope was deposited by the murderer, don't you?' the pressman breathed.

Fulton ignored the question. 'I need everything you were sent,' he snapped. 'And I mean everything.'

McGuigan slipped a hand inside his anorak and produced an A4-size envelope, folded in two, which he slid across the table towards him. 'Got it all here for you. I was going to give it to you anyway.'

Fulton stared at the envelope in disbelief. 'You've been carrying this around with you ever since? How the hell could you have known you'd run into me?'

McGuigan grinned. 'I found out you were the SIO, so I sat on your tail when you left your bungalow for police HQ this morning. Not difficult to spot your battered Volvo on the double yellow lines outside this place.'

Fulton lumbered to his feet. 'You cheeky bastard.'

'True, but cheeky is my middle name. So, do we have an arrangement?'

'Arrangement? You've got to be joking.'

McGuigan's hand shot out to retrieve the envelope, but Fulton's meat hook was quicker and snatched it away. 'The only arrangement you should be thinking about,' he grated, 'is under the plea-bargaining process when they throw the book at you for impeding a police murder inquiry.'

The journalist sat back in his chair and studied him as he swung for the door. 'You always have been an awkward sod to deal with,' he said.

'Yeah, well awkward is *my* middle name,' Fulton threw back over his shoulder. 'And I'd rather go back to issuing parking tickets than doing a deal with you.'

McGuigan chuckled. 'Well, at least that's better than receiving them,' he sniped, 'I saw a nice young lady in uniform sticking one on your windscreen when I came in here just now!'

CHAPTER 4

SADDLER STREET POLICE station was an ugly Victorian building, dating back to the 1880s, which had once accommodated the business of 'H Cotton, Upholsterers and Saddlers', going by the faded lettering still visible on the brickwork above the arched entrance. The place was due for closure when the new police station opened for business on the outskirts of town, and for those who for far too long had had to put up with its shabby, draughty rooms, flickering lamps and dirty leaded-light windows – which admitted only a greyish light but could not be replaced because of a misguided preservation order – closure could not come soon enough.

However, while the building would ordinarily have passed into total obscurity without a soul shedding a tear when that auspicious day actually arrived, a lot had changed in the last twenty-four hours. Due to the gruesome murder of Herbert Lyall, Saddler Street nick had suddenly achieved a level of notoriety that assured it a small but permanent place in the annals of crime history and when Fulton finally returned to the station, he was faced with an aggressive, clamouring throng of reporters and camera units camped outside its doors like a besieging army.

The office of the LIO (or Local Intelligence Officer), which was buried in the basement and sandwiched between the found-property store and archives, was Fulton's first port of call and he burst into the office with characteristic aplomb, all but removing the door from its hinges.

PC George Oates looked up quickly from his computer and swung his swivel-chair round to meet his visitor, almost dislodging a pile of papers on the corner of his desk as he did so. 'Guv,' he acknowledged, his shrewd brown eyes studying Fulton as the big man dropped into a chair in the corner, mopping the perspiration from his forehead.

Oates had been LIO for close on ten years and had become part of the antiquated furniture on the police area, earning a reputation for himself as one of the best intelligence gatherers in the force. Not that there was much about him to suggest greatness. Short and bald, with protruding ears and a permanent lugubrious expression that had earned him the nickname *Gollum* after the notorious creature in Tolkien's *Lord of the Rings*, his talents were pretty well hidden, but they were there all the same. His razor-sharp brain and photographic memory, coupled with a local knowledge that was second to none, had put many a villain away. Consequently, he was an indispensable resource to any investigating officer and Jack Fulton did not believe in wasting resources.

'Long time, no speak, George,' he said, getting his breath back at last.

Oates nodded slowly. 'Heard you were SIO on this one, guv,' he said. 'Bit off your usual manor though, aren't you? You usually cover the northern end of the force.'

Fulton grunted. 'Yeah,' he agreed. 'But they ran out of SIOs down here, so they had to scrape the barrel.'

Oates tried to affect a smile, an unusual facial contortion for him. 'Hardly scraping the barrel where you're concerned, guv,' he replied, making no effort to conceal his respect for him. 'How's Janet?'

Fulton threw him an old-fashioned look. 'You must be the only one who hasn't heard. She's run out on me.'

'I *had* heard; I was just asking you how she was.'

Fulton shrugged. 'Who knows – or cares?' he lied and changed the subject quickly. 'How long is it since we last worked together, George?'

'The Meldrew killing – you were a DI then.'

'As long ago as that. Must be all of—'

'Twelve years,' Oates finished for him. 'I was acting DS.'

'Yeah, I remember. Never made it to skipper, then?'

Oates sighed. 'Nope and not interested now anyway. This job'll suit me fine until I pack it in in a couple of years' time.'

'As soon as that, is it? Doesn't seem possible. Still fooling around with an oval ball, are you?'

'Hardly. My days playing rugby ended a long time ago.' Oates's gaze dropped to Fulton's ample stomach. 'As I suspect yours have. Too old and too many injuries along the way. Just a spot of fishing now.'

Fulton chuckled, his eyes more alive than they had been for a long time. 'Happy days though, George, eh?'

Oates didn't answer, but glanced at his watch. 'Look, is this just a social visit, guv, only…?'

Fulton scratched his nose. 'I need a favour, George.'

'Ah, thought you might. What sort of favour?'

'I need a PNC check on a car reg.'

Oates frowned. 'Why don't you ask one of your own team to do it?'

'Not strictly their bag, George. It's sort of unofficial. And it might raise a few questions if I did the job myself as head of a high-profile murder inquiry. This way, it will be just another vehicle-check from your office.'

Oates shook his head firmly and held up one hand to emphasize the point. 'No go, guv. You should know that as well as anyone.'

'It's just a bloody car number, man.'

Oates leaned forward in his chair. 'Look, guv, my own boss has specifically told me not to get tied up with your inquiry, but to remember that I'm an area – not a headquarters – resource. She said I am to help where I can—'

'Well, there you are then.'

'But only if absolutely essential. What you're asking me to do is well out of order anyway. It's a breach of force regulations, using the police national computer for private purposes, *and* probably Data Protection as well. It could cost me my job. No thanks.'

'You owe me, George,' Fulton said bluntly.

Oates's eyes narrowed. 'I'd hoped you wouldn't rake that up again. It was a long time ago.'

'Yeah, but I still stuck my neck out for you, didn't I? We lost a target criminal because you fell asleep on that surveillance job. If my boss had had her way, you would have been off the department there and then.'

Oates stared at the floor for a moment. 'Is what you're asking me to do connected with Janet?' he said at last.

'Best you don't know.'

Oates groaned, 'Oh, *Guv'nor*!'

Fulton produced a piece of paper and scribbled down the number of the sports car he had noted outside his home and handed it to him. 'George, it's nothing illegal, OK? I just want you to find out an RO for me. Simple as that.'

Oates looked at the number and shook his head wearily. 'So what reason do I give for the check? Tell them I'm just returning a favour?'

Fulton grinned at the jibe, but before he could answer, an attractive young woman in superintendent's uniform poked her head round the door. 'George ...' she began, then froze when she saw Fulton sitting in the corner behind the door. 'Hello, Jack,' she said. 'What's all this? Not leaning on my LIO, I hope?'

Fulton hoisted himself up out of the chair. 'Afternoon, Dee. Just a social visit. George and I go back a long way.'

Superintendent Dee Honeywell looked unconvinced, her blue eyes studying his face suspiciously. 'Got a minute, Jack?'

He nodded, considering the slim blonde appreciatively. One of the new breed of senior officers, this one, almost straight out of university and already starred for future chief officer rank. Maybe he had been born much too early. 'Anything for a lovely lady like you, Dee, you know that.'

Out in the corridor she nodded towards the stairs and cornered him in the stairwell. 'Do you have to make such overtly sexist innuendoes in front of my staff?' she snapped.

His jaw dropped. 'Sexist … what? Dee, it was a joke, OK? A joke!'

'Maybe,' she agreed, her expression hard and unsmiling, 'but those sorts of jokes have no place in today's modern police service and you should know better. Now, I've given our LIO strict instructions that he is not to get bogged down with incident room enquiries – you have your own team to do that. He can provide local knowledge as and when you need it, but that's all. Do we understand each other?'

Fulton grunted. 'Understanding a woman is something I've never been very good at,' he retorted.

She frowned, but chose to ignore the remark. 'So, how's the inquiry going?'

He shrugged. 'It isn't at the moment. But we have one lead your lads might be able to help us with.'

She raised her eyebrows. '*Lads*? That's not very equal ops, is it? You mean personnel, don't you? There are women on this police area as well, you know.'

Fulton caught his breath quickly. 'I'm investigating a bloody murder, Dee, all right?' he grated. 'I haven't got time to worry about all this political correctness crap.'

She compressed her lips into a tight line. 'The chief constable might not look at it that way.'

Fulton's face darkened. 'Then he can come down here and do the job himself,' he snapped. 'And while he's about it, maybe he can explain why his marvellous SOCO team was so short-staffed that they turned up late and we had to borrow floodlights from traffic just to see the bloody corpse!'

'Still no reason to forget the niceties.'

'Niceties?' he erupted. 'What bloody planet are you on, Dee? A man is dead. Have you got that? D-e-a-d! Save your politically correct niceties for the officers' mess or one of your focus groups. I have to live in the real world.'

Her eyes glittered. 'You've made your point, Jack. I think you've said quite enough.'

He emitted a short, unamused laugh. 'Oh, I haven't said anywhere near as much as I'd like, Dee, but I think I'll save it all for another day – or maybe for your next grammar school class.'

Her face was ashen now. 'Anything else we can help you with, *Detective Superintendent*?' she breathed.

He nodded, unabashed. 'Yeah, there is as a matter of fact. One of your area cars was seen in Merchant Street at around 00.45 hours. I need to find out who it was and whether your *personnel* saw anyone there on foot. OK? That's if you can tear yourself away from your GCSE studies!'

'We have a problem, Jack,' DCI Gilham said, closing the door carefully behind him.

Fulton looked up from the pile of newspapers on the desk in his temporary office. He looked haggard. His hair was dishevelled, his coat lay over the back of his chair and one of his red braces was hanging over his arm. 'What, apart from the press?' he snapped, pushing himself away from his desk. 'I gather they're all over the crime scene as well as camped outside this place. I've had to get more troops down to the rec.'

'Best way of dealing with them is a press conference, Jack – give 'em something to keep the hyenas happy. I'll set one up tomorrow morning, if you like. Might cool things down a bit.'

Fulton shook his head, a stubborn set to his jaw. 'Not a chance – not yet, anyway. HQ press office have given them a prepared statement and they'll have to be satisfied with that for now.'

He peered curiously at the manila folder the DCI was carrying. 'So what's this other problem then?'

Gilham carefully laid a portfolio of photographs on the desk and bent the file cover back to reveal one of the prints.

It showed a pair of wrists photographed at close quarters. Even before Gilham said anything, he noted the groove-like indentations in the skin.

'Handcuffs, we believe,' Gilham continued. 'SOCO did a magnificent job getting these to us so soon, but Eddie Hutch thought you ought to see them straight away.'

'I bet he did. He needs to do something right after the cock-up his lot made of getting to the scene.'

Fulton glanced at his watch. Seven o'clock. He'd forgotten all about the time. The incident-room briefing had taken up at least an hour and a half and produced little but speculation from his team. Nothing found in the recreation ground, apart from a half a dozen car keys and double that number of used condoms in the undergrowth of the copse, and so far there were no witnesses from the ongoing house-to-house enquiries. It was like walking in treacle.

'Handcuffs,' he said eventually. 'So, what are you saying?'

Gilham raised his eyes to the ceiling. 'Come on, Jack, you *know* what I'm saying.'

'You can pick up handcuffs in any military surplus shop.'

'True, but they're mainly the old hand-bolts we used to use and they wouldn't have left those marks. Only the new ratchet cuffs applied very tightly would fit the bill – and why remove them and tie up the wrists with cord afterwards anyway?'

'Maybe the killer wanted to keep the cuffs as a souvenir – only had one pair.'

'Or maybe he didn't want us to know he had used them, which suggests all sorts of possibilities.'

'Like, maybe our man was a copper, eh?'

'It's possible and it would certainly explain why Lyall was prepared to let him into his place. Nothing like a police uniform to reassure an elderly security-conscious judge.'

Fulton scowled and lit a cigarette. 'Maybe,' he agreed, 'but I don't want us jumping fences before we can smell the fox. And I don't want this getting to the press. It's the only thing we've got that they don't seem to know about.'

'So, what about the rest of our team?'

Fulton agonized for a few moments, then took a long pull on his cigarette and exhaled with an asthmatic wheeze. 'They don't need to know yet. Warn Eddie Hutch to keep shtum.'

'And when they find out later? They won't be very happy that we've kept something back.'

'Tough. I'm not into counselling and anyway, there are more important issues to worry about than a handful of bruised egos – like why Lyall was topped in the first place, for instance. There's got to be something in his background that made him a target. Find that out and we're well on our way to catching his killer.'

Gilham shrugged. 'Being a judge would be enough. There must be a fair few villains around who have him to thank for a nice helping of porridge.'

'So look into it then. I want to know everything about him: friends, hobbies, where he went at night, any threats he may have received – everything.'

'Could be a mite sensitive, considering who he was.'

'Just do it and if anyone doesn't like it, refer 'em to me.'

Gilham was plainly still far from happy. 'There could be something else to worry about, though.'

'Go on.'

'Maybe our man kept the cuffs because—'

'He intends using them again?' Fulton crushed his cigarette in the ashtray on his desk as if he suddenly found the taste unpleasant. 'Then we'd better pray we catch him first,' he replied grimly. He hauled himself to his feet and grabbed his coat off the back of the chair. 'Now, it's time I went home, I reckon.'

Gilham nodded. 'Yeah, me too. I'm meeting Emily Ford, Lyall's daughter, at the morgue for formal ID of his body at just after nine.'

'And the PM?'

'We're hoping for around two o'clock. Oh, by the way' – he rummaged in his pocket to produce a computer printout – 'LIO asked me to give you this.'

Fulton practically snatched the printout from him and studied it with an air of triumph.

'Something to do with the inquiry?' Gilham queried, hovering curiously, with one hand on the door handle.

'Eh?' Fulton looked up and quickly stuffed the printout into his pocket, inwardly cursing Oates for being so indiscreet. 'No, just a little job he was doing for me.'

Gilham's eyes narrowed. 'Jack,' he began.

Fulton held up one hand to stop him continuing. 'Don't go there, Phil, OK?'

His number two sighed heavily. 'Jack, we're in the middle of a murder inquiry. If you're doing something on the side, maybe to do with Janet—'

'I said forget it. My business.'

'It won't be if it gets out. Listen, Jack, I've heard all about your run-in with Miss PC—'

'Miss who?'

Gilham made a face. 'Dee Honeywell; they call her Miss PC. She's not very popular on this police area.'

Fulton made to push past him into the incident room. 'Why doesn't that surprise me? Now, are you going or not?'

Gilham didn't budge. 'She'll have your "testimonials" if she hears about this, you know that, don't you?'

Fulton reached past him and pulled the door open, forcing him to one side. 'I doubt whether she knows what balls are, Phil.'

Gilham called after him as he strode purposefully past the banks of computers. 'You need to get your head down, Jack.'

Fulton half-turned. 'Don't we all, Phil. See you in the morning.'

Gilham watched him lumber through the door into the corridor and shook his head slowly. 'Damned fool,' he muttered to himself. 'I just hope she's worth it.'

CHAPTER 5

THE ROAD CUT into the closely packed pines like a shaft, dropping away so steeply that Fulton found himself constantly tapping his brakes to keep the car from overreaching itself and skidding off into a ditch. He was very tired and he knew he should have gone home and got his head down as Gilham had suggested. There was a lake of acid churning round in his stomach, his head felt as though it were cracking open and his eyes were so gritty and inflamed that he had to lean forward in his seat to see the road properly. Irresponsible? Yeah, what he was doing was that all right, but he couldn't help himself. He had to find Janet and bring her back.

He didn't try to kid himself that his motives had anything to do with love – that emotion had died a long time ago, shortly after he had found out about her affair with one of the control room inspectors – but he knew how vulnerable Janet was and in spite of all she had done to him over the last few months, he still felt responsible for her. Maybe a lot of what had happened was his own fault anyway. He had always put the job first, working God knew how many hours on the trot and spending far too much of what leisure time he had left down the police club or in a back street pub with the troops in order to keep the team together. He'd been so busy keeping things going at work that he just hadn't seen the problems building up at home, especially after Janet had lost the baby and her depression had set in. Always too tired for anything when he got in, he had failed to appreciate that she had needs too – particularly the physical side of things. They hadn't sat down and talked together properly for a long time now and sex had become anathema to both of them.

She had started drinking heavily a few months ago and became violent towards him soon afterwards. Trouble was, he had tried to deal with the problem on his own and that was a big mistake. Self-inflicted injuries to her face and arms, and accidental bruising caused when he had been forced to hold her off in the middle of one of her attacks, had been misinterpreted by her friends and he had ended up as the villain of the peace – the wife beater – a reputation that she made sure stuck to him. He'd even had a visit from the force welfare officer, a pompous little man who suggested that *he* was the alcoholic and needed help. He hadn't earned himself any favours by giving his visitor some help of his own – straight out the front door and into the flowerbed – and had only avoided court action for assault occasioning actual bodily harm on Janet because she had refused to pursue her malicious complaints afterwards.

Everything was a mess and with the top brass breathing down his neck, he knew his private life needed sorting before it fell apart completely, forcing him into early retirement. Confronting Janet with her new man was probably not the cleverest strategy, but he had always tackled problems head-on and he couldn't think of any other way.

He almost missed the entrance to Staple Farm Cottages – the sign was practically buried in the hedge – and his nearside wing clipped one of the gateposts as he swung into the narrow entrance. The pair of red-brick semi-detached cottages stood at the far end of a large unkempt garden. The further cottage was in darkness, but a single light burned in the upstairs room of the one nearer to him and he pulled up behind a familiar red MG sports car parked by the front door, its hood still down. He smiled grimly. So they were home then. Good.

His feet crunched on the gravel as he strode towards the front door, but the curtains drawn across the upstairs room remained closed and he guessed Janet and her boyfriend were too preoccupied to have heard either the approach of his car or the sound of his footsteps. But the two of them were not long kept in ignorance and his balled fist hammering with considerable force on the front door did more than stir the curtains of that cottage; out of the corner of his eye he saw an upstairs light spring into life next door.

It was Janet who came down and he guessed she must have realized who the caller was even before she opened the door.

For a moment she stood there in the living-room light, her knee-length dressing-gown open provocatively to the navel, revealing that she was wearing nothing underneath, and a mocking smile on her face. 'Hello, Jack,' she said. 'So you got your tyres repaired then?'

He had intended trying to reason with her, to persuade her to come home and start afresh, but the sight of her blatant nakedness in another man's house ignited the spark that was already smouldering in him. 'Cover yourself up, damn you,' he blazed, pushing past her into the living room.

'Well, come in, why don't you?' she shouted after him.

He wheeled to face her, clumsy and awkward. 'Do you have to walk around like that?' he said, almost choking on the words.

She laughed without humour. 'Like what, Jack?' she mocked. 'Like a tramp, you mean?'

He ignored the taunt and scanned the room. A log fire burned low in the grate and a man's suede jacket lay across the seat of one of a pair of tattered armchairs set on either side of the hearth. 'So where is he?' he demanded. 'Too frightened to answer the door himself, is he?'

She allowed the dressing-gown to fall open completely. 'Probably exhausted, Jack,' she replied. 'We were actually—'

Grabbing her by the arm, he pushed her towards a half-open internal door. 'I don't want to hear what you were doing,' he grated. 'Now go and get your clothes on. I'm taking you home.'

'You bastard!' Without warning, she turned sharply and launched herself at him, eyes blazing and fingers curled like talons, raking his face before he had a chance to defend himself. As he staggered back against the wall, she went for him again, but this time he was ready for her and slapped her hard across the face. The force of the blow must have temporarily dazed her, for she sank in a heap on the floor, sobbing hysterically, her dressing-gown slipping down over her shoulders.

For a few moments Fulton just stood there, clenching and unclenching his fists uncertainly. He should never have hit her – he had never done that before – but what was he supposed to do? The woman had flipped and would have had his eyes the second time. But he still felt ashamed and frustrated. He hadn't come here to have a domestic, but to get her to come home. Now it had all gone wrong.

'What the bloody hell's going on?'

Fulton hadn't heard the door open behind him and he turned quickly. The speaker, also wearing just a dressing-gown, was young and muscular, with the sort of tanned face and designer stubble that would not have looked out of place in a television commercial for men's deodorant. This had to be the boyfriend, Doyle, he mused grimly as he dabbed the scratches on his cheek with his handkerchief.

'Bastard hit me again,' Janet sobbed. 'He forced his way in here and hit me.'

Doyle stepped forward a pace, his own fists clenched. 'Is this true? You hit her?'

Fulton threw him a contemptuous glance, but didn't bother to answer him.

'Janet,' he said, bending down beside her. 'Look, I'm sorry. I only came here to get you to come home.'

The burning hatred in her tear-filled eyes made him flinch. 'Home?' she sneered. 'With you? What, so you can use me as a punchball again?'

Fulton straightened up, shaking his head slowly. 'I've never ever hit you before,' he said firmly, 'and you damned well know it.'

She turned her head to smirk at him, her triumphant expression hidden from Doyle's gaze. 'That's not what everyone else says,' she retorted with just about the right amount of feeling in her tone, 'and this time you've gone too far.'

'I think you'd better leave.'

Doyle's hand clamped firmly on Fulton's shoulder and that was a mistake. With an oath, the big man swung an arm outwards in an angry gesture that was intended to shake him off. He did that all right, but instead of simply breaking the other's grip, he sent Doyle crashing back into the wall, where he must have struck his head on a low-hung mirror, for he immediately slumped to the floor in a shower of glass shards, leaving a bright-red smear down the plaster.

In a second Janet was at her boyfriend's side, tugging a handkerchief from her dressing-gown pocket to try and stem the bleeding. 'You really have done it this time,' she almost spat at Fulton over her shoulder. 'This'll cost you everything.'

The policeman had gone white. 'I didn't mean that to happen,' he gasped. 'I just pushed him away – I'll call an ambulance.'

'Just get out!' she screamed as he jerked his mobile from his pocket. 'Get out and don't come back!'

Swaying unsteadily in a state of shock, he turned for the door and stumbled out into the cold night air, heading for his car and the freshness of the open road. He hardly noticed the elderly woman standing in the porch of the next cottage, staring after him, or the dark figure that had been watching the drama unfold through the kitchen window at the side of Doyle's cottage and who now ducked down behind a conveniently placed water-butt as Fulton reversed in a swirl of gravel and roared off down the driveway.

CHAPTER 6

FULTON WAS LATE again. He had slept in, thanks to his traumatic late-night encounter with Janet and the three double whiskies he had downed before turning in at around 1.00 a.m. DCI Gilham was waiting for him, a reproving look on his face when he lumbered into the incident room office.

'Rough night, Jack?' he said.

Fulton deposited himself in his swivel-chair with characteristic disregard for the gas-lift mechanism. 'Thought I'd have a lie-in,' he retorted.

Gilham turned his head to study the scratch marks on his face. 'About time you changed your razor though,' he went on. 'It seems to have developed a serrated edge.'

Fulton glared at him. 'I can do without the funnies this morning, thank you,' he said.

Gilham hesitated. 'You found her, then?'

'Found who?'

'Janet.'

Fulton took a deep breath. 'Let's just stick to business, shall we, Phil?'

Gilham shrugged. 'As you wish. Headquarters have been on the line. They think we should hold a press conference pdq as they're being inundated with calls they can't answer.'

'Tough. I've got nothing to say to that pack of jackals yet. When I have, the press office will be the first to know.'

Gilham hesitated. 'We should try and use them, Jack. And it would take the heat off everyone a bit. Even the incident room is getting call after call.'

'I said no; now what else is on the agenda?'

'PM's set for eleven this morning – they pushed it through ahead of schedule.'

'In half an hour then. What about Lyall's movements? Anything?'

'Nothing as yet, though enquiries are still ongoing. We've checked out the local taxi and private hire firms and so far no trace of any pickups at his home.'

'Which means he *must* have been collected by someone he knew or trusted.'

'Like a copper, you mean?'

Fulton studied him for a moment, but ignored the dig. 'And what about the enquiries I asked for into his background?'

Gilham shrugged. 'Ben Morrison is liaising with senior crown court staff to see if he can turn anything up and I've got a team going over the old boy's house again to see what we can find there. So far though, Lyall seems to have been an A-OK sort of a chap. A bit reclusive, but someone who moved in all the right circles. Ex-army man too, with quite a distinguished record, serving in Suez and various other hotspots, then during the "Troubles" in Northern Ireland around 1975. Got the DSO in Armagh for rescuing someone under fire. Not a whisper of anything that could be a motive for murder.'

'Nevertheless, I want you to keep on top of it. People don't get their balls chopped off for nothing. There must be a skeleton somewhere.'

Gilham gave a wry smile. 'And we all have those, don't we, Jack?' he sniped. 'Which reminds me, you had a visit from the early-turn inspector. Apparently you asked Dee Honeywell to trace a plod patrol seen in Merchant Street around midnight last night.'

'And?'

Gilham made a grimace. 'Be nice, Jack, if you'd told me about that. I felt a right prat when he dropped by.'

Fulton sighed. 'Yeah, well, I've had a lot on my mind.'

'I realize that, but if we are supposed to be a team—'

Fulton held up a hand apologetically. 'OK, OK, don't throw all your toys out of the pram. I should have told you, yes. The journalist who blew the story – a reprobate by the name of Ewan McGuigan – buttonholed me yesterday and said the SP on the murder, together with the photo of Lyall's body in the rec, was pushed through his letterbox in a sealed envelope around 00.45 hours – which was before Lyall was even found by Derringer.'

Gilham whistled softly. 'Then the nocturnal postman must have been the killer.'

Fulton nodded. 'McGuigan said he saw no one in the vicinity after the delivery except a police patrol car cruising past. I thought the plod in it might have clocked someone out and about in the area.'

'And the envelope and contents?'

'Already en route to the lab, but I doubt whether there'll be anything on them of use to us.'

'Ah, so that's why the SOCO team were sent to Merchant Street this morning?'

'Yeah, I thought they might come up with something off the letterbox. Long shot, but there you are.'

'Well, talking to Eddie Hutch a few minutes ago, I gather there were just a few smudged marks – nothing of any real value, and they could belong to anyone.'

'Doesn't surprise me, but at least we can't be criticized later for not doing something.'

Gilham nodded, but he was still far from happy. 'Jack, I have to say that all this "secret squirrel" stuff is not like you. We've done lots of jobs together in the past and you've always been right up front with me. If you don't snap out of this business with Janet—'

Fulton's aggression returned with a vengeance. 'I've told you before, Phil, Janet is my business, so keep out of it! Now, what's the SP from the early-turn inspector?'

Gilham started to say something, then changed his mind. 'Merchant Street is on Area 3's beat,' he said, his tone now cold and resentful. 'I'm told Alpha Shift were on nights when Lyall was murdered and their Area 3 is normally a PC Jenny Storey.'

'Then we'd better have her interviewed pronto.'

'No point. She was apparently in the nick with a prisoner from 23.00 until about 01.30 hours.'

Fulton was losing patience. 'So who the bloody hell *was* it in Merchant Street?'

'Area 4 – PC Derringer – would seem the most likely candidate. We can account for the locations of the rest of the mobiles through the control room log, but he hardly reported in all night – until he found Lyall's body, that is.'

'Derringer?' Fulton breathed the word as if it were an expletive. 'Our illustrious plod! That bugger seems to be popping up everywhere on this investigation.'

'At least he seems to be out and about.'

'Yeah, and well off his area this time.'

'Probably poaching for collars. He has a good arrest record, don't forget.'

Fulton looked unconvinced. 'So, when is he next on duty?'

'That depends. He reported sick today.'

'Then we'll have to get him seen at home.'

Gilham shook his head. 'Not the done thing nowadays, Jack. It could be seen as harassment by the welfare lobby – even an infringement of his human rights.'

Fulton released his breath like an explosive charge. 'Phil, this is a bloody *murder* investigation. Has anyone in this nick cottoned on to that yet? All I've heard about so far is political correctness and human sodding rights.' He waved a hand angrily in the air, as if clearing away irritating tobacco smoke.

'Let's just get to this PM, shall we? And when we get back, *I*'ll handle Mr John Derringer's human rights personally!'

The red-brick building was almost hidden behind a row of strategically placed conifer trees in the grounds of the local hospital and a big green van was parked outside, its rear doors open.

Fulton recognized the undertaker's wagon at once. These days ambulances no longer carried bodies to the mortuary, so the undertakers did the job with one of their less conspicuous vehicles, saving their sleek black hearses for the funerals.

Two men in shabby suits were leaving the mortuary as he and Gilham approached. 'Business booming then, is it, gents?' Fulton grunted as he stood to one side of the double doors to let them pass.

'Never better,' the older man chuckled. 'A drowning and a drugs OD in the last four hours. Things are looking up.'

Gilham threw him a critical glance. 'Wonderful,' he replied as he followed his boss inside the building. 'Long may your good luck continue.'

Fulton's face wore a tight apprehensive frown as they crossed the small foyer to the inner doors. He had never got used to post-mortems, even though in his line of business he spent a fair amount of his duty time in mortuaries watching them, and he was keen to get the butchery over and done with as quickly as possible.

Abbey Lee looked up from the stainless steel examination table as her visitors walked in and gave a perfunctory nod. Her green overalls were spattered with dark stains and her gloved hands were carefully probing the chest cavity of the corpse in front of her. A number of bloody organs had already been removed from the cadaver and sliced into sections. The scalp had also been peeled back from the now opened skull to allow access to the brain, creating the horrific illusion that the face itself was just a mask, which could be removed and replaced with another whenever required, like some science fiction nightmare.

It had always struck Fulton that the most terrible thing a post-mortem did was to destroy the human identity. What had once been an individual human being, with virtually unique facial characteristics and personality, was reduced to just an object – an android, which had suddenly stopped working and was about to be consigned to the scrap heap.

'There are no rights in death, Jack,' Abbey said, as if reading his mind.

Acutely aware of the raw nauseating smell forcing itself up his nostrils and the dismembered organs littering the examination table, Fulton could not help thinking of his local butcher's shop and his stomach heaved. 'Started without us then, have you?' he said in a strained voice, trying to shut his mind to what was going on.

Abbey removed her hands from inside the corpse and nodded to the attendant hovering nearby. 'You happen to be late,' she retorted, peeling off her bloodstained gloves and dropping them into a waste-bin.

'Other things to sort out,' Fulton retorted without apologizing.

She gave him a curious glance. 'Been fighting with the cat, have you?'

'What?'

'You've got some nice scratches on your face.'

Out of the corner of his eye he spotted the sudden grin on Gilham's face and his mouth tightened. 'Just stick to business, will you, Ab.'

She sighed. 'Well, we're all done here now anyway. Coroner's officer and forensic photographer have been and gone.' She retrieved a pocket cassette recorder from the corner of the table and tapped it with her other hand. 'You'll get my report just as soon as I can get my observations typed up.'

Gilham watched the attendant unceremoniously dump bits of mutilated organs back into the cavity from which they had been removed and bend over the abdomen with a needle to begin the gruesome task of stitching it up. 'Nice job, you lot have got,' he observed, shaking his head in disgust.

'*We* like it,' Abbey replied, with a brief smile. 'Interesting examination, too.'

'Oh?'

For reply she bent over the corpse and pointed to one of the arms. 'See the pinch marks on the wrist? Dead giveaway.'

'Yes, we saw them in the SOCO pics,' Gilham said, missing her unintentional pun. 'Ratchet handcuffs, we think.'

She nodded. 'And very tightly applied. The state of both wrists suggests that the circulation must have been almost cut off. There are also marks on both ankles, suggesting these were bound with some form of sticky tape – and then there's this....'

She went to the other end of the examination table, waiting a moment while the attendant skilfully pulled the scalp of the corpse back over the severed lid of the skull, then ran a finger lightly across the forehead of the corpse. 'See?'

Fulton and Gilham almost collided with each other in their eagerness to look closer, but it was not difficult to spot the indented band of bruising that seemed to encompass the head at this point.

'Something was applied to the head almost as tightly as the cuffs on the wrists,' she explained. 'In my opinion it was some sort of clamp or restraint to hold it rigidly in position.'

Gilham looked puzzled. 'And what would be the purpose in that?'

She shrugged. 'I can only point out the physical marks I've found and what, in my professional judgement, is likely to have caused them. It's up to you to decide the whys.'

Fulton shot her a keen glance. 'But you do have a theory of your own, don't you, Ab?'

She pursed her lips. 'Well it's pretty obvious your man was secured to a chair or something similar to severely restrict his movements, but the presence of the band mark to the forehead suggests to me that your killer wanted to ensure his victim's gaze was focused on one particular spot – that he couldn't look away.'

'Like into a mirror?' Fulton suggested.

'So, you haven't lost your touch after all then, Jack?'

Gilham looked totally nonplussed now. 'I have to admit I'm confused,' he put in. 'What are we saying?'

'He wanted his victim to watch his own throat being cut,' Fulton answered with brutal frankness.

'Now that really is sick.'

'Yeah,' Fulton replied, 'and so is chopping off someone's balls.'

Gilham closed his eyes briefly at his chief's crudity, darting a reproving glance in his direction, then reddening under Abbey's half-amused gaze. 'Strange though,' he went on quickly, 'how our killer seems to have managed to kidnap and subdue his victim so easily.'

Fulton raised his eyebrows. 'We don't know it was that easy.'

'Well, there were no signs of a struggle at his home, were there? And I take it there were no other marks of violence on the body?'

Abbey shook her head. 'Not indicative of a struggle, no. He had some deep cuts – no doubt from the weapon – to his inner thighs, which I was coming to in a moment, but, apart from those and the other injuries I've already pointed out, nothing else that I could see.'

'Yet you would have thought that a man like Lyall would have put up some kind of resistance,' Gilham persisted. 'After all, he was ex-army and probably quite a tough old bird. Any chance he could have been drugged in some way?'

She nodded. 'Very possible, I would think. I've taken the usual samples and we should know one way or the other following toxicological analysis.'

'And the murder weapon? Any ideas on that?'

'As I said to Mr Fulton at the scene, judging by the wounds inflicted, I would say it was a very thin blade with an extremely sharp edge – something like a cut-throat razor.'

She frowned. 'Your man was not that competent, though. Did a clean job with the throat – sliced right through the carotid artery – but he made a bit of a mess removing the testicles. Very much a hacking job there, hence those deep slashes to the inner thighs where he evidently tried to manoeuvre the weapon.'

'Our killer is a bit of an amateur, then?' Gilham summarized.

She treated him to a grim smile. 'At the moment, yes, but we all improve with practice, don't we?'

The implication of the remark was not lost on the two policemen, but before either got the chance to pursue the subject further, all conversation was interrupted by the melodic ring-tone of a mobile.

Gilham hurriedly jerked the offending telephone from his pocket, wincing his embarrassment.

The call did not last long and after a series of nods and grunts, he rejoined them. 'Someone wants to see me,' he said.

Fulton raised a quizzical eyebrow. 'Someone?'

Gilham glanced at Abbey and she took the hint and moved away. 'We may have a witness,' he went on.

'Then we'd better get to him pdq.'

'Sorry, Jack, it has to be just me this time.'

The big man caught on in an instant. 'One of your snouts, is it?'

'Used to be when I was a DI here. Seems he found out I was back and wants to trade.'

'You'd better get off then, but keep me informed.

'But how will you get back? We came in my motor, don't forget. Do you want me to call the nick for one of the lads to pick you up?'

Abbey was obviously paying more attention than they had appreciated. 'I can drop him back, Phil. I'm through here now anyway.'

Fulton grunted. 'What sharp little ears you have, Ab,' he said. 'I hope your eyes are as good if you're driving me.'

She smiled sweetly. 'You can always walk, Jack.' she retorted. 'And you sure could do with the exercise.'

CHAPTER 7

LENNY BAKER WAS the archetypal low life, the epitome of a petty criminal who would have delighted any caricaturist or film director looking for a suitable subject. In fact, he could not have looked more like a crook if he had tried. Built like a sparrow, with sparse ginger hair, gold-capped front teeth and sharp blue eyes which were always on the move, he wore a grubby fawn anorak and scuffed suede shoes that even Oxfam would have rejected, and carried a copy of a racing newspaper in one hand, which he constantly slapped against his thigh as if swatting some invisible fly.

Gilham had just about tolerated the mouthy little cockney during his time as DI at the Saddler Street nick, even though he knew his principal source of information was breaking into houses at the same time as he was grassing to the police. Trouble was, Lenny's information was usually pretty reliable, so he was someone to be listened to and that meant turning a blind eye to his own dodgy activities, where possible.

The meet was at a disused cement works close to the railway line; dramatic enough for Lenny and his obsession with gangster movies. The little man looked a lot older than Gilham would have expected in the three years that had elapsed since he had last clapped eyes on him and he now wore a livid mauve scar down the left side of his face. 'The O'Leary brothers,' Lenny said with pride. 'A warnin' for poking me nose. Risky business I'm in, you know.'

Gilham looked around him at the derelict machinery, black and stark in the watery sunlight, and nodded, unimpressed by the uninvited explanation. 'So what have you got for me?' he said with undisguised impatience.

Baker grinned. 'That depends on how much it's worth.'

Gilham shook his head. 'No, Lenny, it depends on how much I *think* it's worth.'

The other moved away and lit a cigarette with as much Humphrey Bogart aplomb as he could manage. 'A monkey is what it's worth.'

Gilham sighed. 'If you're going to be stupid, Lenny … For five hundred pounds, I'd expect to get the Queen's telephone number.'

Lenny chuckled. 'I could give you the numbers of lots of queens, if you was interested.' He hesitated. 'OK, a ton then an' no less.'

'A pony and that's only if it's something we don't know already. I don't want to hear some regurgitated press report.'

Lenny's face darkened. 'Listen, boss, what I saw is worth a lot more than twenty-five bleedin' quid.'

'OK, so forty then and that's it – provided what you tell me is kosher.'

'Now come on, Mr Gilham, would it be anythin' else? I've got me reputation to think of—'

The little man broke off and darted a swift frightened glance towards a ruined concrete building a few yards from where they were standing. 'What was that?' he breathed.

Gilham followed the direction of his gaze. 'I heard nothing.'

'You sure you came alone?'

'You know I did. You saw me arrive.'

'And you weren't followed?'

Gilham sighed, used to Baker's sense of the dramatic. 'No, I wasn't followed, Lenny,' he replied. 'And this isn't the film set of *The Godfather* either, all right?'

As he spoke, a ginger cat materialized from the shadows of the building and streaked off across the scabby concrete apron in front of them, disappearing into a patch of scrub several yards away.

Baker gave a sheepish grin and relaxed. 'Sorry, Mr Gilham, I'm a bit on edge at the moment. Goes with the job, see.'

'Can we get on, Lenny?' Gilham said, his impatience showing.

The little man nodded. 'Fact is, I was out for a walk two nights ago – the night your man got stiffed—'

'A walk? Looking for somewhere to screw, you mean?'

'Actually, I'd been to a mate's house for a poker game, OK? Anyway, I decides to take a short cut across the rec. Then I sees this geezer sitting on one of the kiddies' swings.'

Gilham's heart lurched. 'You saw the dead man?'

Baker shrugged. 'Didn't know he was brown bread then. Thought he was some nutter out from somewhere or a queer waitin' for a punter. A lot of 'em gets down the rec at night.'

'What – sitting on a swing stark naked?'

'Well, there's some funny people about, ain't there? Anyway, all I saw of him was a sort of silhouette, 'alf buried in shadow. Didn't know he was starkers 'till I read the papers.'

'What time was all this then?'

'I left Larry's place at just after midnight, so it must've been around twelve-fifteen or twelve-twenty.'

'And you weren't curious enough to take a closer look at the man?'

'No bleedin' fear. I didn't like the look of him – all still and hunched up like – and besides, he 'ad company.'

Gilham's heart was pounding hard now. 'What do you mean by company?'

'There was a motor in the car park, almost hidden under some trees.'

'Anyone in it?'

'Dunno, I just scarpered. Left by the side entrance into Milton Avenue.'

'Why the panic?'

'It was a cop car.'

'It was a *what*?' Gilham stared at him. 'You sure about this?'

The little man nodded, a triumphant gleam in his eyes. 'Yellow and blue squares all over it an' a nice police sign on the front an' back. It was a cop car all right.'

'And you're positive about the time?'

'Definite. I know I was home by twelve-thirty. I'd made a point of getting back for the start of one of them adult films on the telly. It was down for twelve-thirty-five an' it started just after I hung me coat up. Thing is, papers are sayin' some flatfoot found the stiff just after one a.m. So how come this other copper didn't report it earlier?'

Gilham was not in a position to answer that question, but the implications of Baker's revelations sent an icy chill down his spine and after paying him off, he made his way to his car in a semi daze – which is probably why he failed to appreciate that his meeting with Lenny had not been quite as private as he had imagined.

Abbey Lee lived in a neat mews terrace, which reflected taste and style – from the reproduction Picasso paintings on the pastel-painted walls to the various sculptures positioned carefully in wall niches and glass-fronted cabinets.

She poured Fulton a coffee from a stainless steel percolator after waving him to a chair. 'Don't you light that damned weed in here,' she snapped over her shoulder, sensing his hand moving towards the packet of cigarettes in his pocket.

He made a face as she set the bone-china coffee cup and saucer in front of him. 'Haven't you anything stronger?'

She gave him an old-fashioned look. 'I said we'd drop by my place for a coffee and this is it. You drink too much anyway.'

'My business.'

'Maybe, but this is *my* flat, so it's coffee or nothing, OK?'

He took a couple of sips and appraised her from under hooded lids. Out of the green mortuary overalls, she looked nothing like the sort of girl who spent most of her working life dismembering corpses. Although in her mid-thirties, she obviously looked after herself, probably through regular workouts in the gym. Her breasts were small and rounded beneath the thin white blouse and the tight black trousers showed off her narrow hips and firm rounded thighs to perfection. Even the shoulder-length black hair had a healthy vitality about it and the smile that could light up those big green eyes in a second now hovered uncertainly over the slightly crooked mouth, as if embarrassed by the focus of his gaze.

'Do you have to keep staring at my boobs, Jack?' she said, glancing down at herself.

He jumped, startled at the directness of the question, and slopped some of the coffee from his cup into his lap.

She shook her head with cynical amusement, tossing him a linen serviette. 'You ought to have a bib, Superintendent,' she said.

'Sorry about your chair,' he blurted. 'Hand just slipped and—'

'Bathroom's first on the right,' she cut in, indicating the short corridor to the front door.

For several minutes he stood in front of the wash-hand basin, staring at himself in the mirror. The heavy-jowled face that stared back revolted him – particularly with Janet's nail marks now adorning one cheek like some aboriginal self-mutilation. What had he become? A few years ago it had been rugby, football – any sport available. As a detective constable, he had even boxed for his department. But a lot of the muscle had turned to fat over the years, assisted by greasy takeaway meals and booze, and now he hated the sight of himself. No wonder Janet had lost interest in him. He was just an overweight nicotine junkie, married to a job that had wrecked his health and domestic life and now didn't give a damn about him anymore. Just for a second there was a tear in one eye, but then he blinked, tightened his jaw and it was gone. The machismo image was all he had left – no sense losing that as well.

'Jack, you all right in there?'

He heard Abbey's anxious call and splashed some cold water over his face before returning to the sitting room. 'Just taking stock, Ab,' he replied, without intending to say that at all, 'just taking stock.'

There was concern on her face. 'Taking stock of what, Jack?'

He shook his head, angry with himself for the Freudian slip. 'Nothing, Ab. Now, I've got to get back.'

She placed a restraining hand on his arm. 'If there's something you need to talk about, I'm a good listener.'

He firmly removed her hand. 'There's nothing *to* talk about,' he retorted, his tone sharper than he had meant it to be. 'Thanks for the coffee.'

'But you've barely touched it.'

He took a deep breath. 'Look, I shouldn't have come here at all. It was a bad mistake.'

'Why?'

He turned for the door. 'Just run me back, will you, Ab – or do I have to call the incident room for a car?'

She stepped in front of him. 'Jack, listen to me. I know that behind all this hard man front you put up, there's a decent sensitive person desperate to get out. So why do you put so much effort into frightening people off? What are you afraid of? That someone will actually get to like you?'

He jerked out his mobile telephone and flicked open the cover. 'I haven't got time for all this,' he snapped. 'I've got a murder to investigate.'

'And a wife to sort out.'

It was a cheap shot and she regretted it as soon as she had made it, but she didn't get the chance to take the remark back, for the phone in his hand chose that precise moment to end their conversation.

'Jack?' Phil Gilham's voice sounded strained and apprehensive. 'We need to meet up pdq. Suggest your office. Ben Morrison will be there too.'

'Sounds like bad news?'

'The worst.'

Fulton threw Abbey a questioning glance and she made a grimace in response. 'Damn it!' she muttered under her breath as she scooped up her car ignition keys.

On the other side of the street opposite the house, Ewan McGuigan was a lot happier than either Abbey or Fulton as he raised his camera and took several shots of them walking towards Abbey's four-by-four. 'Gotcha!' he murmured as they drove away.

Ben Morrison's legendary habit of gum chewing was in overdrive when Fulton joined the stocky ex-marine and his own number two in the little incident room office. Morrison was more hyped up than Fulton had ever seen him. The veins in his muscular temples were corded like the taut strands of a tent's guy ropes as he leaned against the radiator, while Gilham, propped uncomfortably on the corner of the desk, looked pale and shaken.

'So, what have we got?' Fulton demanded, falling into his chair.

Gilham nodded towards Morrison and the DI shifted the gum to one side of his mouth, his eyes darting from Fulton to Gilham, then back again. 'PC Derringer, guv,' he said. 'Seems to have disappeared.'

'What do you mean, disappeared?'

Morrison shrugged. 'Didn't turn up for duty last night. Tommy Lester, shift inspector, rang him to find out why and couldn't raise him.'

Fulton glanced at Gilham. 'But I was told he'd called in sick.'

Morrison nodded. 'Tommy was just trying to protect Derringer's arse, guv,' he said. 'Looking after one of his own – you know the score.'

'I'll have his balls for this.'

Morrison chewed furiously for a few seconds. 'Can't blame him, guv,' he defended. 'We all look after our own, don't we? Sort of unwritten rule. You sort out your own problems, not spread 'em around 'less you have to.'

'So how do we know Derringer's done a bunk?'

'We don't, but when Tommy got no reply on the phone, he left it till shift change from nights to late turn today. Came on an hour early and went round to his home. Derringer lives on his tod in basement flat in Quarry Street. Never married. One of the neighbours – Emily Stewart – saw him leave in his Jag at about 08.30 yesterday morning. Ain't seen him since.'

'A Jaguar?' Fulton echoed, thinking of his humble Volvo.

'Yeah, new three-litre something job apparently.

'How the hell does he manage to run that on a bobby's pay?'

Morrison shook his head. 'Dunno. It's raised a few eyebrows in the nick though.'

'And you've checked out Derringer's address?'

'Not yet. Only spoke to Tommy half-hour ago. He said place was dead.'

Fulton lit a cigarette. 'Derringer's a deceitful little bugger by all accounts. Maybe he's just swinging the lead and has gone off somewhere for the day.'

'Could be,' Morrison acknowledged, 'but it don't look good.'

'And it gets a lot worse, Jack,' Gilham put in. 'The snout I went to see was apparently out and about the night Lyall was murdered and he tells me he crossed the rec at around 00.15 and 00.20 and actually saw Lyall slumped on the swing, though he swears blind he didn't know he was dead then.'

'Why should that make things worse for Derringer? We know Lyall was done sometime around 23.00 hours and must have been dumped in the rec between then and the time our man stumbled on the corpse.'

'True, but there's something else. My informant tells me that at the time he saw the corpse, there was a marked police car parked in the rec, almost hidden under some trees.'

Fulton gaped at him for a second, the cigarette stuck to his bottom lip. 'You sure this man of yours is not having a laugh?'

'Positive, Jack. He's always been a hundred per cent reliable and if he started telling porkies, he knows I wouldn't use him again.'

'Could he be wrong about the time? After all, there's only an hour between his alleged sighting and Derringer's reported discovery of the body at 01.15.'

'He's adamant it was between 00.15 and 00.20. He'd just left a poker game and was home by 00.30 in time to see the beginning of some soft-porn crap on TV, which apparently started at 00.35. Anyway, if it *was* Derringer who was parked up, why did it take him an hour to report his find? Also, why was his car tucked away in the shadows the way it was?'

Fulton closed his eyes for a second, then stubbed out his cigarette with an air of finality. 'OK, I agree it all looks pretty suspect. So, first thing we do is get hold of the car Derringer was using. If Lyall was transported in it, there are likely to be DNA traces on the carpets or the boot mat and—'

'Already in hand, guv,' Morrison interjected. 'SOCO are on to it as we speak.'

Fulton nodded his approval. 'And I want you, Ben, to pull Derringer's personal file from personnel. Get hold of any other contact addresses and discreetly check that he's not at one of them. Admin should have the number of his car if he's been parking it at the nick—'

'Do we circulate him as missing?'

Fulton hesitated, fully aware of the ramifications of doing that. 'Not yet. I don't want anyone – not even the incident room – to know about this until we're on solid ground, so tell SOCO and Lester to keep their mouths shut too. I think Phil and I will take a look at Derringer's basement flat first.'

Gilham raised his eyebrows. 'Search warrant, Jack?'

Fulton snorted. 'Don't be silly, Phil!' he replied.

CHAPTER 8

QUARRY STREET WAS in a rundown part of town made up of terraces of late Victorian properties, which were now predominantly used as student bedsits. Derringer's flat was well hidden below the pavement and reached by a flight of stone steps, which crept down between stubby stone pillars to a tiny stone-flagged courtyard.

The front door was old and shaky, with paint peeling from its panels and a taped diagonal crack in the small window at the top. There was no response to Fulton's thunderous knocking and, peering through the dirty glass, he could see only part of an unlit hallway. He frowned and shook the door handle hard.

Gilham's unease was palpable. 'Jack,' he cautioned, touching his arm, 'we can't just go breaking in.'

Fulton threw him a scathing glance and produced his credit card, ignoring his deputy's groan of despair as he bent over the antiquated lock with the plastic. Seconds later the door swung open and despite Gilham's hoarse protest, he disappeared inside. Left with no real alternative, Gilham reluctantly followed.

The exterior of the flat might have looked shabby, but inside was a completely different story. The short hallway was surprisingly well decorated, smelling clean and fresh, and Gilham spotted air-fresheners plugged into the wall in at least two places. Fulton pushed open doors to the left and right and found the bathroom and a sparsely furnished bedroom. Both were empty, as was the live-in kitchen at the end. He put his hand on a coffee percolator on the work surface. It was cold and, lifting the lid, he saw that it contained just dregs.

Gilham's uneasiness was getting worse. 'Jack, we ought to leave,' he advised. 'What if Derringer comes back and finds us in here?'

Fulton grunted. 'Found the door open and thought we'd check it out, didn't we?' he growled, inspecting a pile of unwashed crockery in the sink. 'Doesn't look as though our missing bobby has been here for quite a while. Sounds like the nosy neighbour was right about last seeing him go out at about 08.30 yesterday.'

Gilham shrugged. 'Maybe he doesn't wash up very often. You know, single man and all that.'

Fulton thought of his own kitchen sink and grunted again. 'Yeah, well it could also be that he left here in a hurry.'

'But why? Unless–'

'*That* is the big question.'

Fulton crossed to the large upright fridge-freezer and jerked open the refrigerator door. Inside, it was packed but well ordered, with a couple of bottles of French white wine in the door compartment. The freezer was the same, but he pulled out a couple of frozen parcels and studied their neatly written labels closely for a second before returning them to their basket and closing the freezer door again.

'Lives well, anyway.'

'Why do you say that?'

'Premium French wine in the fridge, pheasant and fillet steaks in the freezer. And we already know he drives a bloody Jag. Doing well for a humble beat bobby, I'd say.'

'Unmarried. What do you expect?'

Fulton treated him to a wolfish grin. 'That's the solution then, is it?' he retorted. 'Stay single? I'll bear that in mind. But in the meantime, let's take a look at matey's bedroom, shall we?'

The bed in the bright, tastefully decorated room had not been made and a police uniform lay in a heap on the floor, as if it had been left where it had been dropped. Gilham stood in the hallway, partly watching his boss and partly keeping an apprehensive eye on the open front door. 'Are we done here, Jack?' he breathed.

Fulton was carefully checking inside the wardrobe and grunted. 'Now that *is* interesting.'

Gilham stepped into the room, his curiosity overruling his uneasiness. 'What is?'

Fulton opened both doors wide. 'Look at this.'

His colleague moved closer, studying the suits and shirts hanging from the rail with obvious puzzlement. 'I don't see—'

The big man cut him off with a snort of irritation and crossed the room to a large chest of drawers. He opened each drawer in turn to glance briefly inside. Then, leaving one of the drawers open, he grabbed a chair and climbed on to it to peer at the top of the wardrobe.

Gilham was totally mystified and checked out the chest of drawers for himself. The open drawer contained just underpants and T-shirts arranged in neat rows.

'Aha!' Fulton suddenly exclaimed, making him jump. 'Suitcase still here.'

Gilham glanced across at him. 'He may have had another.'

'True, but this one appears new and it's good quality smooth leather, covered in a nice layer of dust, which would suggest that nothing has been placed on top of it for quite a while.' He clambered down off the chair, brushing his hands with a handkerchief. 'Furthermore, if he left with a suitcase, why didn't our nosy neighbour, the Stewart woman, mention it? Pretty significant going out off nights at 08.30 hours, carrying a suitcase, wouldn't you say?'

'So you don't think he's done a bunk?'

'Oh I think he's done that all right – and he seems to have been in one hell of a hurry.'

'Why do you say that?'

'They obviously didn't teach you much about observation when you were at university.'

'Sorry?'

Fulton sighed heavily. 'Didn't you see the suits and shirts hanging in the wardrobe? Apart from being expensive designer brands, all are neatly arranged, with the jackets protected by polythene. Then there's the chest of drawers. T-shirts, and underclothes – all carefully folded, without so much as a single crease out of place. And the bathroom I glanced in earlier – towels carefully folded corner to corner on the towel rails, face cloth a neat square on the basin tray and toiletries in perfect rows on the glass shelves above it. No man this fastidious leaves the kitchen in the state it was in, the bed unmade and his uniform – which even has stitched-increases – in a pile on the floor, unless he was off on his toes.'

He produced a cigarette and lit up. 'Oh, our man was certainly running, Phil, and very fast indeed.'

'So you think he's our murderer?'

'I didn't say that, but he seems to have had one hell of a guilty conscience about something.'

'Oh, he's got a guilty conscience all right!'

Gilham wheeled round as the rough unfamiliar voice spoke from the doorway behind him.

The elderly man in the black leather jacket had entered the hall very quietly, catching them both unawares. 'Well, well, well,' he said, 'Mr Jack bloody Fulton.'

Fulton's face was bleak. 'Hello, Mickey,' he said quietly. 'It's been a long time.'

Cold blue eyes appraised them from a death's head face and the new arrival came slowly into the room. Another thickset man, with a completely bald head and the ruined features of the professional pugilist, followed, his faded blue suit straining at every movement.

'What are you doing here, Mickey?' Fulton rasped, then glanced quickly at Gilham. 'Mickey Vansetti, Phil,' he said. 'A disease from my crime-squad days.'

Vansetti looked pained. 'Now that's not very polite, Mr Fulton, is it? Especially seein' as me an' you goes back such a long way.'

'You're on private property,' Fulton responded.

Vansetti grinned. 'So are you, Mr Fulton.' He jerked a thumb over his shoulder. 'Interestin' how you got in though.'

Fulton turned away from him to answer the strident call of his mobile and engaged in a short earnest conversation with someone at the other end.

Vansetti produced a silver cigar case and lit up a slim black panatella. 'Does you like a flutter, Mr Gilham?' he said.

Gilham started, wondering how he knew his name. 'Not for me,' he said.

Vansetti nodded. 'Very wise, Mr Gilham, very wise. See, your Mr Derringer now, he likes a flutter. Wins quite a bit too; talented sort of bloke. Trouble is, he don't play fair an' square.' His smile faded. 'Owes me at least a couple of grand, Mr Gilham. Perhaps you'd pass on my compliments when you finds him. Tell him Mickey was asking after his 'ealth, eh?'

Treating Gilham to an extravagant wink, he turned on his heel and left, his minder shuffling after him.

Gilham breathed a heavy sigh. 'Nice beauty,' he commented.

Fulton closed the cover of his mobile and returned it to his pocket. 'Local hard man,' he said. 'Used to own quite a few backstreet card schools and knocking shops. Was actually a squad target criminal till he got sent down a few years ago. Didn't realize he was back in business.'

'At least we now know why Derringer was running.'

'Maybe,' Fulton replied, his face grim. 'But there could be another reason. That was Ben Morrison on the phone.

SOCO have found stains in the boot of Derringer's area car that look like blood.'

'Gordon Bennett!'

'I can think of a much stronger phrase to use and I reckon ACC ops will too when he receives the glad tidings.'

The afternoon incident room briefing was a sombre affair. Word had already got out that a local officer was high on the list of suspects and had gone missing. Consequently, Fulton faced a shocked, disgruntled team who waited on his every word and studied him warily through the fog of tobacco smoke that choked the room, as if he had suddenly become the enemy.

After a cold hostile reception from ACC Norman Skellet – who had had to authorize the national all-ports circulation on Derringer as 'wanted for interview' and sacrifice a pre-booked evening dinner engagement into the bargain so he could brief the chief constable and be on hand to deal with the anticipated fall-out – Fulton's own mood matched theirs. But now was not the time for holding back and despite his earlier intentions to keep some information about the progress of the inquiry to himself, he took the decision to divulge everything that had come to light so far, reasoning that his team probably knew most of it from the grapevine anyway.

His strategy seemed to pay off, too, and when at last the briefing ended, his troops were in a much better frame of mind. But his sense of achievement took an abrupt nosedive as he left the incident room.

He had spotted Superintendent Honeywell tucked away in a corner of the room while he was talking and had sensed an impending problem in the grim set of her face. He was not long kept in doubt, either.

'I understand from my LIO that you instructed him to carry out an unauthorized vehicle check?' she snapped, buttonholing him in the corridor outside the incident room.

Fulton scowled, inwardly cursing George Oates for his treachery. 'Did I?' he said.

She stood her ground. 'I shall have to report this, Jack. It's a clear breach of the rules.'

He sighed. 'Well, you do what you think best, Dee,' he replied. 'I've got more important things to worry about – and so have you, with one of your own men AWOL.'

'I am well aware of the possible implications attached to PC Derringer's absence, thank you,' she replied, 'and with my DCI on leave and my area chief inspector on the sick, I have quite enough to do running the police area, without having to check up on what you are doing all the time.'

Fulton shrugged. 'Then don't,' he retorted.

Her jaw tightened. 'This is a very serious matter, Jack,' she persisted. 'You do realize that, don't you?'

'So is murder,' he retorted, angered by her dismissive attitude towards Derringer's disappearance. 'And you'd do better putting more effort into finding your own officer than hounding me over trivialities.'

'Trivialities?' she choked, but was abruptly silenced by the blast of the police station Tannoy above her head: 'Detective Superintendent Fulton, please contact control room immediately.'

Anxious to pursue her point, she followed him as he ducked into an adjacent office and picked up the telephone to dial the appropriate extension number. 'You've set an appalling example,' she continued, 'and you just don't give a damn, do you?'

But he was not listening. 'Fulton,' he barked into the receiver, turning his back on her as he listened intently to what he was being told by the control room operator.

'Give me fifteen minutes,' he said, and slammed the receiver back on to its cradle.

'And what was all that about?' Honeywell demanded.

Fulton stared at her as if he were contemplating a scaly insect. 'Nothing much, Dee,' he said, pushing past her for the door. 'Just another murder, that's all!'

Dusk was already shadowing a watery sun when Fulton swung his Volvo into the entrance to the old cement works and Gilham, sitting tensely beside him, flinched instinctively as the woodland crowding the narrow rutted track seemed to close in on the car and a stray branch scraped across the windscreen like a claw. A hundred yards further on a line of red-and-white cones forced them to come to a halt and a uniformed constable appeared at Fulton's window – only to step back to kick two of the cones aside and wave them through when he saw who was behind the wheel.

Beyond the temporary security barrier the track opened out into a vast concrete apron, bordered at the far end by derelict brick buildings. Several police vehicles were parked on a broken section of hard-standing to their left and Fulton pulled up sharply behind a dog van, sending the Alsatian inside into a fit of frenzied barking and snarling. 'Shut up!' a coarse voice yelled from the driving seat, silencing the dog immediately, and a balding constable in blue uniform overalls poked his head out of the window. 'Sorry, guv.' He grinned, nodding towards the low growls now coming from the rear of the van. 'Trouble is, Satan can't tell the goodies from the baddies.'

Fulton cast him a cynical glance. 'Maybe you should get him some glasses then,' he commented. 'Who's in charge here?'

The dog man leaned further out of the window, yelling at the Alsatian again when it resumed its barking, and pointed towards a small group of people standing a short distance from an old Mercedes car parked about thirty yards away. 'DS Prentice, guv. He's over there with Sally Ojibwa, the local area beat unit, talking to the guy who found the stiff.' He grinned, adding: 'Sally's the one with the dreadlocks!'

Prentice came to meet them as they approached the car, his face cold and impassive as ever.

'Guv,' he acknowledged and jerked his head back towards the elderly man he had been talking to. 'That's Mr Duncan Hayes. He found the body.'

Fulton grimaced. 'Bully for him,' he commented. He went to the car and bent his head to peer in through the side window. The dead man had fallen sideways and now lay across both front seats, his face turned towards them to expose the grinning gash in his throat, which appeared to have almost decapitated him. Much of the front interior of the car, including virtually the entire windscreen, was plastered in blood, as if someone had sprayed it with a high pressure paint gun, and some of the thick sticky juices had already begun to solidify.

'It's Lenny Baker,' Gilham breathed. 'My informant.'

Fulton raised an eyebrow. 'Well, he won't be passing on any more grubby gossip, that's for sure,' he said. 'No doubt that's why he was done.'

Gilham straightened up and ran a hand through his hair in a gesture of frustration. 'Damn it!' he exclaimed. 'Lenny said he heard something, but I just put it down to his usual dramatics.'

Fulton stared at him. 'What do you mean?' he said sharply.

'He asked if I'd heard a noise and if I'd been followed. Then this cat emerged from the place over there and I thought …' His eyes widened. 'Gordon Bennett, Jack, the swine that did this must have followed me here. He coolly waited until I left before …' He broke off again and gestured towards the car in resignation.

Fulton walked away from him in the direction of the building he had indicated and peered in through the doorway. Even in the diminishing light, he could see the grass and weeds poking through the broken concrete floor. The place smelled like a urinal and he made a grimace as Gilham joined him.

'We'll get SOCO to give the place the once over,' he said. 'Might find a fibre or two, you never know.'

Prentice coughed discreetly from behind them. 'Mr Hayes was out walking his dog when he came across the car, guv,' he explained. 'Dog ran off and—'

'Anyone else in the vicinity?' Fulton interjected, turning to eye the DS quizzically. 'Or maybe another vehicle driving away?'

Prentice shook his head with the weary patience of the experienced professional being taught to suck eggs. 'Just the car and the dead man. He rang us on his mobile.'

Fulton nodded. 'Grateful to him for his help. Get his details and take a statement. We can always speak to him later. Pathologist and SOCO en route?'

'All in hand, guv.'

'Good.' Fulton cast a roving glance around him. 'Hopefully they'll turn up before the press get wind of what's happened.'

Prentice shook his head. 'Already been, guv.'

'What?'

'Yeah – just one of them though. Some smarmy creep calling himself Ewan McGuigan. Said he knew you.'

Fulton's jaw dropped. 'McGuigan? How the hell did that bastard get on to this one so fast? You didn't let him anywhere near the car?'

'Not a chance.' The DS gave a rare smile. 'He didn't get much opportunity anyway.' He nodded towards the dog van. 'Jimmy Talbot was exercising Satan and the Alsatian took a bit of a dislike to your man. Tell you, I've never seen anyone in such a hurry to get back to his car.'

Fulton's eyes gleamed. 'Nice one. Pity the bloody dog didn't sink his teeth into his arse. Anyway, I'll get some extra units up here to help you secure the scene.' He inclined his head towards his number two. 'DCI Gilham will remain here too until they arrive.'

Gilham rewarded his boss with a sour grimace, but said nothing until he was seeing him to his car. 'Thanks for that, Jack,' he said.

Fulton smiled again. 'My pleasure, Phil,' he replied. 'But don't let the damp spoil that tan of yours, will you?'

Gilham didn't acknowledge the jibe and there was a frown on his face as he opened the driver's door for him.

'Who the hell are we dealing with, Jack? Surely Derringer wouldn't have...?'

There was the double click of a lighter and cigarette smoke trailed in the still air. 'Who can say what anyone would do under the right amount of pressure?' Fulton replied. 'And we don't know whether the same person did both jobs anyway – although, apart from the fact that Lenny seems to have hung on to his balls, the two MOs are very similar.'

'Both had their throats cut, certainly.'

'More than that. Didn't you notice the rear view mirror?'

'The mirror?'

'Yes, it was twisted at an unnatural angle.'

Gilham thought about that for a second. 'Could have been knocked when Lenny fell across the seats,' he suggested.

'Unlikely, the way he was lying, and it wouldn't have ended up at that sort of angle anyway. Don't forget what Abbey Lee said about Lyall.'

'So are you saying Lenny was forced to watch his own throat being cut, just like our late judge?'

'Something like that. It's possible that the killer was in the back seat, waiting for your man, and that he forced his head back against the headrest with one hand while he did the job with the other. He would have already worked out the best position for the mirror and no doubt adjusted it just before Lenny climbed behind the wheel.'

Gilham shivered. 'A nice beauty.'

Fulton climbed into his car. 'I can think of a better description. And one thing is very clear: whoever he is, he seems to be keeping very close tabs on us.'

Gilham glanced quickly into the surrounding woodland as his boss drove away and shivered again, feeling the mist that was rising through the gathering dusk settle on his shoulders like a clammy dead hand.

CHAPTER 9

FULTON MADE A point of dropping into the LIO's office when he returned to Saddler Street police station. George Oates was already packing up for the day, one hand on his computer mouse as he bent over his desk to shut down the demanding beast that dominated his working life. He winced when Fulton's shed-like bulk darkened his doorway.

'Thanks a lot, George,' the big man drawled, studying him with open hostility. 'Dee Honeywell and I had a real heart to heart over my vehicle check.'

Oates straightened and held up both hands in a defensive gesture. 'What could I do, guv?' he pleaded. 'She *is* my boss and she had already sussed that you were up to something. I had to tell her in the end just to get her off my back.'

Fulton ignored his obvious preparations for the 'off' and dropped into the chair he had occupied on his previous visit. 'Well, you can make amends by doing me another little favour,' he growled.

Oates raised his eyes to the ceiling. 'Guv, look—'

'And this time it's official.'

Oates sat down heavily in his swivel-chair. 'But I was about to go home.'

Fulton snorted. 'What, at this hour? Wish I had your job.'

'You wouldn't. I've been at an LIO conference all afternoon. Likely to put you off criminal intelligence for life.'

Fulton leaned forward. 'What do you know about a lowlife called Lenny Baker?'

Oates raised an eyebrow. 'The guy who's just had his throat cut?'

'How did you know about that?'

'It's my job to know what's going on and there are such things in police stations as personal radios.'

Fulton ignored the sarcasm. 'So, what about Baker then?'

Oates shrugged. 'Local tea leaf. Likes – liked – to think of himself as a supergrass. Came up with some useful snippets from time to time though. Maybe your serial killer thought he'd seen too much and decided surgery was necessary.'

Fulton pursed his lips for a moment. 'We don't know he *is* a serial killer,' he reminded him, 'or that he stiffed both Lenny as well as the judge.'

'OK, but from what I hear, the MOs are pretty similar anyway.'

'Not quite. There doesn't appear to have been any other form of mutilation this time.'

'Both victims had their throats slit in the good old Sweeney Todd tradition though, didn't they?'

'Maybe, but two hits don't necessarily make a serial killer.'

'Let's hope you're right.'

Obviously tiring of the discussion, Oates started to get up in his chair, only to sit down again when Fulton continued. 'Where did Baker live?'

'He had a bedsit, I believe, over on Caledonian Row by the canal – number 22.'

Fulton produced a cigarette and lit up. 'Then we shall have to give it a spin, won't we? Might be something there that will lead us to our killer.'

'You've discounted John Derringer, then?'

'Hardly, but he seems to have disappeared into thin air and anyway, I like to keep my options open.' Fulton studied him keenly. 'Know Derringer well, do you?'

'Not particularly. He keeps very much to himself. Good thief-taker, but not much of a team man.'

'What else do you know about him?'

Oates hesitated. 'Look, guv, I'm going out tonight. Can we continue this conversation tomorrow?'

Fulton's eyes narrowed. 'My gut tells me you know quite a lot about PC Derringer, but you don't want to say.'

'Well, he *is* a colleague.'

'He's also a key suspect in a murder investigation – maybe two murder investigations.'

Oates wriggled in his seat for a moment, plainly torn by indecision. In the end, however, he had no choice but to capitulate. 'OK, so he liked a little flutter.'

'Just a flutter?'

'Well, the word is he was in over his head with one of the local villains.'

'Mickey Vansetti?'

Oates nodded, looking down at his feet. 'John likes the good life, anyone will tell you that – designer suits, fast cars and expensive birds. Bit of a problem on a bobby's pay.'

'Do you think that's why he went missing – Vansetti came after him?'

'Could be.'

'Could be – *but*, eh?'

Oates made a grimace. 'He had a bit of an axe to grind with Lyall. Said he was bent.'

'Oh?' Fulton was very interested now. 'And why would he think that? From what I hear, Herbert Lyall was an absolute pillar of the community.'

Oates gave a disparaging snort. 'They're often the worst kind.'

'Maybe that's true, but why would a simple plod like Derringer have a thing about a crown court judge? Despite his extravagant lifestyle, I doubt that he and Lyall moved in the same circles.'

'They didn't have to. Derringer's twenty-year-old sister, Mary, was killed in a nasty road accident at Claverslea a few months back and—'

Fulton snapped his fingers, his eyes gleaming. 'Remember it! The car was driven by Lyall.'

Oates nodded. 'He always maintained that the girl stepped out in front of him and the hospital autopsy did later reveal she had knocked back a fair few glasses of claret before the accident.'

'And Lyall got off with it.'

'Totally exonerated. Thing was, a witness said that his car was being driven a bit erratically immediately prior to the accident, yet he was never breathalysed.'

'Fix?'

'Derringer thought so, especially as Lyall was a mate of both the Lord Lieutenant and the Lord Chief Justice. Derringer was obsessed with conspiracy theories and said Lyall needed to be punished.'

'Enough of a reason to kill him?'

'I can't answer that.'

'So how do you know all this?'

Oates sighed. 'John used to drop by my office for a chat every so often. We're both loners, so I suppose he felt he could trust me.'

Fulton stood up. 'Well, he obviously couldn't if you're telling me all this now.'

Oates glared at him. 'That's not fair, guv'nor,' he snapped.

Fulton paused briefly with his hand on the door frame. 'Being fair is not something I've ever aspired to, George,' he said, his face suddenly grim. 'Just being right suits me.'

The special thanksgiving service had finished ten minutes early; a real rollercoaster ride of short hymns, short readings and an even shorter sermon that left the congregation feeling disgruntled and cheated. After all, what was the point of sacrificing the night's soap episode on television and raiding the wardrobe for the suit or dress that would impress the most, only to find an unsmiling twitchy vicar who could hardly wait to say the magic words 'Go in Peace' and get rid of everybody?

Not surprisingly, the handshakes of the Reverend Andrew Cotter's flock were less than enthusiastic as they filed past him through the north door of the little country church and hurried to their parked cars, muttering and shaking their heads in righteous indignation. But Cotter was hardly aware of their dissatisfaction. He had a much more important problem on his mind, something that threatened to destroy his career, his marriage – his whole life. And that problem had had the audacity to demand a meeting with him in the church itself, straight after the service.

As he closed the door after the choir and stewards had finally left, he tried for the millionth time since the sealed letter had been placed on the sacristy desk to work out who his tormentor might be, but yet again he failed miserably. He had only been at St Peter's for three years and the skeletons in his cupboard were much too old for any of his present flock to know about. No, the person who had typed that note must be someone who had known him in the old days, someone with a grudge – and possibly a desire for money as well as revenge.

Turning back into the church, he shivered. The lights had been dimmed by the departing verger, and without its worshippers the building seemed suddenly cold and sinister, the twin rows of ornate stone columns that marched so resolutely through the rows of vacant pews, reaching up into the heavy blackness of the vaulted roof as if into infinity, and the brass eagle supporting the pulpit lectern gleaming lifelike and malevolent in the dimly lit gloom.

He crossed himself automatically as he turned down the nave towards the chancel, genuflecting in front of the simple brass cross on the altar before making for the north-east corner. The curtains across the choir vestry stirred on his approach, as if under a draught, and he paused again with a frown, peering over his shoulder at the north door. It appeared to be securely shut and he shook his head a couple of times in puzzlement, wondering where the draught could have come from. Then he shrugged, mentally reproaching himself for his stupidity. For heaven's sake, man, he thought, the church is 700 years old. You can hardly expect it to be vacuum sealed.

The low door to the sacristy at the far end of the choir vestry was ajar, the bunch of keys still dangling from the lock where he had left them earlier, and he ducked his head as he went through. The lamp burned brightly on his desk, casting fantasy shadows up the bare stonework, but not all were illusions and he froze when one peeled itself off the wall behind the desk and came towards him. 'Good evening, Father,' the figure said quietly. 'That was a nice short service.'

Cotter's mouth tightened and the worms immediately started crawling around his insides. 'I am not a *father*,' he snapped, trying to take command of the situation, but finding himself let down by the nervous quaver in his tone. 'This is an Anglican church.'

His visitor chuckled. 'Well, whatever, Andrew,' he replied, continuing to advance slowly towards him. 'Let's not split hairs, shall we?'

Cotter clenched both fists by his sides. 'What do you want?' he whispered. 'Is it money you're after?'

The other laughed harshly. 'Money, Andrew?' he echoed. 'Money? Oh, I think you'll need a lot more than mere money to clear *your* debt.'

'I don't know what you mean.'

'Now, now, Andrew, no more playing games, eh? You did enough of that in the old days, remember?'

Cotter shook his head quickly as he backed away from his sinister visitor. 'I haven't the faintest idea what you're talking about.'

Feeling the top of the low arched doorway touching the back of his head, he suddenly ducked under it and out into the choir vestry, grasping the iron ring in the door and pulling it shut behind him. Then, after turning the key in the lock, he scurried through the curtains of the choir vestry in a panic, his cassock flapping around him as he ran down the aisle towards the porch doors.

Virtual silence accompanied his flight, a silence broken only by the ringing thud of his shoes on the flagstones, and for a moment he was surprised that there was no sound of angry banging from the sacristy he had just left as his visitor tried to force the door open. Then, with an icy twist in his gut, he remembered the external door, which gave access to the church from the churchyard itself; he realized that his 'prisoner' must already be out and was no doubt pacing him along the outer wall, ready to confront him when he burst through.

Changing direction at the last minute, he stumbled through the pews to the nave and headed for the west door, only to find it locked. Fumbling for the keys in his cassock pocket, he suddenly remembered they were still in the door of the sacristy. He was trapped. With a very non-Christian exclamation, he spun round and raced back down the nave, darting suddenly into the nearest row of pews and crouching down on both knees as he heard the loud 'crack' that indicated the heavy iron latch on the north door had been raised.

Next came the sound of the door opening, followed by a familiar bang as it struck the stone pillar just inside, then heavy footsteps advancing along the stone-flagged aisle to the nave. Silence for a few moments before the footsteps resumed, walking slowly down the nave towards the west door. Cotter pressed closer to the back of the pew behind which he sheltered, freezing as the footsteps passed by his hiding-place and praying that they would not stop.

But even the prayers of the Almighty's chosen ones are not always answered and he was still crouching there with his eyes tightly closed, waiting for a miracle, when the apparition appeared in the pew behind him and leaned over to tap him gently on the shoulder. As he jerked his head round with a terrified cry, a powerful hand grabbed him by the hair, hauling him back on to the seat of the pew, while a soft pad soaked in some sort of strong anaesthetic was pressed tightly over his mouth and nose. His last recollection was of hearing the clock in the church tower begin to strike the hour before a heavy, all-consuming blackness swallowed him whole.

CHAPTER 10

FULTON COULD NOT settle. He had gone home with the intention of putting his feet up for a while, but things kept racing around inside his head like an erratic DVD trailer. The brutal murders of Herbert Lyall and Lenny Baker, the disappearance of John Derringer, the row with Dee Honeywell and the acid comments of Andy Stoller – a poisonous witches' brew of voices, images and doubts, each one clamouring for pride of place, and there, in the midst of it all, the podgy face of Janet glaring at him with all the malevolence of the witch herself.

In the end, hot, sweaty and irritable, he got up and took a shower before slumping into his armchair with a cigarette in one hand and a half-full glass of whisky in the other. Pushing thoughts of Janet, Andy Stoller and Dee Honeywell out of his mind, he concentrated instead on the murder inquiry. He was missing something – a fact so obvious that it was screaming at him to be noticed. Somehow he knew it wasn't visual. It was something he had been told or overheard, possibly in the last twenty-four hours, and it had grated on him like a discordant note at the Last Night of the Proms. But exactly what was it, that was the point?

He had managed to get a warrant for Baker's place, but apart from a stack of dirty magazines, a selection of soft porn DVDs and a pile of racing papers, his search team had found absolutely zilch. Lenny apparently lived alone and his flat was a tip, presided over by a flea-bitten mongrel that had managed to sink its teeth into the leg of a member of the search team before it had been dispatched to the local kennels in the general-purpose Transit.

He took a couple of sips from the whisky glass, then, making a sudden decision, abandoned the rest.

Rain was spattering against the window panes as he left the house and got into his car, and a thick fog had developed by the time he pulled up outside Derringer's flat. The street seemed to be deserted, the cars that were parked on both sides of it just sinister smudges in the gloom.

He had his credit card ready and his torch in his other hand by the time he got to the bottom of the steps and approached the front door, but then he stopped short, his senses tingling. The door was ajar.

He listened intently for a moment, but heard nothing, save the sound of a distant train. He was positive he had secured the door properly at the end of his last visit with Phil Gilham, but there was no denying it was open now.

He switched on his torch, grinning to himself as the beam, expertly masked with black tape, pinpointed the lock. Masked torches were usually carried by villains with a penchant for breaking into houses and he wondered what would happen if a passing patrol happened to walk in on him, equipped as he was.

He switched the torch off again, pushed the door wider and peered into the gloom, still listening for the slightest sound. Then he heard it – a soft scraping noise from the bedroom to the right of the door as if a drawer were being carefully closed. A second later, a glimmer of light showed, then died. Someone else, it seemed, was using a masked torch as well.

He poked his head round the corner of the room. His heart made strange squishing noises as he tried to control his heavy breathing and his mouth tightened as a floorboard cracked under his weight. The bedroom was in total darkness now. The intruder knew he was there.

He fumbled for the light switch, but at the same moment a big solid shape, blacker than the darkness he was peering into, came at him from nowhere, briefly knocking him off balance and lunging for the front door. Instinctively, his balled fist struck out and he had the satisfaction of feeling the crunch as it connected with flesh and bone, but although the intruder cried out in pain, the blow failed to diminish the speed of his departure. He was out through the front door before Fulton even managed to swing round and the thud of his flying feet on the steps up to the street quickly faded as he vanished into the fog, leaving behind the smell of cheap aftershave.

Cursing under his breath, Fulton flexed his bruised fingers, but made no effort to go after his antagonist. He had to accept that his bulk was not built for speed and anyway, matey-boy would have been long gone by the time he even got to the top of the steps.

Instead, he contented himself with a look round the flat and when he eventually found the light switch he wasn't surprised by what he saw. The whole place had been ransacked; the bed stripped and slit open with a sharp blade to expose the springs, drawers pulled out and their contents dumped unceremoniously on the floor and the expensive shirts and suits he had noticed on his previous visit ripped from their hangers and left in piles in front of the wardrobe.

The kitchen had not escaped attention either, with cupboards and drawers emptied on to the floor and bags of sugar and flour slit open, then tossed among the litter of pots and pans, crockery and food which had preceded them. Even the freezer had been emptied and grisly-looking parcels of red meat, fish and packets of frozen vegetables lay everywhere.

For a moment Fulton leaned back against the kitchen wall, studying the mess while he lit a cigarette. When he had first disturbed the intruder, it had flashed through his mind that maybe Derringer had sneaked back for a change of clothes, but the man who had crashed into him was of a much heavier build than the weasel-faced beat bobby, and besides, why would Derringer want to trash his own flat? It didn't make sense. No, whoever was responsible for this job, must be someone other than Derringer, but who, that was the point? And, more important, what the hell were they after? This latest inquiry was turning out to be a lot more complicated than he had at first expected and the conviction was growing on him that, aside from the killer, there were other players involved in the business, each one working to a different agenda. As he jerked his mobile from his pocket and put in a call to the police control room to summon the cavalry, he knew it was time he paid one of those players a visit.

It was after ten by the time Fulton rang the bell at the Vansetti house in Grove and, when the muscular thug in his tight blue suit answered the door, he could not help grinning.

Bruno Dodd had never been particularly handsome, but the swollen cheekbone and black eye gave him a kind of grotesque comic book appearance, which Fulton was delighted to see.

'Screwed any basement flats lately, Bruno?' he sniped, quite sure how he had sustained his injuries.

The dead eyes studied him like those of a lizard. 'Hello, Mr Fulton,' the other said politely. 'You come to see Mickey?'

'You're sharp this evening, Bruno.'

'It's late.'

'So what? Has he had his Horlicks already, then?'

'I'll ask him if he's in.'

Two minutes later Fulton was shown into a thickly carpeted lounge, furnished with a gilt-leafed bar and several green-leather chairs. Carlo Vansetti was sitting in one of the chairs, propped up by cushions. Old and eaten up with cancer, his days as head of the family were nearly done, but the jaundiced eyes still missed very little and the grey emaciated face turned towards the policeman when he entered the room, nodding slowly without speaking.

Mickey was at the bar with his back to the door, but he turned to greet his visitor with two half-filled glasses in his hands. 'Well, this is a pleasure, Jack,' he said. 'Scotch?'

Fulton accepted the drink and took a sip. 'You should get a minder for Bruno,' he said. 'Then, when he gets caught breaking into basement flats, he won't get hurt.'

Mickey chuckled. 'Gettin' old, Jack – like the rest of us.'

Fulton took another sip of his drink and deposited himself in one of the chairs. 'OK, Mickey, let's cut the crap, shall we? Tell me about John Derringer.'

The death's head smile returned, but the eyes were cold and hard. 'Been a naughty boy, your Mr Derringer, Jack. Needs a slap.'

'How much has he taken you for?'

Now even the pretence of a smile vanished. 'No one takes me for nothin', Jack, you knows that. Let's just say he's made an unauthorized withdrawal.'

'Meaning what exactly?'

'We speaking off the record? No wire nor nothin'?'

'Depends what you tell me, but I'm not wired, you have my word on that.'

Vansetti drained his glass and stretched his thin lips over his teeth. 'Your Mr Derringer ain't a very nice man, Jack,' he said. 'Shafted one of my little girls, then used her to get his hands on my money.'

'One of *your* girls?'

'She were a croupier at a sort of unofficial club I owns in Pilstone, just down the road. Derringer liked to play blackjack most nights he were off duty and he persuaded her to come in on a little scam he had cooked up. Managed to cream off a couple of grand over a few weeks, too.'

'You must be making a few bucks if you didn't notice that. I'd miss twenty quid from my bank account.'

The grin returned. 'Said you was in the wrong job, Jack. Anyway, the little tart took off when my manager finally sussed what was going down. Bruno managed to find her an' bring her back, but by then she had tipped off your Mr Derringer, who did a runner.'

'And you thought Derringer might have a stash somewhere in his flat?'

'I can see why you're a detective, Jack, and I'm just a poor entrepreneur.'

'I could haul you and Bruno in for burglary.'

Mickey sighed. 'You'd have to prove it first, my son.'

'Maybe I *am* wired and I have what you said on tape?'

'I doubt it, Jack. You're old school like me. You give me your word. And anyway, you ain't interested in me. You wants your bent bluebottle. Murder, they tells me. Always knew he were a wrong 'un.'

Fulton leaned forward in the chair. 'So where is he?'

Vansetti poured himself another drink. 'If I knew that, I wouldn't be tellin' you now, would I?'

Fulton stood up, sensing he had got as much out of his old antagonist as he was going to. 'If I find you're holding out on me, Mickey, your little club at Pilstone could come in for some real heat. Do you savvy?'

The death's head wore a bleak expression when Vansetti turned to face him again. 'Oh I savvy all right, Jack, but I'll tell you one thing.'

'Go on.'

'I don't reckon John Derringer's got the guts to whack anyone. But someone else in your nick has. So if I was you, I'd watch my back, me ol' mucker.'

The Reverend Cotter awoke with a splitting headache in almost total darkness – almost total because there was a lamp of some sort just above his head, which cast a small circle of light around him, but revealed nothing beyond it. It was like being in the middle of a stage spotlight, though he was quite sure he was not in any theatre. He was conscious of a rhythmic chugging sound close by, like that made by a labouring engine, and there was a strong smell of diesel, cloying and nauseating.

He was sitting in a high-backed leather chair, but that was all he could tell, because he could not move. His wrists were handcuffed to the arms in such a way that the metal bit viciously into the flesh, while his ankles seemed to be secured to the chair by some sort of sticky tape, which crackled slightly when he futilely tried to wriggle the circulation back into them. Most frightening of all was the tight, inflexible band that gripped his forehead, pulling his head back against the headrest so that his gaze was directed upwards at an angle and he could only see the lower part of his body as far as his wrists by forcing his eyeballs down in their sockets in an unnatural, painful contortion.

'Ah, you're awake then, Andrew?' The voice seemed to come from somewhere over to his right. 'Sorry we couldn't get together before, but I gather you were away on some sabbatical or other.'

Cotter tried to turn towards the voice, but the band gripping his forehead like a huge crushing hand prevented virtually all movement. 'Who in God's name are you?' he said, his mouth and throat so dry that he could only manage a croak.

His captor made reproving clucking noises with his tongue. 'Profanity, Andrew, profanity. The bishop would be shocked if he heard you taking the Lord's name in vain like that.'

Cotter swallowed hard several times. 'Why are you doing this to me?'

More spotlights blazed into life behind him and he found himself looking at his own reflection in a long mirror suspended on chains from somewhere in the darkness above. As he stared into it, a hard face with dark brooding eyes appeared in the bottom right hand corner, peering over his shoulder from behind his chair.

'You mean you really don't know?' the other breathed close to his ear.

'How can I? I'm a man of God. I've done nothing to anyone.'

A sneering laugh. 'Oh come, come, Andrew, don't tell me you've forgotten the old days already? Maybe this will remind you.'

More lights blazed to reveal a small square room. Because of his restricted vision, Cotter could only see a small part of it, but what he did see drew a sharp gasp from his trembling lips.

His captor laughed again. 'Know where you are, Andrew? You ought to. What happened here should haunt your Christian conscience every single waking hour.'

Cotter's eyes widened in horror. 'It cannot be,' he whispered. 'The place was sealed up.'

He felt and heard a loud 'clonk' and the chair spun round fifty degrees, so that he was staring directly into the dark eyes of his tormentor.

'You're quite right, Andrew, it was, but I *un*sealed it, as you can see. You really should have destroyed everything instead of hiding it away and I'm surprised you didn't. After all, you were pretty good at destroying other things in those days, if I recall – like people's lives, for instance. Your conscience hasn't bothered you though, has it? Or those others you conspired with. The lot of you simply buried those nasty memories and walked away as if nothing had ever happened.

'You've all done pretty well for yourselves too. Money, position, civic honours, you've had it all – and I believe I am right in saying that the Reverend Andrew Cotter is actually tipped for an MBE in the New Year's Honours list because of his tireless work with disadvantaged children. Now that really is a success story, isn't it?'

The chair swung back to face the mirror again and his captor's face was once more reflected in the glass below his own. 'Well, Andrew, the time has come for you to pay – just like Herbert Lyall and those others I have yet to chastise.'

A flicker of understanding showed in the clergyman's eyes and his tongue flicked along dry trembling lips. 'Please, you've got it all wrong,' he whispered.

There was a click and a hand appeared in the mirror, holding a thin blade between long violinist's fingers. 'Oh no,' the other said softly, 'I've got it exactly right. But I wanted us to have this little chat first, so there are no misunderstandings and you know precisely why you are being punished.'

'Punished?' Cotter's voice rose to a choking scream. 'Why, what are you going to do?'

'Do?' the other said. 'Why, I'm going to emasculate you, my dear Reverend, and then exhibit your shame to the world. But before that, I'm going to very slowly cut your throat – and you can watch the whole thing as it happens, just like on television.'

CHAPTER 11

THE MEDIA SIEGE of Saddler Street police station was still in full swing at eight the following morning when Fulton, early for once, drove into the police station car park on the opposite side of the road and reversed into a tight space between a CID car and a flashy BMW saloon that he knew, belonged to Superintendent Honeywell.

Pushing through the crush, he headed straight for the incident room, surprised to find not only Gilham waiting for him in his office, but Andy Stoller as well.

'You're up early, Andy,' he said, shrugging himself out of the heavy woollen coat he was wearing. 'Shit the bed or something?'

Stoller turned away from the window he had been facing for the best part of five minutes and thrust a copy of the regional daily towards him as if it had been a dagger. 'Think you'd better read this, Jack,' he said grimly. 'You may not feel quite so humorous afterwards.'

Fulton raised an eyebrow and cast a brief enquiring glance at his number two, but was treated to just a warning frown in reply. Sensing imminent meltdown (detective chief superintendents did not normally put in a personal appearance in incident rooms at just after eight in the morning), he dropped the newspaper on to his desk in an effort to maintain a protective air of indifference and draped his coat over the back of his chair. 'Don't tell me,' he said conversationally, 'Al Qaeda have blown up my favourite whisky distillery?'

Stoller treated Gilham to a curt nod, but the DCI knew when it was time to go and he was already heading for the door. 'Just read the front page, Jack,' the headquarters man grated as Gilham closed the door behind him.

With a reluctant sigh, Fulton retrieved the newspaper and held it up in front of him, only to tense noticeably when he read the headline and first few lines of text.

SLICER STRIKES AGAIN

Police hunting the killer of crown court judge, Colonel Herbert Lyall, are investigating the brutal murder of another local resident, who was found by a dog walker in his car at a derelict cement works with his throat cut. The dead man, who has yet to be formally identified, is believed to have been a valuable police informant and, according to an inside source, police believe both crimes were committed by the same man, whom local residents have nicknamed the Slicer....

'They've given the swine a *nickname*?' Fulton almost spat. 'Whose bloody idea was that?'

'The press themselves, I should think,' Stoller replied. 'A dramatic nickname always helps a story like this along. Remember the Yorkshire Ripper?'

Fulton shook his head several times, his anger practically boiling over once again. 'But how the hell did they get hold of all this info?' he snarled. 'It's just like last time. Some bastard on the team is leaking stuff – has to be.'

Stoller did not disagree. 'Maybe they are, but you know as well as I do that it is next to impossible to keep something like this under wraps,' he said. 'Anyway, I wasn't referring to that story, though heaven knows it's bad enough – I meant *this*!'

He pointed to a smaller boxed piece at the foot of the front page and this time the headline and opening paragraph made Fulton cringe.

SUPER'S TIME OUT

Despite leading the investigation into the grisly murder of an eminent crown court judge, Detective Superintendent Jack Fulton (otherwise known as *The Grunt*), still had time to relax yesterday afternoon. And what better way of doing that than with a nice cup of tea poured by the fair hand of Dr Abbey Lee, the forensic pathologist in the case, at her mews terrace home in the upmarket Grove area of the city. Who said crime investigation was dull?

Beside the story was a photograph of himself leaving the house with Abbey, which bore the caption 'Suitably refreshed'.

'ACC ops has done his crust over this,' Stoller went on, trying to keep calm, but failing miserably. 'Damn it, Jack, why the hell did you have to go *home* with her? The SIO in a murder case fraternizing with an expert witness? It's totally out of order and you know it.'

Fulton glanced at the newspaper again and stabbed a finger at the boxed story. 'Bloody McGuigan! How was I to know he was lurking around outside?'

Stoller raised his eyes to the ceiling. 'Jack, this isn't about McGuigan. You're missing the whole point. If we catch our killer, Abbey Lee will be providing vital forensic evidence. Any cute brief is bound to try and use your association with her to discredit that evidence, don't you see?'

'Yeah, of course I see. But there was nothing in it. We didn't even discuss the case.'

'That doesn't enter into it. The implication is enough and when the press find out our key suspect is a serving officer who has gone missing, how do you think that will look – especially if he turns out to be innocent? They'll shout "fix" from every newspaper stand in the country.'

Fulton suddenly looked drained and his hand shook slightly as he settled heavily on the corner of the desk and stared down at his scuffed shoes. 'So what happens now?' he said after a pause, raising his head to peer at Stoller.

Stoller turned to face the window again. 'Nothing – yet,' he replied with his back towards him. 'By rights you should be off the case, and that *has* been considered, believe me, but it would send out the wrong message and play right into the hands of the media. So you're staying with it for the time being, but,' and his expression was bleak as he turned to face Fulton again, 'one more cock-up and you might as well grab your pension and run while you still have it to look forward to. Do I make myself clear?'

Fulton hesitated a second, thinking of Dee Honeywell's report about his unauthorized vehicle check and his errant wife's possible complaint of assault. 'Totally clear,' he replied.

Stoller looked unconvinced, but left it there. 'Good. Now, any further developments on the inquiry itself?'

Fulton quickly got a grip on himself and brought his boss up to date, including details on the murder of Lenny Baker, though he guessed that the head of force CID would know most of it by now anyway.

'And anything new on this missing PC Derringer?'

'None. He seems to have vanished off the face of the earth.'

'Looking at his background, he seems an unlikely suspect.'

'Yeah, but then why run?'

'Maybe he was carrying other baggage.'

Fulton thought of Mickey Vansetti and nodded. 'Something I'm looking into.'

'ACC operations thinks you should be looking into holding a press conference too.'

'Oh, he does, does he?'

'Yes, he feels we should be using the media rather than ignoring them. Appeals for witnesses, that sort of thing.'

'Well, I don't, not at this early stage anyway. We have nothing more we can tell them other than what they have got hold of already and HQ press office has already put out a press release, asking for witnesses.'

'Maybe, but television has more of an impact, especially when the SIO is in front of a camera.'

'There's no way I'm doing that until I have something worthwhile to say. Besides, it would be daft for me to stick my head above the parapet just after that story about Abbey Lee and myself has hit the front page – I'd be hung out to dry.'

Stoller looked uncomfortable. 'Well, I'm afraid you're having a conference, whether you like it or not.'

Fulton's face froze. 'What did you say?'

Stoller shrugged. 'ACC ops has instructed the press office to set one up here at ten-thirty, straight after your morning incident team briefing. Caroline James, the force press officer, is coming over to hold your hand.'

Fulton lurched to his feet, his fists clenched angrily. 'Like hell! Who does Skellet think he is?'

Stoller raised an eyebrow. 'The assistant chief constable operations, I believe,' he answered. 'And as such, he outranks both of us.'

'*I*'m SIO. *I* decide if and when to hold press conferences.'

Stoller shook his head. 'Not this time, Jack.' He retrieved his newspaper from the table and turned for the door. 'Oh, by the way, Mr Skellet also asked if you had considered using the services of one of our criminal profilers yet? Seems appropriate under the circumstances. You know, two stiffs, no leads – that sort of thing.'

Fulton looked about ready to explode. 'Any other advice *Sherlock* Skellet might want to pass on?' he grated. 'Like which eggs I should suck first?'

Stoller chuckled, more than a glint of mischief in his eyes. 'Nothing that comes to mind, Jack. No, that's about it, I think. Oh no, tell a lie, there is one more thing I should mention before I head back to the "big house". Arrangements have been made for one of the press office liaison assistants to be on hand here from now on to deal with all press enquiries. Find a suitable office, for them will you?'

The press conference, which had been set up in the police station's old parade room, was a total disaster, just as Fulton had predicted. After being virtually ignored for the best part of two days, the media were in an ugly vindictive mood and very definitely out for blood. Once they found Fulton had nothing new to tell them and that what he did have he wasn't prepared to divulge, they got personal and concentrated instead on his relationship with Abbey Lee.

After a tense, totally unproductive incident room briefing, he needed this kind of hostility like a hole in the head. Nevertheless, at first he tolerated the insinuations as to be expected under the circumstances, but when the questions got more and more vitriolic, he started to lose the small amount of patience he possessed. In the end, sensing that things were about to fall apart on them, Caroline James brought the conference to an abrupt close and ushered him from the room.

But Fulton's problems were not over even then, for his mobile phone rang as he headed back to his office. It was Abbey Lee and he grimaced when he recognized her voice.

'What the devil's going on, Jack?' she demanded. 'Have you seen the newspapers?'

He cleared his throat. 'Wouldn't help if I said no, I suppose?' he replied.

'Jack, do you realize what they're implying? I'm damned furious.'

'I'm not best pleased either, Ab.'

'Coroner's been on to me and he's not a happy man – especially as I gather the opening inquest on Lyall is likely to be on Monday next.'

'It's all down to a little creep called Ewan McGuigan …' he began, then tensed as Phil Gilham appeared through the double doors at the end of the corridor, obviously in something of a hurry.

'I don't care who's responsible, Jack. What are we going to do about it?'

'Nothing we can do, Ab. Just keep our heads down and think of England. See you at the inquest when it's confirmed, OK?'

Before she could say anything else, he ended the call by snapping the cover of his mobile shut and turned to meet his number two, raising an expectant eyebrow when he saw the agitation on his face. 'Problem?' he queried.

Gilham nodded. 'Derringer,' he replied.

'Don't tell me the DNA result on his car is back already?'

'Hardly that quick – not even for a judge – but apparently, since SOCO found the stained carpet and sent it off to the lab, the car was stripped out and something even more interesting was found under one of the rear seats.'

Fulton motioned him into an adjacent office. 'Which was?'

'Torn bit of an old-style driving licence in the name of Herbert Benjamin Lyall. The car's a hatchback, so the piece of paper must have slid under the seat from the boot when it fell out of Lyall's pocket.'

Fulton lit a cigarette and stared unseeing at the uniform patrol beat plan pinned to the wall. 'So, even without the DNA result, Derringer is well in the frame then?'

'Got to be.'

The big man shook his head, his frustration evident. 'I don't think it's as simple as that, Phil. There's more than one thing going down here.'

'What do you mean?'

Fulton quickly told him about his encounter with the intruder at Derringer's flat and his visit to Vansetti. Gilham's mouth dropped. 'You're still doing it, Jack, aren't you?'

'Doing what?'

'Your own thing – going it alone.'

'Don't talk bollocks! Something was nagging at me. I had to follow it up.'

'So you took off on a one-man raid?'

Fulton ignored the sarcasm. 'At least we know what Derringer was up to.'

'And you think that's the only reason he bolted?'

'Well, it seems a good enough one to me.'

'Despite everything pointing to the contrary then, you don't think Derringer is our murderer?'

'I can't say that. I just think the whole thing is a lot more complicated.'

'Then how did Lyall's driving licence get in the boot of Derringer's patrol car? Come on, Jack, it isn't like you to look for things that aren't there.'

Fulton scowled. 'Something's been playing on my mind, Phil, ever since we found Lenny Baker, but I can't put my finger on it. Something I saw or something someone said.' He shook his head. 'It's been bugging me ever since.'

'OK, so let's humour you for a moment. If Derringer isn't our man, who the hell is?'

'I'm a copper, not a clairvoyant.'

'OK, so maybe we should consider calling for more specialist assistance – like a profiler, for instance?'

Fulton visibly started, his eyes narrowing suspiciously. 'What made you say that?' he snapped. 'Someone been talking to you?'

Gilham looked bewildered. '*Talking* to me?' he repeated. 'No, not at all. I just thought – well, it's early days yet, I know, but we've nothing to lose and we *have* used profilers before.'

The big man grunted, stubborn pride making him dig his heels in almost up to his neck. 'Don't go there, Phil, OK?' he retorted, his face hard and uncompromising. 'Just don't go there.'

Gilham had known his boss for far too long to try and pursue something when he was in this obstructive frame of mind, but he was determined to make his point anyway. 'OK,' he said with a resigned shrug, 'forget the profiler for now then, but with Derringer on his toes, local enquiries so far turning up little of value and the results of forensic analysis still awaited, maybe you can tell me precisely what else we *should* be doing?'

Fulton didn't answer the question, but snapped his fingers as another thought occurred to him. 'What about the vehicle mileage book? All police vehicles have them to record who drove where and when. That should narrow things down a bit.'

There was the suggestion of a smirk on Gilham's face now. 'Already tried that. Book's gone walkabout.'

'What?'

'Yeah, we've done a thorough search of the nick and all that, but so far, nothing.'

Fulton propped himself on the edge of a desk. 'Then either Derringer dumped it or …'

Both men exchanged glances.

'Someone else did,' Gilham finished for him. 'Which means if Derringer isn't the killer, another of our finest is.'

Fulton nodded, his expression bleak. 'And either way, we've got a psycho cop on the loose,' he said. 'I can't think of anything worse, can you?'

Before Gilham could answer, his own mobile rang and his face was ashen when he turned to face his boss. 'Control room, Jack,' he said simply. 'Apparently we've got another stiff. And, by all accounts, it's worse than the last two.'

Fulton stubbed out his cigarette. 'Got any more good news up your sleeve, Phil?' he commented drily.

CHAPTER 12

THE REVEREND Andrew Cotter had not had a good death – that much was reflected in the bulging eyes and the terrified expression on the grey contorted face – and as Gilham tore his gaze away from the horrific spectacle, he desperately tried to hold his quivering stomach in check to prevent it from jettisoning everything it contained.

The small market town of Axton, just ten miles from Maddington, had witnessed more than its fair share of blood and violence over the centuries. The soldiers of Henry VIII had put a score of its residents to the sword on the steps of its Norman church for opposing the dissolution of the monasteries and Oliver Cromwell had left his own bloody mark on the town during the Civil War because of its Royalist connections. In World War II Hitler's Luftwaffe had bombed Axton as part of an attack on the nearby airfield and, more recently, an armed robbery at the local post office had left two people dying from shotgun wounds when the postmistress had sounded the alarm and the gunman had lost his head, blasting the customers at close range as he fled.

But for sheer premeditated savagery, the latest atrocity took some beating and it had been left for all to see in the playground of the local Church of England nursery school, a few hundred yards off the ancient paved square.

Like Herbert Lyall, Cotter's throat had been slashed open by a sharp blade and his naked corpse – wearing just his clerical collar and mutilated in exactly the same way as the late judge – had been dumped on a swing, the wrists and thighs lashed to it by rope to keep him in a grotesque sitting position.

Fortunately the police had got to the scene quickly, putting up screens borrowed from the school itself to hide the corpse from public view until the SOCO tent could be erected, and as it was the autumn half-term, the school was closed for the week, sparing the children a sight which would have traumatized them for years to come. Nevertheless, word had got round and the uniformed bobbies present were having a hard time keeping onlookers at bay as the newly arrived scenes-of-crime team unloaded their kit in the playground nearby, closely watched by a stern-faced Barbara Molloy, the crime scene manager.

'Likes his swings, our man, doesn't he?' Gilham murmured, coughing discreetly into his handkerchief.

Fulton ignored the comment, his attention drawn towards the crowd of onlookers beyond the gates and the familiar figure standing at the front, with his camera aimed in their direction. 'Bloody McGuigan,' he said. 'On the ball as usual. Wonder if he got another sealed envelope through his letterbox last night?'

'Got here even before local plods, guv,' Ben Morrison's gruff voice commented at his elbow. 'Skipper had to turf him out of playground.'

Fulton glared at the pressman, his fists clenching involuntarily when McGuigan waved back. 'So who found the body?' he said, turning to face his DI.

'Caretaker, guv,' Morrison replied. 'Name of Tom Sykes. Come in to check place at ten. Does it every morning when school's closed. Saw matey on swing, but from gate he couldn't see who it was. Thought it might be a nutter or one of local lads stuck there by his mates as a prank after a boozy night out. Went over to him to tell him to clutter off, then saw it was Cotter.'

Fulton looked back at the knot of spectators in the street outside the iron gates. 'So which one is this Tom Sykes?'

'None of 'em, guv. Gone home. In a right state he was too.'

Fulton glared at him. 'You let him go home?'

'No choice. He was out of it. Anyway, I had a good chat with him before he went and one of team is already on way round to interview him and take a statement.'

'And do we know who the dead man is?'

'Local clergyman – Reverend Andrew Cotter. Well known hereabouts, according to Sykes. Vicar of both St Peter's in Studley Gorton down the road and St John the Baptist in square here. Tipped for an MBE in New Year's Honours list.'

'So why dump his body here, I wonder?'

'Dunno, but seems he was a school founder and is – was – chairman of governors.'

Fulton started. 'The hell he was!' he grated. 'And Lyall was a founder of the recreation ground where *he* was dumped, wasn't he?'

'Now that *is* a bit of a coincidence,' Gilham commented.

Fulton snorted. 'Coincidence? It's a damned sight more than that, Phil. Both victims castrated, both with their throats cut, both tied to swings in places they were personally associated with and both left bollock naked except for the insignia of their bloody offices? There's a message here for us and we need to find out what it is.'

He turned back to Morrison. 'So where did our vicar live?'

'Rectory, just behind church over there.'

Fulton stared back along the lane towards the imposing Norman spire. 'Anyone been over to it yet?'

'Yeah. Got place covered by uniform until we can get inside for a look-see. Cotter's wife's away in Bournemouth visiting sister and house is locked up like Fort Knox. Local Bill's trying to trace her as we speak.'

'So who identified him?'

'Only Tom Sykes so far, though there don't seem any doubt about it. Sykes doubles as sexton at St John's and St Peter's, so he works with Cotter a lot. Mrs Cotter should be able to do a formal ID when we get hold of her to break the news.'

Fulton grunted. 'I wouldn't like to be the poor sod delivering that death message.'

Morrison shrugged. 'Know what they say, guv? If you can't stand a joke, you shouldn't have joined.'

Fulton shot him a scathing glance, but ignored the insensitive remark. 'And when was he last seen?'

Morrison reddened under his gaze. 'Er – special service at St Peter's last night. Seemed a bit jittery, according to Sykes – anxious to finish. Said he would lock up afterwards, which was a bit unusual for him – especially as job is normally done by verger. Also, rectory is in Axton so he'd have had to drive back here anyway when he'd finished.'

Fulton's eyes narrowed. 'Sounds like St Peter's might be worth a visit when we're done here.'

Morrison nodded towards a group of uniformed officers assisting with the assembly of the SOCO tent. 'Nothing more can be done here now anyway, guv. Babs Molloy has everything under control and Abbey Lee, Home Office pathologist, already en route.'

'Abbey Lee?' Fulton made a rueful grimace and turned back towards the school gates. 'Then it's the church for us, Phil – and the sooner the better, I think.'

Gilham gave a mischievous grin as he followed his boss from the scene. 'Don't you want to hang on for her, Jack?' he said. 'She might like to talk to you about your next newspaper feature?'

Fulton threw a venomous glance at him over his shoulder. 'Quit while you're ahead, Phil,' he warned. 'Or it could be fatal!'

St Peter's was cold and dank, in stark contrast to the fragile sunlight outside, and an atmosphere of hostility was very evident as soon as the heavy porch doors were opened, almost as if the ancient building was a living thinking creature that knew its loyal custodian was now dead.

Gilham shivered as he closed the door behind him and followed Fulton along the tiled floor to the nave. 'Exactly what are we looking for, Jack?' he queried, instinctively lowering his voice to just above a whisper, his uneasiness palpable in this unfamiliar environment.

'How should I know?' Fulton growled. 'Sacristy would be a good place to start though, I fancy.'

Gilham stopped to peer up into the gloom of the vaulted roof. 'So where is this sacristy then?'

Fulton glanced about him for a moment, then waved a hand towards a curtained archway in the far corner. 'Probably in there, behind the choir vestry.'

Gilham threw him a quizzical look. 'You seem to know a lot about churches, Jack.' He grinned. 'Choirboy once, were you?'

Fulton ignored the jibe, instead moving on ahead of his companion, tight-lipped and uncommunicative. The last thing he needed was for his past links with the church to get out. He would never live it down and it would certainly put paid to the hard man image he had so carefully cultivated over the years.

The choir vestry was empty, the sacristy door at the far end closed with the key still in the lock. Fulton tried the heavy iron ring which served as a handle, but the door wouldn't budge. 'Locked,' he declared unnecessarily and turned the key sharply to one side. The door opened easily then and as he stepped into the small room beyond he raised his eyebrows in surprise. A table lamp burned brightly on a small desk opposite and another door behind the desk stood ajar, admitting a trickle of sunlight. 'Seems someone was working late and forgot to turn off the lamp,' he added.

Gilham crossed to the other door and pushed it wide, revealing a gravel path separating the church from the encircling graveyard. 'Forgot to shut the door after them as well,' he replied.

Fulton frowned. 'This is a funny business,' he said. 'I can accept the light being accidentally left on in here, but why would the door to the choir vestry be locked, with the key on the other side? Surely Cotter would have robed up in the sacristy, then gone through the choir vestry to take the service?'

Gilham nodded, this time failing to pick up on the big man's apparent familiarity with devotional procedure. 'If you say so. And I can't understand why the external door was left open, either. I don't know a lot about churches, but isn't the sacristy the room where all the sacred artcfacts are kept? Looks like the cupboard for them over there in the corner. It doesn't make sense for the outside door to be left open, inviting any passing tea leaf to pop in.'

Fulton dropped into the chair behind the desk, rubbing his face with one large hand, as if trying to wipe his frustration away with his own perspiration. 'Nothing about this case makes sense. To start with, why the hell is our killer obsessed with swings? What's the crazy bastard trying to tell us? And why does he snatch his victims, top them and then take the trouble to dump their mutilated bodies in some public place or other like a sodding Turner art exhibit?'

He jerked open the topmost of the three drawers, absently flicking through the bundles of papers inside. Finding nothing of interest, he turned his attention to the second drawer.

Gilham watched him a moment from the doorway, a curious expression on his face. 'What *are* we looking for, Jack?' he said for the second time since their arrival.

Fulton slammed the second drawer shut and went for the third, tugging hard on the brass stud, then swearing when it stayed closed. 'Blast the thing,' he snarled. 'Locked.'

Gilham closed his eyes in resignation as his boss produced a small penknife and inserted the blade into the top of the drawer. A sharp 'crack' and it slid open. 'Jack!'

Fulton looked up briefly, then began leafing through the contents. 'I reckon Cotter may have been meeting someone here,' he said.

'Where on earth did you get that idea from?'

'Elementary, my dear Watson.' The big man grinned. There was nothing he liked better than baiting his number two. 'Think about it, Phil. Our victim was jittery, wanted to get the service over quickly and then volunteered to stay on to close up. Had to be because he had an appointment with someone.'

Gilham nodded approvingly. 'Very good, Holmes, but it still doesn't answer the mystery of the locked door. Why would he lock the sacristy door from the other side, then come all the way round the church to meet someone in here, using the external door?'

'Maybe he didn't – maybe he was running.'

'Running?'

'Yeah. It's just possible that he locked the door to prevent someone going after him.'

'But they only had to go round the outside of the church to one of the other doors to head him off.'

'Perhaps that's just what they did. That's why Cotter ended up with a slit throat.'

Fulton slammed drawer number three shut and sat back in his chair with a sullen face. 'Bills, Bibles and bugger-all else,' he grated.

Gilham shrugged. 'What did you expect to find in a vicar's desk?'

Fulton lurched to his feet and stared out into the graveyard. 'I'm not even sure myself,' he replied. 'Maybe a diary, a note – anything to move this bloody inquiry on.'

Gilham bent down beside him and retrieved a crumpled piece of paper from the carpet. 'Will this do?' he queried after studying it for a second. 'I thought I saw it fall out of one of the Bibles you picked up.'

'Eh?' Fulton turned quickly and leaned over his shoulder. The note was in block capitals and was unsigned, but the message got Fulton's heart going in a very big way.

REMEMBER DREW HOUSE? I SHALL NEVER FORGET IT! MEET ME TONIGHT AFTER THE SERVICE SO WE CAN REMINISCE – UNLESS YOU'D RATHER TALK TO THE POLICE?

'Nice one!' Fulton breathed and, snatching an envelope from a rack on the desk, opened it wide for Gilham to slip the note inside.

'A nice present for the lab,' Gilham observed.

'Yeah, and maybe SOCO will find something even better when they give this place the once over – like a few prints on the desk that shouldn't be there, for instance.' He cleared his throat. 'Apart from mine, of course.'

Gilham stared at him. 'We can't turn over a church sacristy.'

Fulton snorted. 'Why not? It's just another room.'

'But you'd have to close off the whole church while the team did their stuff. There'd be an outcry.'

'I'm used to outcries, remember?'

'And you'd need to speak to the church authorities anyway. We can't just walk in here.'

Fulton pushed past him through the open door. 'We did just now,' he retorted, pausing for a second on the gravel path. 'Anyway, you're going to have to stay here for a while to keep people out until I can get SOCO and some uniforms on site to relieve you. Meantime, I'll get control to dig out a member of the parochial church council – or whatever they're called round here – so we can make everything all nice and legal.'

'You mean you're actually going to dump me here without any wheels?'

Fulton shrugged. 'Can't avoid it, Phil. Scene needs preserving.' He grinned for the first time with something akin to real humour. 'Anyway, you could always say a prayer while you're waiting. In fact, you could even try and say one for me.'

George Oates froze, the cheese-and-pickle sandwich halfway to his mouth. Not again, he thought.

'Morning, George,' Fulton said curtly, then looked at his watch. 'Or is it afternoon now?'

Oates got the message and set the sandwich down on a pile of criminal-record forms on his desk, watching the pickle dribble down between the slices and trail across the topmost report. 'It's lunchtime actually, guv,' he replied.

Fulton ignored the hint and dumped himself in his usual chair. 'Drew House?' he snapped. 'Heard of it?'

'No. Should I have done?'

'I thought you LIOs knew everything?'

Oates sighed and pushed himself away from his desk. 'What is it you want this time, guv?'

'Quite simple really. I want to know about Drew House.'

Oates thought a second and shook his head. 'Then I can't help you. I said I've never heard of it.'

Fulton lit a cigarette, ignoring his grimace. 'Nothing on your wonder box then? Or do I have to ask someone else to look it up?'

Oates turned back to his computer, firing it up and playing with the mouse for a few seconds. 'Told you,' he said after some moments. He swung back on his swivel-chair towards his visitor. 'Nothing there.'

Fulton lurched to his feet and bent over the machine, catching the search name at the top as Oates closed the page down. 'Spelling never was your strong point, George, was it?' he growled. 'The name is spelled D-r-e-w, not B-r-u-e. And it's Drew House, not *Place*! Do it again.'

Oates took a deep breath and tapped the keys, his patience obviously wearing thin, but this time his search did at least produce a result. The name Drew House snapped into place above a black-and-white etching of a sombre-looking Victorian mansion set in extensive grounds.

Fulton scanned the full page of text beneath, reading selected bits aloud: 'Drew House ... Little Culham ... Built 1846 by Sir Henry Havers-Price on site of 'plague' hamlet of

Drew, which was razed by Cromwell's troops in 1653 after allegations of witchcraft ... Norman church only building left standing and absorbed by estate ... House itself home of Havers-Price family for four generations ... Bequeathed to Leister Heritage Trust in 1957 after death of Sir Charles Havers-Price, reclusive last in line ...'

He skated over the rest of the text to the penultimate paragraph, then continued reading aloud, but in a much more precise tone. 'Opened June 1958 as Drew House Academy, an independent school for boys ... Closed May 1974 and six years later utilized as a boarding clinic for rehabilitation of young people suffering from drug addiction ... Closed after arson destroyed building November 1993 ... House and church earmarked for restoration by Leister Heritage Trust, but project currently suspended due to ongoing legal dispute with church commissioners over ownership of church ...' He straightened up. 'Is that all the Internet has?'

'Well, it *is* a site dedicated to English country houses, as you'd see on the other pages – pure National Trust type stuff.'

'OK, so come out of the Internet and try your local box. Place was torched, so there should be a crime report somewhere in there.'

Oates tapped away again. The screen produced a blue-tinted page this time and after a few minutes' searching, the relevant report appeared. Fulton leaned over the LIO's shoulder, his eagerness palpable. 'Drew House Clinic, Little Culham,' he recited, picking out the salient points in the crime report. 'Arson ... Between 0005 hrs and 0015 hrs 6 October 1993 ... Time of report 0010 hrs ... Reported by senior nurse, Angela Grange.'

He continued to read on: 'Fire believed to have been started in library by former patient, Edward Heath, who broke into premises whilst under influence of lysergic acid. Both Heath and principal psychologist, Julian Score, perished in blaze.'

He made a waving motion with one hand. 'Take it down to the bottom. I want to see who the officer in the case was. Maybe he can put some flesh on the bones.'

Oates complied and Fulton whistled. 'Detective Superintendent Nick Halloran? Now *there's* a name to get the nose twitching.'

The LIO nodded. 'I remember him. Bent, wasn't he?'

The big man emitted a grim laugh. 'You can say that again. Bastard was well on the take. Got five years' porridge for trying to bury evidence on some tom he was seeing to. They found him hanged in his cell. Alleged suicide, but I was never too sure about that. He had a lot of enemies in the nick.' He shook his head. 'Well, that's one avenue of enquiry we definitely can't pursue.'

He stared at the screen for a little longer, as if willing something to appear that wasn't there, the fingers of one hand tapping out a rhythm on the desk. 'OK, get me a copy of everything you have anyway.'

Oates shrugged. 'Only the information you've just seen is available on our local box. The crime was categorized as "detected", so you'll have to go to the old archived microfiche records for more detail – if the case wasn't wiped off the system when everything was computerized.'

'I'll have what's here anyway – plus your country-house stuff.'

'You're the boss.'

Fulton stepped back to light a cigarette and watched as the copies spilled out of the printer's maw. 'Do we have a full address and how to get there?' he queried, leafing through them. 'Just says Little Culham here.'

Oates sighed again, casting a regretful eye at his cheese-and-pickle sandwich. 'Place has gone now, guv,' he replied. 'What's the point in an address?'

Fulton's gaze hardened. 'The *point*, George, is that I want the address, OK?'

Oates returned to the previous English Country House site, his skilful fingers producing another page, which he scanned quickly before printing it. 'Place will be just a ruin now – tenanted by ghosts.'

Fulton nodded. 'Well, maybe it's time to do a bit of ghost-hunting, eh? Even ghosts sometimes have a tale to tell.'

CHAPTER 13

THE RUINS THAT had once been Drew House hid behind a seven-foot-high brick wall on the outskirts of Little Culham; only the nest of tall Victorian chimneys was visible from the road. Vandals had sprayed the green-and-gold sign with black paint, but the name was still just visible and, peering closer, Fulton was able to read the proud inscription underneath: 'Free the mind and lighten the soul.'

The rusted iron gates, though pulled across the entrance, opened easily on well-oiled hinges and he saw tyre marks in the track which cut through the trees. 'Not as abandoned as you pretend, are you?' he murmured to himself as he got back into his car.

The track was at least a quarter of a mile long and it ended in a wide paved courtyard with a derelict fountain in the centre. The charred overgrown shell behind it would have delighted the location manager of any Gothic horror film; its empty windows staring at him coldly like the rotted eye-sockets of something unclean, and he shivered as he climbed out of his car and headed for the main entrance.

Vandals had been here too. Crudely painted swastikas and obscene spray-can drawings plastered every available patch of bare stonework. Inside the building electric wiring hung down in liquorice-like festoons and ivy and other parasitic climbers sprouted from the broken floorboards and twisted their way up through the few remaining rafters, making their way out through the gaping holes in the roof.

Glass crunched under his feet as he picked his way through the debris and the familiar sour smell he always associated with derelict buildings welcomed him like a poisonous miasma.

He had no idea why he had come, no idea what he expected to find and as he made his way from room to room, he began to realize the futility of it all. Something had happened at Drew House a very long time ago, something undoubtedly connected with the fire which had consumed the building. But why had that 'something' driven a deranged mind to kill after a gap of fifteen years? And where did Cotter and Lyall fit into the puzzle? There were so many questions that needed answers. Yet there was nothing to see among the ruins, except darkness and decay.

Pausing in a long corridor below a collection of blackened spars that had obviously once been a staircase, he lit a cigarette and leaned against the wall, thinking of the sinister note Phil Gilham had picked up in the sacristy of St Peter's Church. REMEMBER DREW HOUSE? I SHALL NEVER FORGET IT!

'Why won't you forget it?' he said aloud, jumping at the sound of his own voice in the silence. 'What won't you forget?'

Then he stiffened to the sound of a loud 'bang', like a door slamming or something heavy falling over, which seemed to come from the back of the house.

He eased himself off the wall and advanced further along the corridor, wincing every time he crunched glass or other debris underfoot, but grateful for the shards of pale sunlight probing the gloom around him, enabling him to negotiate the more dangerous obstacles ahead without using the torch he had brought with him.

He found a large square hall, now almost completely open to the sky, which had no doubt once served as the dining room, going by the few remaining bench seats and tables that were still in evidence. Then, just beyond it, the kitchens, still with the shells of the rusted but dismembered gas ranges *in situ*. He paused to listen again, remembering his close encounter in Derringer's flat and anxious not to be caught unawares this time – particularly if that meant getting another lecture from Phil Gilham on going it alone.

He heard no further banging sounds as he ducked through the back door, but glimpsed a ghostly stab of light in the window of a small church on the far side of a derelict kitchen garden. He hesitated. Big and ugly as he was, he knew he was not invincible and just now he was breaking every rule in the book by not calling for back-up. But curiosity, coupled with pride in his toughie reputation, spurred him on regardless.

The spectral light did not reappear as he crossed the garden. Reaching the church itself he began to ask himself if he had actually seen it at all or whether that momentary flash had been just a figment of his imagination or a trick of the dying sun.

By the look of it, the grey stone building was as much a ruin as Drew House itself, even though it had at least escaped the fire that had engulfed the Victorian mansion. The stained-glass windows at the front – or south wall, according to the Ordnance Survey map he had brought with him (this church seemed to have been built facing in the traditional direction, unlike St Peter's) – had been totally destroyed, probably by the bricks of the same vandals who had daubed their graffiti on the house walls. The ragged holes in the slate-tiled pitched roof also bore testimony, not only to the ravages of time, but the energies of other unscrupulous desecrators who had stripped away much of the lead that had once sealed the building against the elements.

On the face of it there did not seem to be much to commend this pile of holy bricks and certainly very little to attract a casual visitor, save perhaps a wandering tramp or a teenage runaway looking for shelter. Yet Fulton's nose had developed a significant twitch that he could not ignore.

Trying the double doors in the entrance porch, he found that both opened with less resistance than he would have expected. He ran a hand down one hinge and smelled oil on his fingers. So, despite the apparent dereliction of the place, someone had thought it necessary to ensure ease of access, had they? Now that *was* interesting.

The gloom inside the church seemed to be much more dense than that in the house and something – probably a bat – flapped past him and up towards the weak strands of sunlight filtering through the holes in the roof. He pulled out his torch and directed the beam down the nave, touching on the dismembered pews on either side and fastening on the elaborately carved rood screen within the chancel arch. Seeing nothing, he picked his way through small piles of debris, past the bare stone pulpit, and paused before the entrance to the choir stalls and chancel itself. The marble altar was still intact, though split in places, but the cross had long since gone and the branches of a mature tree now reached through the empty chancel window like a demon hand groping for prey.

Silence, except for the nervous flapping of wings high up in the vaulted roof. He frowned, conscious, not for the first time over the last few days, of the rapid thudding of his heart. Something had been going on in here, something he had interrupted – he could feel it in his water – but what?

Turning, he shone his torch back down the nave. Again, zilch. No lurking figures or signs of movement. Just the rows of pews, hunched up in the gloom like broken teeth. OK, so if there *had* been an intruder, where had he disappeared to?

He trailed the beam along the south wall, picking out half-obliterated texts inscribed on inset stone tablets. He started briefly when a headless statue seemed physically to lurch into view from a dark corner. More stone tablets on the north wall, with ivy cramming another empty window, but still nothing to suggest that anyone other than himself had disturbed the sepulchral stillness of the place for a very long time.

He was about ready to give up then – ready to put his suspicions down to an over-fertile imagination and head back to his car – and he would have done just that had his curiosity not been aroused by a low archway just feet away, almost buried in the gloom of the north-east corner. Moving closer, he discovered a short flight of stone steps going down into the archway, no doubt affording access to some sort of chapel, but further progress was prevented by a large wooden chest, bound with iron, which blocked the entrance.

The chest was obviously very old and though his knowledge of ecclesiastical things was pretty limited despite his background, he guessed that it had probably once been the church's strongbox, containing the priest's vestments and possibly such things as the churchwarden's accounts and parish registers – now likely to be on sale at a car boot somewhere or forming part of a local historian's illicit collection. Plainly, the box was empty, for it was missing its lid, and it struck him as a little strange for someone to have taken the trouble to drag the thing across the archway steps when they could quite easily have left it in the north aisle with the rest of the rubbish.

It only took a few minutes heaving at the chest – which was still fairly heavy despite being reduced to a shell – for him to make his surprise discovery. The archway, it seemed, had once held a recessed door and the reason for its appearing so low was that it opened off a square paved area some six feet below the level of the church floor. Like many of the north doors found in old churches, this one had for some reason been bricked up, but someone had evidently decided to *un*brick part of it. There was now a ragged hole in the base of the cement-faced stonework, a hole which would not have been visible from the aisle above even without the presence of the chest.

The hole itself was large enough to crawl through, but he chose to check out what was on the other side before chancing his arm. The beam of his torch streamed down a second, much longer flight of stone steps, which dropped away at a forty-five degree angle into a heavy claustrophobic blackness laden with the earthy smell of the grave.

He made a face in the darkness. The steps almost certainly led to a crypt, but if that was the case, why had someone taken it into their head to seal up the entrance door? Even more mystifying, why had someone decided to break it open again? Maybe he would find the answer when he got down there.

Crawling through the opening on his hands and knees, he straightened up gingerly on the other side, expecting his head to connect with the roof, but to his relief he discovered that there were several inches to spare. Raising one hand against the wall to steady himself, he began a cautious descent, his torch thrust out in front of him as if it were the cross of an exorcist seeking to ward off evil spirits.

There was a heavy wooden door at the bottom, which proved to be closed but unlocked, and although the iron ring that served as a handle turned easily enough, it released the latch with a sharp 'crack' that set a score of echoes reverberating and could not have announced his presence more effectively than if he had actually fallen down the steps.

As it turned out, however, there was no one to announce his presence *to*, anyway, for the room on the other side of the door proved to be completely deserted, but any disappointment he might have felt over the absence of any intruder was instantly eclipsed by what he was confronted with instead. He had expected to find himself in a crypt, which was logical under the circumstances, but, whilst the place might originally have been constructed for the interment of the dead, it had more recently been adapted for an altogether different, more chilling purpose; a purpose clearly revealed by the nature of its contents. There were no tombs here anymore, but what was in their place had the effect of anaesthetizing his brain with the blinding intensity of an acetylene flame.

Phil Gilham had had just about enough of the musty gloom of St Peter's church and the pious indignation of church warden, Ernest Clapper, who had arrived on the scene unannounced just after Fulton had left and had shown more interest in preserving the sanctity of his pile of stones than helping the police detect the murder of the incumbent minister. Not surprisingly, the hard-pressed DCI could hardly conceal his relief when the SOCO team arrived and Clapper was banished to the other side of the blue-and-white crime-scene tape, allowing him to be chauffeured back to the relative normality of Saddler Street police station in a local area car.

But his anticipated appointment with the incident room's coffee machine was kicked into touch when Ben Morrison waylaid him en route. 'Derringer's turned up,' the DI announced through a wodge of pink chewing gum.

Gilham felt a new rush of adrenaline. 'Turned up where?'

'Casualty Department, Middle Moor hospital.'

'You mean he's injured?'

'Yeah, sounds like he got a pasting from someone. Anonymous call made to Ambulance Control who picked him up from a motel near Helmscott airfield. Been trying to fix up a private flight to Ireland with local flying school apparently.'

'So he *was* doing a runner?'

'Looks like it – and someone took exception to it.'

'Is he badly hurt?'

Morrison frowned. 'Bit of a going over, I hear. Busted face, couple of cracked ribs, but not life-threatening. Hospital keeping him in overnight for obs.'

'Do we have someone there?'

'Yeah, local plod babysitting him for us.'

Gilham glanced round the incident room. 'So where's the guv'nor?'

'Dunno. Stuck his head round door a while ago to ask me to check some microfiche records, then cleared off somewhere. Been gone a couple of hours.'

'Microfiche? That's going back a bit. What records were those?'

'Some fire – arson – place called Drew House. Said he wanted to look at statements, press reports and other docs.'

Remembering the note he had found in the church, Gilham started. 'A fire, you say? So the place was torched, was it? Now that *is* interesting.'

'Is it? Buggered if I know why. Seems it happened around fifteen years ago so local box ain't got much on it.' The DI shrugged. 'Not that archives could do any better. Hard-copy file has gone walkies and old microfiche records have been wiped. Just a copy of crime report on system now.'

'I don't like the smell of that.'

'Nor will guv'nor when he finds out – especially as he already knows IO in case was Nick Halloran.'

'What, *the* Nick Halloran? The one they called *Corkscrew*?'

'The same.'

Gilham made a face. 'And you haven't let Mr Fulton know about the file yet?'

'Did me best. Mobile *and* home number, but no response. Control still trying to get hold of him.'

'You mean he's gone AWOL?'

'Don't ask me.'

'So what the hell do we do about Derringer? Boss'll want to see him first, you know that.'

Morrison shrugged. 'Your call, not mine.'

Gilham wrestled with the implications of this for a few moments. 'OK, tell control to keep at it. Then meet me in the car park. We'll just have to go and see Derringer ourselves.'

'Guv'nor won't like it.'

'Guv'nor's not here, is he?'

Morrison chewed furiously for a second. 'Your funeral,' he said and grinned. 'Glad I'm only a DI.'

The Marquis de Sade would have felt entirely at home in the crypt under Drew House's small church. In the dank decaying atmosphere Fulton could practically smell the pain and misery of the pitiful souls who must have suffered here at the hands of their perverted tormentors.

He saw the wire cage first: a sinister-looking device shaped like the torso and legs of a man, suspended from steel chains bolted to the roof. He didn't need a history degree to know what it would have been used for and he jumped when it stirred slightly in the sudden rush of air that accompanied him into the room, as if the ghost of the last emaciated wretch who had been clasped in its cruel embrace was still present and mischievously trying to set the thing swinging.

Moving cautiously round the room, his torch probing the Stygian darkness, he found other devices tucked away in alcoves and deep corners – among them, an oblong mediaeval style rack complete with rollers, chains and winding handle, an overturned brazier which had been burned right through at the bottom and a long wooden table fitted with a series of leather straps and set with rows of retractable iron spikes operated by a small wheel at one end.

Exactly when the instruments of torture had replaced the tombs of the deceased was a matter of conjecture – if there had ever been any tombs in the crypt in the first place. Perhaps the Havers-Price family had installed the things themselves to satisfy some penchant for depraved thrills. And there again, perhaps not. He had no idea precisely how old the church was. The Internet write-up he had scanned in the LIO's office had indicated that it pre-dated Drew House by several hundred years and though it was unlikely from the apparent condition of the devices that they had been *in situ* that long, they could still have been put here before the mansion was built.

Whoever *was* responsible, however, they had obviously not felt it necessary to destroy the evidence when they tired of their depraved sport; no doubt because they had not thought anyone would ever break through the bricked-up archway and discover what they had abandoned anyway. As a result, everything had just been left to rust or rot away beneath the floor of the church, pulleys and chains silent, screws and bolts seized; a chilling legacy buried in the haunted blackness of a real-life chamber of horrors.

He would have been content to leave things as they were, too; prepared to accept that what he had stumbled upon was nothing more than old history; an assortment of hideous relics of past sadism, which had no relevance to the present day or the current murder investigation. But then the beam of his torch penetrated further into the vault and he was confronted by cold reality.

He saw the spotlights first, a tight cluster rigged on a metal tower behind a high-backed chair – unlit, but still glittering in the torchlight. The scene reminded him of a programme he had once seen on television, where the contestant being questioned sat in a pool of light in an otherwise blacked-out room, but here, instead of a camera, there was a large mirror suspended from the ceiling on two chains just in front of the chair – a mirror in which, he knew instinctively, the hapless Herbert Lyall and Andrew Cotter had witnessed their own executions.

For several minutes he simply stood there, staring fixedly at what had to be the most significant and macabre discovery of his career, noting the thick black cables running from the tower to a small generator in the corner and detecting for the first time the strong odour of diesel, which provided a key indication of just how much planning must have gone into the Slicer's murderous operation.

Closer inspection of the chair reinforced this fact, for like the spotlights and generator, it belonged very much to the twenty-first century and as such, must have been installed only recently. It appeared to be made of black leather and was of the swivel type with an elongated section extending from the seat to the floor to support the legs. It looked very much like one of the chairs used in his local barber's hairdressing salon, but there the similarity ended. This particular chair had a unique piece of equipment attached to its modified headrest, consisting of a sinister-looking leather harness, obviously designed to fit a human head, with a wide band at the top and adjustable straps at the side. A pair of ratchet handcuffs dangled from each of the padded arms and he noted the tattered remains of light-coloured plastic tape still attached to the foot of the elongated section, which fluttered slightly in the draught from the open door.

Now he knew how the marks on Lyall's limbs had been made, and if any further confirmation were needed that he had stumbled on the butcher's lair, he got it when he turned away from the chair and his right shoe peeled off a soft sticky deposit in which he had been inadvertently standing.

Retching and coughing as a stream of hot acid spurted up into his gullet, he fumbled for his mobile phone, but even as he dialled the police control room number, he heard the unmistakable sound of footsteps ringing eerily on naked stone in the darkness above his head, footsteps that grew ever closer as they clumped their way down the flight of steps that he had just descended.

CHAPTER 14

DERRINGER WAS SITTING up in bed in the tiny side room off the top-floor corridor. He was propped up on pillows and looked as if he had been used as a punchbag by someone who liked to play rough. The uniformed constable sitting beside his bed closed his reading book with a bang and jumped to his feet as Gilham and Morrison appeared in the open doorway.

'Go and get yourself a coffee,' Gilham told him, flashing his warrant card, then dropping into the vacated chair. Morrison propped himself on the windowsill and probed a nostril with one podgy finger.

'What, no grapes?' Derringer wisecracked through his swollen lips, but winced as he attempted a grin.

'You can save the funnies for the crown court,' Gilham said. 'But somehow I don't think they'll laugh.'

'So this isn't a welfare visit then?' Derringer sneered. 'Don't know what the force is coming to. No interest in their staff anymore.'

'You little turd,' Morrison growled, but turned away to examine his other nostril when Gilham threw him a warning glance.

'So who did this to you?' Gilham continued. 'One of Vansetti's boys?'

'Shouldn't you be cautioning me or something?'

'You wanted welfare? I'm giving you welfare. OK?'

Derringer eased his neck into a more comfortable position. 'Maybe he thinks I was too successful on one of his tables and wants some of his dosh back.'

'Is Vansetti why you were doing a runner?'

Derringer gave a disparaging snort, then immediately raised a hand to his chest with a sharp cry of pain. 'Well, you can't seriously believe I had anything to do with those murders, can you?' he said through gritted teeth.

Gilham shrugged. 'Jury's out on that. But you're in deep poo anyway.'

'What, because I decided to quit the job without a formal resignation?'

'No, because part of a driving licence with Herbert Lyall's name on it was found in your patrol car, plus what looks suspiciously like bloodstains.'

For a few seconds Derringer just stared at him. 'But that's ridiculous.'

Gilham hesitated, thinking of PACE[1] and the rules of interview he was legally obliged to follow. 'John Derringer,' he began. 'I have reason to believe that—'

'Oh *p-lease*,' Derringer cut in.

Gilham carried on regardless, adding: 'You do not have to say anything, but it may harm your defence if—'

'I don't need that crap!' Derringer forced himself up off the pillows, his teeth gritted even more tightly against the pain. 'And anyway, for your information, I wasn't even driving my bloody car that night.'

Gilham foundered in the middle of the caution and Morrison started to ease himself off the windowsill. 'You what?'

Derringer slumped back in the bed, his eyes half-closed, his breathing harsh and irregular. 'Listen, when I went to get my keys after briefing, they were missing. You know the nick. All the vehicle keys are left hanging up on a board in the briefing room. Everyone has access to them. Spares are kept in the sergeants' office.'

'I'll need to check that out.'

'Surprised a super sleuth like you hasn't done it already. And while you're doing your checking, speak to Sergeant Andy Dunn. He couldn't find the spares either when I went to see him.'

'So why is it he hasn't reported them missing?'

'Why don't you ask him? Maybe it's because they turned up later, I don't know.'

'So you're saying you took another vehicle?'

'You really are catching on, aren't you? Fact is, someone had already pinched my usual area car – I checked the car park to make sure – so I took one of the two spares we've got.'

'Yet no one happened to notice your vehicle being driven by someone else? Bit odd that, isn't it?'

'Not when there are cars in and out of the car park all day and night and the car park itself is on the other side of the road to the nick. Who's to see? And anyway, who's going to bother checking the registration number of another police vehicle to verify that the right copper is behind the wheel of the right area car? A patrol car is a patrol car, for flip's sake.'

'So why would someone else take your car in particular?'

'Maybe because it was already fuelled up.' Derringer sighed. 'Look, we're supposed to fill up at the end of every tour so that the cars are ready for instant deployment by the following shift. Some lazy bastards don't bother and it's common practice to pinch someone else's motor if yours is nearly out of gas.'

Gilham sat back in his chair, clearly deflated.

Derringer's eyes gleamed. 'Got it wrong, Detective Chief Inspector, haven't you?' he sneered. 'Question is, if not me, then who, eh? Could be anyone at the nick, couldn't it? Even someone on your own team. Now that's a thought, isn't it?'

'Any copper other than you, you mean?' Morrison growled. 'That's convenient.'

Derringer turned his head towards him a fraction. 'Not necessarily another copper either, Mr Morrison. Could be anyone with regular access to the nick: social worker, civvy control-room operator, community support officer, maybe even an *ex*-bobby who knows just where everything is and how Saddler Street ticks.'

'Oh come on,' Gilham snorted. 'Dream up another fantasy, will you? You won't get yourself off the hook with crap like that.'

Derringer seemed unperturbed by his reaction. 'Think what you like, Chief Inspector,' he said, 'but I know what I know.'

Gilham's eyes narrowed and he leaned forward slightly. 'And exactly what *do* you know?'

'That depends.'

'On what?'

'On what sort of an arrangement we can come to.'

Gilham shot to his feet, his face pale and angry. 'You're in no position to bargain,' he said. 'We've got enough on you to go to the CPS now.'

The mocking gleam returned to Derringer's eyes. 'Then be my guest,' he replied, 'but what happens when the Slicer decides to total someone else after you've charged me, eh? Could be a tad embarrassing for the force, don't you think?'

Gilham's expression was suddenly bleak. 'Could be a tad worse for you,' he said, 'if you are the innocent you pretend to be and the killer thinks you could finger him!'

Then he turned for the door, brushing past Derringer's uniformed minder as he returned to claim his chair, leaving Derringer staring uneasily into the dimly lit passage outside his room.

The adrenaline was surging through Fulton's veins like a miniature Severn Bore as he quickly masked his torch with his hand and edged his way diagonally across the stone-flagged floor towards the half-open door. The approaching footsteps were getting much louder now and he only just managed to take up a position on the hinged side of the door when he heard them come to a halt outside.

For a second there was silence, broken only by his thudding heart and someone else's heavy breathing. Then a hand grasped the handle and the door swung fully inwards, admitting a powerful shaft of light, which exploded in the mirror hanging from the ceiling. Apparently satisfied that the room was empty, a dark, indistinct shape – blacker than the darkness around it, but touched by the flashlight it was carrying – stepped through the doorway and stood there for a second, lowering the beam to illuminate the high-backed chair. It was then that Fulton made his move, drawing on every ounce of energy he could muster and launching himself at the intruder with annihilating force.

The other didn't stand a chance, but slammed into the unyielding floor with a bone-crunching finality, the big man pinning him down like a rock slab from an avalanche. Heedless of the groans from beneath him, Fulton grabbed his prisoner by the hair and, wrenching the man's head sideways, he directed the beam of his torch into his bloodied face. 'Well, I'll be damned,' he rasped. 'Ewan flaming McGuigan!'

'Don't look much like Sweeney Todd, does he, guv?' Ben Morrison commented with a grin as he watched a shocked and battered Ewan McGuigan being escorted from the church crypt by two burly policemen.

Fulton tore his gaze away from the grisly crime scene, now brilliantly illuminated by the cluster of spotlights behind the leather chair as the generator the DI had managed to get going chugged away in the background. 'What did you say?' he rapped.

Morrison's grin faded, sensing from his boss's expression that he had said the wrong thing yet again. 'Er – Sweeney Todd, guv,' he replied and threw an uneasy glance at Phil Gilham. 'Demon barber of Fleet Street. Slit customer's throats with a razor while they was sitting havin' a shave and …'

His voice trailed away, for it was plain that Fulton was no longer listening to him, but had retreated within himself, his face contorted in thought.

'What is it, Jack?' Gilham queried, a slight edge to his voice.

Fulton's eyes refocused and he shook his head with obvious frustration. 'Buggered if I know!' he said heavily. 'As I told you before, something's been bothering me ever since Lenny Baker was sliced.' He stabbed his forehead none too gently with one stout finger. 'But it's buried in here somewhere and I can't get it out.'

'So why would Sweeney Todd be significant?'

The big man smiled grimly. 'Maybe McGuigan will be able to answer that.'

'You think he's our man?'

'Do you?'

'Well, he has to be a pretty hot suspect after turning up here this afternoon, doesn't he?'

'He could have just followed me to Drew House. After all, he's done that sort of thing before.'

Gilham studied him suspiciously. 'You're beginning to sound like his brief, Jack.'

'Nothing of the sort. I just don't see him as a psycho.' Fulton frowned. 'Anyway, why this sudden change of heart? I thought you were hung up on Derringer being the culprit.'

'Not anymore.'

'Oh?'

Gilham took a deep breath. 'Situation's changed, Jack. Derringer is in Middle Moor hospital and looks like being off the hook. Ben and I interviewed him an hour ago.'

'You did *what*?'

Gilham threw Morrison a quick glance and received a frozen 'I'm not here any more' stare in return. 'You were not contactable – again – so what was I supposed to do?'

The anger in Fulton's expression began to fade and he gave a grudging nod. 'At least we have him at last,' he muttered. 'And what crap did he come out with this time?'

Gilham gave him a précis of the interview and he digested the information for a few moments. 'So he thinks he knows who our man is, does he?'

'That's what he intimated, yes, but he wants to cut a deal before he'll say anything.'

'And you think he's legit?'

'No way of knowing, but he did suggest that the killer may not necessarily be someone at the nick.'

Fulton smiled without humour. 'Could be a journalist, you mean?' he said pointedly.

'It *is* possible.'

Fulton shook his head firmly. 'I don't buy that. Only a copper could have borrowed the car in which Lyall's body was carried. There's no way an outsider could have got into the nick, snaffled the keys and driven off without being challenged by someone.'

'I tend to agree with you there, but that doesn't mean our rogue cop was working alone.'

'Two psychos, you mean? Bit far-fetched.'

'Maybe one wasn't a psycho, just someone who saw an opportunity for a leg-up in his journalistic career?'

'Oh come on, Phil!'

Gilham ushered Fulton to one side as footsteps on the stairs outside heralded the arrival of the SOCO team. 'Just think about it. How does McGuigan always manage to be in the right place at the right time? He broke the first story, claiming he was fed the information through his letterbox, and he's been on the scene of all three murders within minutes of our own troops. Then he just happens to turn up here.'

'OK, but that doesn't make him our killer.'

'Well, he's certainly got some explaining to do.'

There was a vengeful glint in Fulton's narrowed eyes. 'That he has and you know what? This is one interview I'm really going to enjoy.'

[1] Police & Criminal Evidence Act. First published by Home Office 1985

CHAPTER 15

EWAN McGUIGAN HAD never been particularly good-looking and his earlier encounter with Jack Fulton had not rearranged his face for the better. The bruising he had suffered was now really starting to come out, with one side of his face so badly swollen that it resembled a huge abscess. There were also a number of deep cuts to the same cheek and he sported a shiner of a black eye. Gilham could not help wincing when he entered the interview room just behind his boss and met the smouldering stare of the dishevelled figure sitting beside his solicitor on the other side of the table. Somehow he did not think this interview was going to be an easy one and things certainly did not start well.

In fact, they barely had time to close the door behind them before the journalist was on his feet with a snarl, glaring at Fulton with his good eye and pointing at his own battered face with one bandaged hand.

'I'm going to bloody well have you for this, Fulton,' he choked. 'Look at my face. And I reckon I've got at least one cracked rib.'

Gilham cut in quickly before his boss could reply. 'Your prerogative, Mr McGuigan,' he said, 'though I gather from the police doctor who examined you that none of your injuries is serious.'

'Not serious?' McGuigan's voice rose several octaves. 'What's that got to do with it? I was beaten up by your bloody guv'nor and he's not going to get away with it—'

'My client will be making an official complaint of assault against you, Superintendent,' the balding representative of Dolland, Kirkby & Harbottle interjected hastily. He tugged firmly on McGuigan's arm until he sat down again.

Gilham waited while Fulton parked himself in the chair facing McGuigan across the table, then dropped into the other one. 'As I've just said, Mr Dolland,' he replied, 'that's his prerogative. But his complaint will have to come later. Right now we're here to interview him about three murders.'

Conscious of the mounting tension in the room, Gilham went straight into the pre-interview formalities, turning on the tape machine and finishing up with a rushed caution that drew a smirk from Dolland and the contemptuous retort from the journalist: 'You must be having a laugh.'

Gilham's eyes narrowed. 'I assure you this is no laughing matter, Mr McGuigan,' he said politely. 'And to start with, perhaps you wouldn't mind telling us what were you doing at Drew House this evening?'

McGuigan scowled. 'Following Jack Fulton,' he replied. 'Been keeping tabs on the arsehole ever since Lyall was done in.'

Gilham's eyes flicked briefly in the direction of his boss, but Fulton was saying nothing. He just sat there studying McGuigan through half-closed eyes; he was, as the DCI knew from past experience, watching, assessing and waiting. 'And you expect us to believe that?'

'Believe what you like.'

'So how did you know the crypt in which you were arrested was there in the first place?'

'I didn't. As I said, I was following Fulton.'

'Without him even noticing he had a tail?'

'I kept well back, but lost him when he went into the church. Then I discovered that bloody great hole in the wall with the steps going down and thought I'd take a look.'

Fulton came to life suddenly. 'Let's cut the crap, McGuigan,' he rasped. 'You're in deep shit and you know it.'

'I'm speaking the truth.'

'Yeah, yeah. So you just *happened* to stumble on the very place in which two murders were committed? That was a stroke of luck, wasn't it? You've been pretty lucky like that all through this inquiry, haven't you?'

'I don't know what you mean.'

'Well, according to your original claim, for some reason the killer specifically chose you to break the news to about the Lyall killing – actually furnishing you with all the details, including a nice photograph – and slipping the lot through your letterbox in the middle of the night.'

'That's exactly what happened.'

'So why would he hit on you rather than one of the big boys in Fleet Street?'

'How should I know? Maybe he wanted someone local.'

There was a cynical glint in Fulton's eyes. 'Oh, that would explain it then. So the killer pre-warned you about the murders of Lenny Baker and the Reverend Andrew Cotter then, did he?'

'No, of course not.'

Fulton bent forward across the table towards him. 'Then how did you know where their bodies were to be found so soon after they had been dumped? You turned up at both locations well in advance of anyone else. You even beat the police to the Reverend Cotter.'

There was more than a hint of perspiration on McGuigan's forehead and Fulton waited for the telltale jerk of his Adam's apple, which, as an experienced interviewer, he knew was a prime indicator of guilt. He didn't have to wait long either and he smiled contemptuously when it happened, keen to press home the advantage he had created.

'Truth is, Mr McGuigan, you knew all about these murders, didn't you – where they were committed and where the bodies had been dumped – because you had committed them? The only thing that puzzles me is why?'

Before McGuigan could answer, Dolland held up one pale hand. 'My client denies your insinuations absolutely,' he snapped. 'Now, are you going to charge him or not? If not, then you have no option but to release him.'

Fulton ignored him and piled on the pressure. 'Well, *Mr* McGuigan, are you frightened to answer the question because you know you are guilty? You must admit, things are not looking too good for you at the moment, are they?'

The journalist studied him over a hastily grabbed glass of water. His expression was no longer belligerent, but had the look of a trapped animal.

'You don't have to say anything,' Dolland breathed close to his ear. 'He has to produce evidence.'

McGuigan glanced at him and then at Fulton, plainly in a gut-wrenching dilemma.

'Think about it, McGuigan,' Fulton persisted. 'Three brutal murders and you have been in the know for each of them. Then you turn up at the principal murder scene – not just in the vicinity, mark you, but on the actual killing ground. I call that a bit too much of a coincidence and I think any jury will feel the same way.'

'I listen to police radios,' McGuigan blurted suddenly and Dolland relaxed with a smirk.

Gilham felt his heart lurch. Damn it, the swine had tossed the ball right back into Fulton's lap, which meant it was put-up or shut-up time. So what did they do now? There was unlikely to be any forensic evidence to back up any charge against McGuigan and there were no witnesses to put the journalist anywhere near the victims prior to their deaths. It looked like they were stuffed, but he had reckoned without Fulton's brass neck and his long experience as an interviewer, and the big man went straight for the wild card without even blinking.

'There *were* no initial radio transmissions regarding the murders of Lenny Baker and the Reverend Cotter,' he said, poker-faced and as definite as a player with a royal flush. 'Both incidents were reported by telephone to Saddler Street nick and officers were dispatched direct from there to each location. You were on the scene of each crime before the responding units had time to radio a situation report.'

Gilham froze, knowing full well that Fulton was bluffing, but then he saw Dolland tense and, to his surprise, McGuigan promptly fell apart.

'I didn't kill anyone,' he said, slumping in his chair with the weariness of someone who had been carrying a guilty secret for far too long. 'I just reported what he gave me.'

Dolland looked horrified and even Gilham was stunned by his sudden unexpected admission.

It was Fulton who seized the initiative. 'What he *gave* you?' he said carefully, keen to ensure there were no ambiguities on the tape. 'You're saying you had some sort of ongoing dialogue with this psycho?'

The other shook his head. 'Not dialogue, no. He – he telephoned me after each of the last two—'

'Murders?'

McGuigan gave a resigned nod, seemingly unaware of his solicitor holding his head in his hands.

'Each of the last two *murders*?' Fulton persisted.

A noticeable grimace, followed by an irritable: 'Yes, murders, damn you!'

'To tell you the locations of the bodies?'

'Yes!'

'Then you made sure he got maximum publicity?'

McGuigan winced. 'I reported the facts as disclosed; that's my job.'

'Very noble of you. And you got an exclusive each time, of course. Not a bad deal, eh?'

Outwitted and demoralized, the journalist cast him a sullen glance. 'There *was* no deal.'

Fulton raised an eyebrow again, a glint of triumph in his eyes. 'How would you describe it, then? You didn't happen to alert the police to the telephone calls, did you?'

'I had no idea who the killer was or that he would kill again after he had sliced Lenny Baker. Also, the calls were kept very short, the voice obviously disguised. So what was the point?'

'The *point*, McGuigan,' Fulton said tersely, 'is that we could have put a tap on your phone; maybe nailed this psycho the next time he rang.'

The journalist's expression registered his contempt. 'And what good would that have done? When he called me about Cotter it was around nine o'clock in the morning. By then the good reverend would already have been dead.'

'Yeah,' Fulton agreed, 'but it would at least have given us the opportunity of trying to trace the call and put a stop to any further killings – and there will be more, you can be sure of it.'

McGuigan hesitated, as if unsure as to whether he should say anything else or not. He glanced quickly at Dolland, but the solicitor gave the indifferent shrug of a man who felt that anything he said now was pretty academic anyway.

'I already did that,' the journalist said at last.

'What?'

'The – the call came from a mobile and though the number was withheld, I managed to get a trace on it through a contact I have in the phone company.'

'And?'

'The subscriber was Herbert Lyall.'

'Lyall?' Gilham exclaimed, unable to contain himself any longer.

'Yes, which means the killer must have stolen the phone from him the night of his murder – and there's more.'

Both policemen studied him warily, sensing from the sudden triumphant gleam in his eyes that they wouldn't like what was coming. 'Go on.'

'There was some background noise when he last rang me.'

'What sort of background noise?' Fulton snapped.

McGuigan now leaned across the table. 'A Tannoy message,' he replied, 'a Tannoy message asking the duty inspector to report to the control room.' His face twisted into an ugly sneer. 'Your psycho, *Mr* bloody Fulton, is not only one of your own, but is actually planning his hits from inside your own nick!'

CHAPTER 16

FULTON WAS SURPRISED to see the sleek blue Jaguar of the assistant chief constable operations in the police station car park when he turned up for work the following morning, especially as it was only just 8.30. Remembering Andy Stoller's previous early appearance at Saddler Street and the bad news it had heralded, he couldn't help feeling distinctly uneasy as he reversed into a convenient space. Something had to be up to get an assistant chief constable out of bed this early. He just hoped it had nothing to do with him or the investigation.

There seemed to be even more press than usual gathered outside the police station and they homed in on him like wasps targeting a fruit salad as he climbed the steps to the front doors. Something had wound them up and Fulton guessed it was the sight of McGuigan being wheeled into the nick the night before. Nothing like concern for your own, he mused, barging through them and ignoring the inevitable barrage of questions.

He spied Norman Skellet's thin figure standing at the foot of the stairs as soon as he passed through the security door into the station and his stomach churned.

'Superintendent!' Skellet snapped, blocking Fulton's path. 'A word please.'

Apprehension settling on him with the force of gravity, Fulton followed the ACC along the corridor to a door labelled Interview Room 1. There were two of them seated at the bolted-down table inside – a wiry grey-haired man in his late fifties with pebble eyes and pallid sunken features, and a much younger colleague, blessed with a thick crop of oily black hair and a full beard.

'This is Detective Chief Superintendent Harringay and Detective Superintendent Nesbitt from the South Thames force,' Skellet announced, his face bleak. 'They have been called in at the request of the deputy chief constable to interview you in connection with a serious criminal matter.'

'A serious *what*?' Fulton tried to conceal the telltale jerk of his Adam's apple, but he could feel the knife twisting in his gut as he thought of Janet and the complaint of assault he had long been expecting.

Skellet ignored his question. 'And after they have finished with you, you will report to me in the superintendent's office upstairs, is that understood?'

Glancing past the ACC, he saw Andy Stoller standing in the doorway and tried to catch his eye, but Stoller chose to examine the floor instead. Before the big man could think of anything else to say, Skellet turned on his heel and left the room, pushing Stoller ahead of him as he closed the door behind them.

'Sit down, Mr Fulton,' Harringay said.

Fulton remained standing, his face now wearing a truculent expression.

'I said *sit*!' Harringay snapped. 'Unless you wish to stand there for the next few hours.'

'Next what?' Fulton retorted. 'Just what the hell is all this about? I have a bloody murder to investigate.'

Harringay rested his elbows on the table and studied him over long, steepled fingers. 'So have I, Mr Fulton,' he said quietly, then added with brutal frankness: 'The murder of your estranged wife and her boyfriend!'

Fulton ignored his doorbell at first. Plagued by the press ever since returning home after hours of interrogation (there had even been one of the hyenas creeping round his back garden at lunchtime), he had eventually taken the telephone off the hook and closed the blinds on the large front window, determined to exclude the world from his misery and humiliation.

He still could not take in what was happening to him and he knew he would never forget his escorted trip to the mortuary to see Janet's body. Both she and Doyle had apparently been beaten to death with a pickaxe handle – SOCO had found it in the undergrowth at the scene – and she wasn't a pretty sight. He could still see her lying there with one side of her head caved in and her eyes starting from their sockets and staring at him through the swollen bloodied remains of her face like some ghastly visitant from a nightmare. There had been no expression of sympathy from Detective Superintendent Nesbitt, who had accompanied him, or the elderly mortuary attendant who had studied him with open hostility throughout the whole process. Why should there be? After all, he was a cold-blooded murderer who had battered his wife and her lover to death with a pickaxe handle – everyone knew that – and murderers weren't entitled to sympathy, or anything else for that matter. He thought about his own career and wondered if *he* had come across like that to those he had interviewed on suspicion of serious crime. Maybe this was his punishment for prejudging others. If so, it was the cruellest punishment that could ever have been meted out.

'Jack?' a familiar voice shouted through the letterbox. 'You in there?'

He stubbed out his cigarette and slouched reluctantly from the room to open up.

'So you *are* in, then?' Abbey Lee snapped, pushing past him into the hall as he slammed the door on the two reporters who had evidently been harassing her on the garden path. 'Thought you could do with some company.'

There was no gratitude in his expression. 'Got plenty of that out there, thank you,' he retorted, waving an arm towards the lounge.

She went ahead of him and stood for a moment in the doorway. The whisky bottle on the coffee table was half-empty, the glass beside it half-full and the air laden with cigarette smoke.

'That's the answer then, is it?' she commented with a grimace and nodded towards the bottle.

Fulton shrugged. 'What else is there?'

She settled on the edge of the settee. 'What about your self-respect?'

He stood in the doorway, scowling and looking uncomfortable. 'If I'd wanted a preacher, I'd have sent for the bloody vicar by now,' he said.

Her lips tightened. 'You're never easy to help, are you, Jack?' she breathed.

'I didn't ask for help in the first place,' he retorted, slumping back into his armchair and reaching for the whisky glass.

She hesitated, biting her lip. 'Look, I'm really sorry about Janet. I heard all about it on the news. You must be devastated.'

He grimaced. 'That's the point,' he replied, 'I'm not.'

'Not what?'

'Not devastated, Ab – *not devastated*. Terrible, isn't it? My wife has been brutally murdered and I should be the grieving husband, but I'm not. Oh, it was a terrible shock when I heard about it, I freely admit that – nearly passed out at the interview – but it was no more of a shock than if the victim had been someone else I knew personally. I pity her, yes, but I haven't felt any gut-wrenching sense of sorrow or loss over her death.'

'Hardly surprising after the way she treated you.'

He stared at her frankly. 'I didn't kill her, Ab, no matter how bad things might look, and I wouldn't have wished such a terrible thing on Janet anyway.'

'I know that, Jack, but someone else did do it and under the circumstances you are bound to be high on the list of suspects.'

He stood up again and took his glass to the window, lifting a corner of the blinds to peer out at the knot of reporters and photographers gathered by the gate. 'I've been suspended, Ab. Can you believe that?' he said. 'Twenty-seven years exemplary service in the force and now I'm on suspension; arrested, bailed – me, *bailed* – and required to report to the nick again in one month, like some bloody villain, while my own DCI is handed my job on a plate as SIO.'

She nodded. 'I know. The whole town is buzzing with the news.'

He stared at her, the shock still etched into his face. 'Do you know, I even had to supply a DNA sample and allow them to search my bungalow for bloodstained clothing. Half my neighbours must have had a grandstand view of the troops arriving. Have you any idea how humiliating that was?'

'I can imagine.'

'No you can't – not even nearly.'

'OK, so I can't. Point is what are you going to do now?'

He turned back into the room and poured himself another whisky. 'What do you *think* I should do?'

'Well, you are a bit limited on options. Best to keep your head down and let things sort themselves out.'

'So just give up, right?'

'I wouldn't put it quite like that, but you'd be a fool to risk attracting more flak.'

'Would I now?' His eyes were hard. 'Well, you just listen to me, Abbey Lee. Someone set me up, I'm convinced of it, and there's no way I'm going to be played for a sap.'

'I don't follow you.'

He set the whisky glass down on the coffee table, untouched, and lit another cigarette. 'I've been doing a lot of thinking since I came home,' he said, starting to pace the room like a caged animal. 'Doesn't it strike you as a bit odd that my wife and her boyfriend should be battered to death at a time when I am leading a serial murder investigation?'

'It's just a coincidence.'

'I don't believe in coincidences.'

'They happen.'

'So does shit.'

'What are you suggesting?'

'I think someone – almost certainly the so-called Slicer – wanted me off the current murder enquiry pdq, in case I got lucky, and framing me was one way of getting the job done.'

'You've been reading too many thrillers.'

'Maybe, but it all fits and the thing is, whoever's behind it must be someone in the know – someone reasonably close to me who is *au fait* with the progress of my inquiry and can keep tabs on my movements without arousing suspicion. He must have followed me to Janet's love nest the night she died, otherwise how else would he have known where she had gone to ground?'

She started. 'Janet's love nest? Are you saying you confronted her at her boyfriend's place?'

He stopped pacing and faced her with a grimace. 'I wanted to persuade her to come home, but we had a bit of a fight and—'

'A fight? That was a damned stupid thing to do. You've laid yourself wide open.'

His expression was suddenly ironic. 'Tell me about it, but, as they say, hindsight is not an exact science.'

'And you think the killer followed you to the address?'

'It's the only explanation I can think of.'

'And he's one of your own?'

'Well, we've been sure for some time now that the Slicer is someone at the local nick and we did have a likely suspect – a bobby called Derringer who was AWOL – but he has turned up in Middle Moor hospital and looks like being off the hook.'

'But I thought you had just arrested someone else in connection with your inquiry? According to the news on the radio, a local journalist is currently in custody.'

He gave an irritable shake of his head. 'I don't think for one moment that he's our man, though it is possible he is part of some sort of conspiracy. I'm not going to get the opportunity of following that up now, anyway.'

'So you're stuck.'

His eyes gleamed. 'Not quite. Master Derringer has indicated that he may know who our killer is and wants to cut a deal in exchange for the information.'

'So?'

'I think I might toddle along to see him.' He gave a fierce grin. 'Use my subtle counselling skills to get the info out of him.'

'What?' She half-rose on the settee. 'Are you mad? The force will hang you out to dry.'

He took a deep breath and nodded. 'Maybe, but I've no intention of just sitting here while the bastards finish stitching me up.'

'Don't you think you should trust your own team to get that sort of information out of Derringer?'

He emitted a harsh laugh. 'And which member of my own team should I trust to do that, Ab? I've already said someone in the know has to be our killer and it could just as easily be someone on the team itself.'

'Surely not Phil Gilham or Ben Morrison?'

'I wouldn't rule anyone out at this stage – especially after what I discovered from a few routine enquiries this morning.'

'This morning? Then you've been poking your nose into things already, have you?'

'Let's just say I've been checking on someone I've had particular doubts about – and it turns out he has been telling me a few porky pies.'

'And who would that be?'

He shook his head. 'Never you mind.'

She shrugged. 'Suit yourself, but whatever suspicions you might have about anyone, I still think you're crazy going to see this PC Derringer when you should be keeping a low profile. And in any event, how do you propose getting away from here unnoticed? Wherever you go, you'll have a posse of reporters chasing after you.'

He studied her for a moment. 'That's where you come in, Ab.'

She jumped to her feet, shaking her head repeatedly. 'Oh no you don't. No way. I'm not getting involved in your suicidal scheme.'

He held up one placatory hand. 'Look, all I'm asking you to do is drop me at the hospital gates after dark this evening. There's a lane behind my garden. If you were to be there this evening at say,' – he glanced at his watch – 'eight-thirty time, I could hop over my garden wall and slip in the back of your motor. No one will bother to follow you even if they do see the car. What press are still around outside will think I'm still indoors.'

'Absolutely not, Jack – and that's final!'

He nodded and treated her to the first genuine smile he had been able to manage for many hours. 'Thanks, Ab, I knew I could count on you. Fancy a cup of tea and a sandwich before you pop home to change?'

CHAPTER 17

'I CAN'T BELIEVE I'm doing this.' Abbey Lee engaged first gear with a horrible scraping noise and crept back along the lane, using the moonlight instead of the car's headlights to guide her between the garden walls of the adjoining houses and the steep ditch on the other side.

'Lights!' Fulton growled from the back seat as they joined the main road. 'We can do without a ticket from some eagle-eyed woodentop.'

It was a clear night and, for once, there was not much traffic about – even the police seemed to have stayed indoors – and Abbey made good time to the hospital, pulling into the large lamplit car park and steering the big four-by-four into a bay partly hidden by the shadows of an overhanging beech tree.

'You'd better stay here,' Fulton said, struggling to extricate himself from the cramped space between the front and rear seats. 'I won't be long.'

Abbey snorted. 'I'll do nothing of the sort,' she retorted and shivered as she glanced round the near empty car park. 'I'm not staying here on my own.'

Fulton placed a heavy hand on her shoulder from over the back seat. 'You'll do as I tell you,' he growled. 'As yet, you have only given me a lift to the hospital. Go to the next stage and you'll be totally compromised.'

She released her breath in an irritable hiss, reluctantly accepting the wisdom of his argument. 'All right, all right, but don't do anything stupid.'

He gave a faint smile. 'Just keep your eyes open for the bogeyman, will you?

'Very funny,' she called after him. Slamming the door and applying the internal locks, she sank down as low in the seat as she could, her eyes probing the car park for the slightest movement.

Fulton found the main reception area of the hospital deserted. Visiting hours had long since ended and the regular administrative staff had all gone home. The uniformed security officer slouched behind the reception counter seemed to be fast asleep and the big man shook his head with cynical amusement as he strode past him to the lift. So much for security, he mused, pressing the call button and slipping into the lift even as the doors slid silently open.

He knew exactly where he was going, having learned from Phil Gilham earlier that Derrringer was occupying a private room on the fourth level. Seconds later he stepped from the lift into a long vinyl-floored corridor with a large Exit sign at each end.

He was greeted by the strong smell of antiseptic and the sound of raucous coughing from somewhere to his left, but the corridor itself was deserted. Room Six was easy to spot; there was a plastic chair positioned to the left of the double doors, a thermos flask beneath it and a paperback book open on the seat. His eyes narrowed. So where was the policeman who should have been sitting outside?

Heart thumping, he gently pushed the doors open, took a few steps into the room, then abruptly froze.

John Derrringer had lost a lot of blood – in fact, most of his allocation by the look of it – and it had exited through the deep slash in this throat, plastering the bed, floor and the inside of the double doors in the same fashion as Lenny

Baker, like paint from a spray gun. It was apparent that he was already dead: his wide open eyes stared fixedly at the ceiling, as if studying something of interest, while the blood continued to drip from the sheets on to the vinyl floor with a hollow 'plopping' sound.

'Looks like it only just happened,' Mickey Vansetti said, emerging from behind the right-hand door. 'Must've missed the arsehole by a whisker.'

Fulton snapped out of his trance and stared at him, but his astonishment at finding him at the murder scene was abruptly cancelled out by a more immediate concern. 'Stairs!' he snarled. He wheeled round clumsily in the doorway and lumbered off along the corridor towards the nearest exit door, ignoring Vansetti's shout: 'Too late, Jack.'

He heard the 'boom' of a slammed door and the clatter of fast-descending feet at least two landings below him the moment he shouldered through the exit door, but even as he started down the staircase, he stopped short, hanging on to the banister rail and panting with the exertion. It was pointless. If that was the killer making good his escape, there was no way he would catch up with him – especially in his present physical state. Cupping his hands round his eyes to shut out the reflection from the fluorescent ceiling-light, he peered through the landing window and saw a shadow emerge from an invisible door at ground level and streak round the side of the building. It disappeared in the direction of the car park at the front.

'He must have dived in somewhere when he heard the ping of my lift,' Vansetti said at his elbow. 'Weren't no one in the corridor.'

Fulton leaned back against the wall, breathing heavily and studying him with predictable hostility. 'Maybe there *was* no one else, Mickey,' he grated. 'Maybe there was just you.'

Vansetti shook his head, disappointment in his expression. 'Come on, Jack, you know that's cobblers. Why would I stiff him? He owed me a bundle and I come here to persuade him to tell me where he'd stashed it.' He gave a dark smile. 'Anyway, you knows me. Don't need to do no heavy jobs meself. Got boys to do 'em for me.'

Fulton chose not to follow up on that one, though he realized deep down that his old antagonist was speaking the truth. 'So where's the bloody copper who should have been outside the door?' he grated.

Vansetti grinned. 'Last time I see him, he was comin' out the lift as I got in an' headin' for the nurses' rest room on the ground floor,' he replied. 'Had a packet of fags in his hand.'

'The bastard,' Fulton breathed and reached for his mobile phone.

Vansetti quickly grabbed his wrist. 'What you doin', Jack?' he said. 'Not callin' up Ol' Bill?'

'What do *you* think?'

Vansetti shrugged and withdrew his hand. 'So what's goin' to happen when you does that, eh? You're already suspended and on sus' for toppin' your ol' lady. You shouldn't even be here. Officially you ain't a copper no more.'

'So?'

Vansetti sighed. 'Jack, they'll crucify you if they knows you been here. How you goin' to get yourself off the hook stuck in a cell?'

Fulton hesitated, the cover of his mobile open and the cold display staring back at him.

'Anyway, you're too late,' Vansetti murmured, holding the exit door open a fraction.

'What?' Fulton peered through the gap and saw a thickset uniformed bobby striding towards Derrringer's room from the direction of the lift.

'Let's go, Jack, before the shit hits the fan.'

For a moment Fulton just stood there.

'Jack!' Vansetti breathed urgently. 'Come on!'

'Why should you give a toss?'

Vansetti pushed him towards the stairs. 'Maybe 'cause I don't like bent coppers no more than you do and your bleedin' psycho is one of 'em.'

'Yeah,' Fulton agreed, reluctantly following him. 'And by killing Derringer, he's also scotched any chance you had of recovering your money.'

Vansetti threw open the door of the lower landing and grinned. 'Psychos is always bad for business, Jack,' he said.

The lights in the car park seemed brighter than before and for the first time Fulton glimpsed the big Mercedes projecting from behind a low hedge in a disabled bay. The powerful engine came to life the moment they appeared and without being summoned, the car eased smoothly out of the bay towards them, a big hunched shape behind the wheel. 'Be in touch, Jack,' Vansetti called as he threw open the rear passenger door and ducked inside. 'Keep your head down.'

Fulton felt sick and giddy as he headed for the four-by-four on the opposite side of the car park. He couldn't believe that he had just walked out on a serious crime scene without doing anything about it. OK, so John Derringer had not amounted to much – he was a completely rotten apple – but was Fulton himself any better? He should never have allowed himself to be persuaded by Vansetti's bent logic to cut and run. At least he should have telephoned the incident room or Phil Gilham – or should he? What would that have achieved? Another nail in his coffin and an ace in the hole for Skellet. No, like it or not, he had to keep a low profile or risk losing any possible chance of clearing his name this side of a pensionless retirement.

First, though, he had to break the bad news to Abbey. He had selfishly dragged her into this business and after the latest horrific development, her position would be totally compromised and she would find herself inextricably bound up in his own continuing misfortune. He dreaded to think how she would react, but there was no easy way of saying what he had to say and he steeled himself for the inevitable heated confrontation as he threw open the front passenger door.

But there was no confrontation. Abbey was no longer in the car. He smelled the strong antiseptic smell first and saw

the piece of paper lying on her seat as he bent inside. The message, written with what looked like lipstick in squat block capitals, was short and chilling in the car's interior light:
I HAVE YOUR GIRLFRIEND NOW JACK SO DON'T DO ANYTHING SILLY. TELL NO ONE UNLESS YOU WANT HER SLICED LIKE THE OTHERS. AWAIT MY CALL.

Fulton passed a fleet of incoming police cars on the hospital's service road as he eased the big four-by-four into the late-evening traffic flow. Obviously Derringer's police guard had found his charge and he could well imagine the mayhem that must have broken out.

Borrowing Abbey's Honda to get home was a risky move, but so was leaving it where it was. The police were bound to check the car park and do a registered owner check on any vehicle there. Then they would be asking where Abbey had gone and what she had been doing at the hospital in the first place. Furthermore, the only other way he could have made it home was by taxi and any good police investigator would check every taxi firm in town for hospital pick-ups as a matter of course.

The rationality of what he was doing didn't ease his conscience, however. He had got Abbey into this thing and he felt as if he were now callously abandoning her to her fate, even though staying put would not have helped her in the slightest.

It had occurred to him to disregard the instructions in the note and contact Phil Gilham direct, reasoning that maybe their combined talents, coupled with the police resources at their disposal, would enable them to find her before it was too late. But then he had dismissed the idea as a total non-starter. He was no longer a member of the force and if he were to reveal Abbey's kidnapping, he would have to admit to finding Derringer's body as well, opening up a whole new can of worms. In addition, if the police investigation team had so far been incapable of catching the killer, there was not much chance of their finding Abbey. And if the man they were after was someone at the nick, as now seemed certain, their quarry would soon learn that Fulton had disobeyed his instructions, with disastrous consequences for Abbey.

He swung off the main drag and headed into the back streets to avoid falling foul of one of the police checkpoints which, he knew, would soon be set up. He had to admit to himself that he had never felt so helpless and alone. Dancing to a psycho's tune was contrary to everything he had ever stood for and the very thought left a nasty taste in his mouth, but with no idea whatsoever as to the identity of his antagonist, what choice did he have? If only he could remember what had been bugging him for the last two days and why the spectre of Sweeney Todd loomed so large in his mind. What the hell was the connection between the demon barber and this sadistic serial killer? He was sure there was one, but his constipated mind still stubbornly refused to give it up, and the more he puzzled over the issue the deeper it sank into the quicksand of his subconscious.

He was still struggling with it as he climbed over the low wall into his back garden after parking the four-by-four in the lane where Abbey had picked him up, but the next second he had something more pressing to think about, for the telephone in his bungalow was ringing.

CHAPTER 18

PHIL GILHAM STOOD for a full minute in the doorway, staring at the bloodstained shell that had once been John Derringer. 'Poor devil,' he muttered. 'He must have seen it coming and couldn't do a damned thing about it.'

Ed Carrick, the Home Office pathologist, straightened up from his examination of the corpse and gave him a keen glance. 'I doubt he saw it coming,' he said. 'At least, not until he was actually attacked. From the angle of the wound and the slightly contorted position of the body, I would say that this was done from the left side of the bed after a heavy blow to the forehead. See the bruising just starting to come out on top of his other injuries?' He smiled grimly. 'Your officer would have been stunned like a bull going to slaughter before the blade sliced through the artery.'

Gilham jumped, startled by the sudden flash of the SOCO photographer's camera. 'Maybe Derringer was asleep and woke up when the killer bent over him,' he suggested. 'Hence the blow to the head.'

'More likely he knew him, guv,' put in DS Prentice, who had materialized at his elbow and was now breathing a heady mixture of stale beer and cigarettes over him.

Gilham turned his head to study the sallow pockmarked face, surprised yet pleased to see the DS already at the scene. 'You're probably right,' he agreed, 'but whoever our man is, how the hell did he get past the plod stationed outside the door? I left strict instructions that no one was to be allowed in here, except duty medical staff.'

Prentice hesitated briefly before answering. 'PC Leighton, the officer on security duty, says he went for a leak and when he got back—'

'Give me strength!' Gilham raised his eyes to the ceiling in disbelief. 'You're telling me he left his post for – for a *leak*?'

Prentice shrugged. 'That's what he told me, guv. Gone just a few minutes, he claimed.'

Gilham snorted. 'More likely he went for a damned smoke. And hospital security? Were they all having a leak as well?'

Prentice shook his head. 'Only one security officer on duty and he was downstairs in reception.'

'Security cameras?'

'None on site as yet. Hospital are currently doing a competitive tender for them. Should be installed next financial year.'

Gilham gave a short cynical laugh. 'Brilliant!' he said. 'It's encouraging to know the NHS is on the ball.'

Prentice made a face in sympathy. 'Do you want to see PC Leighton now, guv? He's downstairs in reception.'

Gilham took a deep breath. 'No,' he said grimly. 'I'll save that pleasure for later.' He glanced along the corridor. 'But I would like to know where my DI, Ben Morrison, has got to.'

Prentice shook his greasy black hair. 'Dunno, guv,' he said. 'Control room have apparently been trying to raise him ever since you called up, but they're getting no reply from his mobile or personal radio.' He grinned. 'Probably gone to bed early.'

Gilham's bleak expression indicated that he didn't think much of the joke. 'Well, you can tell control they can send someone round to get him out of it,' he snapped. 'If I'm still up, I don't see why he shouldn't be.'

As Prentice headed off in the direction of the lift, the pathologist ducked under the blue-and-white security tape fixed across the doorway. 'One of those nights, eh, Chief Inspector?' he said, peeling off his surgical gloves. 'You have an AWOL DI and I have an AWOL pathologist.'

Gilham followed him to the empty bedroom hospital security had placed at the disposal of the police. 'Not your call tonight then, sir?' he queried, watching the elderly man shake himself out of his protective suit.

'Not at all,' the other replied. 'Should have been Abbey Lee, but she seems to have disappeared off the face of the earth. No one can get hold of her.' He smiled mischievously. 'Probably having a sleep-over.'

'Well, it wouldn't be with Ben Morrison, that's for sure,' Gilham replied uncharitably, thinking of his gum-chewing leg man as he stared out of the window into the lamplit car park.

'Ah, but who can tell what's in a woman's mind?' Carrick countered.

'Or in Ben Morrison's,' Gilham murmured, wondering exactly where the ex-marine had got to and why his absence made him feel so uneasy.

He was still lost in thought when Carrick shook him by the elbow. 'They're calling you,' he said, nodding towards the corridor. 'New development by the sound of it.'

Gilham almost collided with a uniformed bobby in the corridor. 'Better come down, sir,' he said, breathing heavily from an apparent sprint. 'Search unit has come up with something. SOCO are already on their way downstairs.'

'This better be worth it,' Gilham threatened, following him to the lift.

The ground-floor fire exit stood wide open, the window smashed, and black masking tape still trailing from some of the jagged pieces of glass left in the frame. A concentration of torches directed at the shrubbery just outside revealed what looked like a white hospital coat rolled up and dumped among the bushes and even from where he stood, Gilham could see the coat was heavily soiled.

'OK, so we know how he got in and away again,' he said. 'That's something anyway.'

'Bit more than that, guv,' a uniformed woman sergeant put in, the triumph in her voice very pronounced. 'That bush is a pyracantha, which has some pretty unforgiving thorns.' She grabbed a flashlight from one of the other officers standing beside her. 'Look you there.'

Gilham bent down to study the prickly branch arching out towards him in the powerful beam and his heart lurched when he saw the patch of discoloured leaves.

'One of my sharp-eyed units spotted it,' the sergeant went on. 'Our man must have torn his hand open when he pushed the coat into the shrubbery.' Her eyes seemed to shine in the light streaming out through the fire exit. 'Your serial killer may have got away, but he made us a very nice present of his DNA.'

Fulton snatched up the phone in the hall and leaned against the wall with his other hand, breathing like a misfiring car engine. There was a clucking sound at the other end of the line.

'Sorry, Jack,' a metallic voice mocked. 'Didn't make you run, did I?'

Fulton couldn't answer for a moment and when he did his voice was strained and unnatural. 'Just cut the crap,' he wheezed. 'What is it you want?'

The caller sighed. 'I've got the greatest respect for you, Jack – always have had – but you're becoming a bit of a pain. Almost caught me tonight, so I decided I needed to buy some insurance.'

Fulton went into a fit of coughing. 'You touch her, you bastard, and—'

'Now, now, Jack, don't go getting yourself all worked up. She's quite safe,' and the voice hardened, 'but she'll only stay that way if you keep your distance.'

Fulton held himself in check with an effort. After years of dealing with people like this, he knew that losing his cool would achieve nothing. If he wanted to help Abbey, he needed to stay calm and focused. 'Why did you kill Derringer?' he said quietly, using the tactic he had employed so often in the past to keep his target talking in the hope that he might let drop something that would help to identify him or his location.

Another sigh. 'Had to, Jack. He was getting a bit too close to things.'

'How do you mean?'

'Pretty shrewd cookie was our John. Always sniffing around, trying to get the dirt on people so he could make a few quid.'

'You're saying he was into blackmail?'

'Oh I think that was coming my way eventually, but he wasn't quite there. Then he fell afoul of the Vansetti family and had to do a runner. Good of them to find him for me, wasn't it? Gave me the opportunity of preventing any little indiscretions on his part.'

'Indiscretions? How did you know that was on the cards?'

'I didn't, but when I heard on the nick's bush telegraph that he had been found, I couldn't afford to take the chance.'

The killer's disclosure about the source of his information seemed like a bad slip at first and Fulton felt a thrill of satisfaction, but then the other chuckled. 'Oh I'm not shy about confirming what you've always suspected, Jack – that I'm a copper – but the problem for you is that you don't know *which* copper, do you?'

'That shouldn't take too long to find out.'

'You reckon? OK, so how many bobbies do you think there are on this police area, eh? Force establishment figures say ninety-three. About a third of those are wopsies, but that still leaves a healthy sixty-two of the male gender – lot of suspects there for you to choose from.'

'I'm gradually getting there.'

'Oh, I know you are, Jack, and it will come to you before long. That's why I needed an edge, just in case.'

'And part of that edge was battering my wife to death, was it?'

'Well, at the start I naively thought it would get you out of my hair, give me a bit of time. And she wasn't a very nice lady, was she? As for her boyfriend – ugh! Insipid little shit, he was. You should be grateful to me for getting rid of the pair of them for you.'

'I'll come after you, you know that, don't you?'

'Quite sure you will, Jack, but once I've finished what I have to do, I won't care anyway. Just need a little more time and then I'm all yours, so be patient.'

'How do I know Abbey's still alive?'

'You don't, but you'll just have to accept a policeman's word, won't you? And she should feel completely at home where she is now anyway.'

'Let me speak to her.'

The caller snorted. 'Oh come on, Mr Superintendent, this is beginning to sound like one of those crime movies – you know, the good guy speaks to the hostage and she slips him the info about where she's being held so he can rescue her. Get real, Jack.'

Fulton straightened up, his face taut and uncompromising. 'Either I speak to her or it's no deal.'

Another chuckle. 'Do you know, Jack, I can practically hear that shrewd little mind of yours going into overdrive, trying to work out where I might be phoning from, listening for any telltale background noises or any giveaway comments. Sorry to disappoint you, but I'm using the mobile I nicked from Lyall, so I could be anywhere.'

'I said I want to speak to Abbey.'

'Patience, Jack, patience. Why don't you give me a tinkle – say, at midnight, the old witching hour, eh? Maybe I'll tell you a bit more about the little lady then – like the colour of her knickers, for instance.'

'I want to speak to her now.'

The other ignored him. 'See, if you had still been in charge of the inquiry, Jack, you could have had this call taped and traced or the conversation broken down by the tech services unit to try and identify my voice. But you're no longer Mr Big Wheel, are you, so you can't call the shots any more. Must be really hard to stomach. Still, we can talk about all this at twelve, can't we? Don't forget to ring me, will you?'

'Either I speak to Abbey or I keep looking for you.'

There was a brief pause and the caller's voice was heavy with menace. 'Get anywhere near me, Jack, and I'll use Abbey's tools of the trade to give her open heart surgery. Got it?' At which point the line went dead.

For a long time after the call Fulton sat slumped in his armchair in the lounge, communing with his whisky bottle and watching the hands of the mantelpiece clock tick inexorably towards midnight as he tried to mediate in the fierce struggle that was taking place between conscience and principles. In the end, however, he had to accept that he was stuffed and had no option but to go along with the killer's demands – but that didn't mean he couldn't try a little subterfuge of his own.

At precisely 11.30 he picked up the lounge telephone and retrieved the details of the psycho's call from the BT 1471 service. Then, tapping in the code to withhold his number, he carefully dialled Lyall's mobile to see what would happen.

The telephone rang for several seconds before there was any response. Then to his surprise there was a click and a voice said cautiously: 'Yeah, who's that?'

He froze, his hand tightening on the receiver and his lips compressed into a thin hard line.

'I said who's calling?'

Very slowly he put the telephone back on its rest and stared at the wall, his brain numb with shock. He had not really expected anyone to answer the call half an hour early or, if they did, that he would be able to recognize the voice of the person at the other end of the line – and he had certainly not expected that that person would be Acting Superintendent Phil Gilham!

CHAPTER 19

SADDLER STREET POLICE station was like a mausoleum when Phil Gilham pushed through the security door from the foyer, curtly acknowledging the station duty officer who had let him in. Most of the night shift were already out on patrol and the local area control room, with its team of civilian operators, was a sealed unit, inaccessible to all save authorized communication staff.

He gave a thin smile as he made for the ornate Victorian staircase. Funny how what should have been the safest place in town had now assumed such a menacing brooding atmosphere. Even the bobbies themselves felt uneasy and vulnerable. The suspicion that one of their own colleagues was behind the spate of murders had had an unsettling effect on everyone, creating a distrust that was working its way through station morale like a destructive worm. Every patch of shadow in the dimly lit corridors and offices had become a threat, every creak and groan of the antiquated building as it stretched its weary sinews something sinister and every member of staff a potential assassin. Saddler Street was a police station teetering on the very edge and it only needed a gentle push to send it right over.

Pausing at the foot of the staircase and peering up towards the first floor landing, still cloaked in heavy darkness, he had to empathize with his colleagues. Even without the Slicer's influence, the place was about as creepy as any building could get and the antiquated lighting system did not help matters either. He reached for the switch and flicked it twice before anything happened. Then it was a case of watching and waiting as the landing globe reluctantly came on, dipped and steadied into a pale watery glow, before he was able to begin his ascent, his leather-soled shoes ringing on the naked stone.

The first floor accommodated the offices of the superintendent, DCI and uniformed chief inspector, plus the area's admin staff, and through the glass-panelled door off the landing he saw that, as to be expected at this time of the night, everything was in darkness. But, hand on the banister rail leading to the top floor, he stopped dead, conscious of the sound of heavy footsteps directly above his head. He frowned. Who the devil could be wandering about on the top floor? There was only a conference room and the police club – now the incident room – on that level and there was no reason for anyone to be up there at such a late hour.

As with the floor below, all the lights on the top floor had been turned off and he opened the landing's glass-panelled door cautiously, freezing in the long corridor on the other side to listen. More noises from his left (the incident room) and the faint glow of a light inside, which was abruptly extinguished. Then further heavy footsteps, muffled by carpet at first, but sharper on contact with the vinyl floor of the corridor. His hand fumbled for the light switch, but he was too late and the heavy thickset man cannoned into him just as the corridor illuminated.

'Sorry, guv,' Ben Morrison mumbled. 'Didn't see you there.'

Gilham stared at his number two in astonishment. 'Where the devil have you been?' he exclaimed. 'I've been trying to get hold of you for at least two hours.'

'Yeah,' Morrison admitted. 'Just checked me mobile and got your message about Derringer. Had an accident, see.' He pulled back the sleeve of his leather jacket to reveal a heavily bandaged hand and forearm. 'Ran over a bloody cat on me way home for some nosh. Soddin' thing clawed me hand when I went back to check it.'

'So why didn't you let me know?'

Morrison shrugged. 'Couldn't use me mobile in Casualty – X-rays and all that – and public phone out of order.'

Gilham looked unconvinced. 'So what are you doing up here at this time of night?'

Morrison frowned. 'What *is* all this, guv – third degree? Came up to see you, didn't I? Thought you'd be back and wanted to apologize.'

'So why didn't you check with the SDO first to see if I'd returned?'

Anger burned suddenly in the DI's dark eyes. 'Dunno what you're on about. Look, time I went home, unless you've any objections. Got a shot at hospital and don't feel so good.'

'Fine. I'll talk to you again in the morning.'

Morrison slammed the exit door against the wall as he slouched for the stairs. 'Look forward to it,' he growled. '*If* I decide to come in.'

For a few moments Gilham stood behind the glass panel of the door and watched him go, his brows puckered in thought and a nasty little bug crawling around inside his head. Then abruptly he turned away from the door and headed off along the corridor in the opposite direction.

The incident room was in darkness, the computer monitors switched off, but green and red lights glowed everywhere and the hum of quietly operating circuits competed with the clatter of an activated fax machine. He glanced at the messages in the fax tray, but it was all routine stuff – mainly press enquiries that should have been directed to the headquarters press office and responses to enquiries made to other police forces. Despite Morrison's very plausible story about the accident and the reason he had given for returning to the police station, doubts still crowded Gilham's mind and he couldn't help asking himself the question: what on earth had the DI been doing in the blacked-out incident room?

The door to the small SIO's office was shut, but it was not locked. He turned on the light inside and scanned the room. Everything appeared to be more or less as he had left it, though a couple of the drawers in the desk were half-open and the catch on the flap of the briefcase he had left in the corner was not engaged. His policeman's nose twitched. What the hell had Morrison been looking for? And what had prompted him to start looking in the first place? Gilham felt uneasy and vulnerable, but, though he did not realize it at that moment, his night of surprises was far from over.

It was cold in the big four-by-four. The engine had only been off for around an hour, but the Honda's polished tin was no barrier to the chill rising from the frozen ground as Fulton climbed behind the wheel. He had decided to borrow Abbey's Honda again as it was less likely to attract the attention of any lurking reporters than his familiar battered Volvo, but he knew he was taking one hell of a risk. If he were to be pulled over for a routine check by a police patrol, he would have quite a bit of explaining to do – especially as Abbey was missing and he was already suspected of murdering his own wife. But what choice did he have? If he used the Volvo, he was almost certain to end up with an unwelcome press entourage all the way to Saddler Street police station and staying at home with the whisky bottle was certainly not an option.

As it was, he got to Saddler Street without incident. He parked the Honda in the entrance to a nearby industrial estate, and to his surprise access to the station was just as easy. The officer manning the front desk obviously hadn't read the local newspapers or force email circulations that referred to his suspension and barred him from police premises, for he let him in with hardly a glance in his direction. Though the lapse was to Fulton's benefit, the big man shook his head in disbelief as he stomped along the corridor towards the stairs. Talk about communication.

He forgot all about the negligent bobby as he panted his way to the top floor, however, for he had more important things to worry about. In fact, his mind was so crowded with doubts and questions that he could hardly think straight. Although it was almost impossible to believe that someone like Phil Gilham – a man he had worked with on so many cases in the past – could be a cold, sadistic killer, he was unable to come up with any rational explanation as to how his former DCI could have got hold of Lyall's stolen mobile unless he was implicated in the murders in some way. Derringer had already suggested that there might be more than just the psycho involved in the serial killings; maybe he had been right after all and Phil Gilham was the accomplice?

But if Gilham were implicated, certain things just did not add up. For example, why would he deliberately indicate he was using Lyall's mobile when he rang earlier, and then not only fail to take advantage of the number withheld facility, but actually invite his old boss to phone him on the number later the same night? And why would he go to all the trouble of masking his voice in the original phone call and yet make no attempt to do so when Fulton rang him back? It was time for some answers and Fulton was in exactly the right mood to demand them.

Gilham was still in the SIO's office, slouched behind the desk, when he lumbered through the half-open doorway. The former DCI's face was pale and drawn, the stress cruelly evident in his expression, and Fulton couldn't help noticing, with a sense of malicious satisfaction, the uncombed hair and rumpled state of the usually immaculate suit.

'How the devil did *you* manage to get in?' Gilham demanded, his eyes widening as he instinctively straightened in the chair.

Fulton towered over him. 'Never mind that,' he snarled. 'What are you doing with Lyall's mobile?'

Gilham picked up the silver-grey telephone from his desk, absently turning it over to reveal the Dyno-tape label,

'H B Lyall', on the back. 'So it was you who rang me just now,' he breathed. 'What are you playing at, Jack?'

Fulton snorted. 'You're the one who should be coming up with the explanations, Phil,' he said. 'McGuigan told us that the psycho was using Lyall's phone, remember? So how come you've got it now?'

Gilham gave a short nervous laugh. 'Oh, hang on a minute, Jack, you're away with the fairies. Believe it or not, this phone was in the top drawer of my desk. I only discovered it when it started ringing.'

'How did it get in your drawer – fly in?'

Gilham's face hardened. 'Someone must have planted it there while the office was empty – and I'm pretty sure I know who that someone was.'

Fulton deposited his massive frame on the edge of the desk. 'Oh? And who's that?'

Gilham looked up at him. 'Ben Morrison,' he said. 'He was buggering about up here when I came back in.'

'You're saying he was actually in this office?'

Gilham pushed the chair away from the desk and stood up. 'I can't say that, but he had just come out of the incident room when I turned up and he looked pretty guilty, I can tell you.'

'But why would he go to all the trouble of trying to stitch you up?'

'He probably thought he needed to divert attention away from himself.'

'For what reason? As far as I know, there has never been any suggestion of him being a suspect.'

'There is now.' Gilham quickly told him about Derringer's murder, the excuse Morrison had made about the injured cat and the significance of his injured hand in relation to the bloodstained pyracantha bush at the hospital.

Fulton was tempted to say that he had first-hand knowledge of Derringer's death, but decided against it, instead exhibiting shock at the news and making the right sort of convincing noises as he lit up a cigarette to cover any visible signs of guilt in his expression.

'We always said it was someone on or close to the team, didn't we, Jack?' Gilham continued, turning to stare out of the window with his hands thrust into his trouser pockets. 'Someone who knew everything that was happening and could wander in and out of the nick at any time of the day and night without attracting suspicion. Who better than Ben Morrison?'

The big man shrugged. 'And who better than you, Phil?' he said, back on the attack. 'Maybe Ben's explanation about the cat clawing his hand is legit – and after all, you *are* the one actually in possession of Lyall's phone.'

Gilham swung back into the room and stared at him in astonishment. 'Oh come on, Jack, you can't really think I'm the killer surely? I mean, look at it logically. If I *were*, I would hardly leave the most incriminating bit of evidence of all in my drawer and answer the first call that came in on it. I'm not totally stupid, you know.'

'Nor is Ben Morrison, but someone put the mobile there.'

'Well, it wasn't me and, on the subject of likely suspects, you forget that I wasn't even here when Lyall was killed. I was on my way back from Jamaica with my partner, Helen. I didn't land at Heathrow until after Lyall's body had been discovered.'

The suspicion in Fulton's eyes did not diminish. 'Cast-iron alibi, you reckon then, do you?' he said.

'It counts me out as a damned suspect, if that's what you mean.'

'Does it? Well, it may interest you to know that, following my suspension, I made a few enquiries about your little holiday trip.'

'You did what?'

'And my contact at Heathrow Airport was very helpful indeed. In fact, she told me there was no record of a Philip Gilham on the passenger manifest for the fourth of October – the night Lyall was killed – but there *was* a Philip Gilham listed for the night before, which means you were actually home around twenty-four hours before the old boy's estimated time of death.'

Gilham had paled significantly and was now gnawing at his bottom lip. 'All right,' he said eventually, 'I'll admit I was home a day earlier than I led you to believe, but certainly not to slit a retired judge's throat.' He took a deep breath and turned back to the window to hide his embarrassment. 'Truth is, Jack, I've been over the side for a couple of months now – an old university girlfriend of mine I dated in my final year. I – I told Helen that I was due back at work the morning after we returned from Jamaica and would be away overnight on a crime conference in the Smoke, but actually I was with – with my ex-girlfriend at her flat.'

'Nice to know integrity still means something.'

Gilham winced at the barb and turned to face him again. 'OK, so I'm not proud of myself,' he admitted, 'but the important thing is that I can prove I was nowhere near Lyall the night he died – I was with the lady in question – and if anyone wants that fact verified, I am fully prepared to give them her details so that they can check with her personally.'

'Even if that means destroying your long-term relationship with Helen?'

'Better that than being in the frame for multiple murder – and anyway, I would hope that any enquiry would be discreet.'

Fulton grunted. 'As discreet as it has been for Janet and me, you mean?' he commented, a bitter edge to his voice.

Gilham flinched. 'I'm sorry about what happened to Janet,' he said, 'and for the witch-hunt that's been mounted against you, I truly am, but that's no reason to accuse me of being a sadistic psychopath.'

'I'm not accusing you of anything, but you have to admit that your behaviour so far has been more than a little questionable.'

'Well, what about yours? For instance, how is it you knew to ring Lyall's mobile in the first place?'

Fulton threw him a cynical glance and stripped the seal off a new packet of cigarettes. 'Let's just say I got a call from a little bird who suggested I should,' he replied, selecting a filter-tip and lighting up.

Gilham nodded grimly. 'Probably the same little bird who sent me a text message, telling me to be in my office at midnight tonight,' he retorted, 'which is how I came to be here when you rang.'

'And I suppose you're going to tell me you've since deleted that message?'

There was a sneer on Gilham's face as he jerked another mobile phone from his pocket and flicked open the flap. 'As a matter of fact, I haven't,' he said, tapping some buttons and thrusting the phone almost into his face.

Fulton didn't react, laconically glancing at the illuminated display. 'Who was the sender?' he queried.

Gilham checked and showed him it again. Fulton nodded, unsurprised. 'Lyall's number,' he said.

His colleague nodded. 'Strangely enough, until you told me that, *I* wouldn't have known whose number it was, but the killer obviously slipped the mobile in the drawer here after making his call to you.' He frowned. 'And what I can't fathom is why the Slicer would give it to you at all. I mean, why would he want to draw you back into the inquiry after taking so much trouble to get you taken off it in the first place.'

Fulton stiffened. 'What makes you think he had anything to do with my suspension?' he said, the suspicion back in his tone.

Gilham snorted his derision. 'Oh come on, Jack, it stands to reason that he was responsible for the murders of Janet and her boyfriend. You may be many things, including a real pain in the bum at times, but a cold-blooded murderer is not one of them.'

'Thanks for the vote of confidence.'

Gilham raised an interrogative eyebrow. 'Which brings me back to my original question,' he persisted, instinctively sensing he was on to something. 'Why would the killer choose to rattle your cage at all?'

Fulton affected an indifferent shrug. 'Maybe it's more a case of *his* cage being rattled rather than the other way about,' he replied, thinking of his own refusal to give up on the case even after Abbey's kidnapping and the killer's threats. 'Could be he wanted to muddy the waters a little and create a rift in the team, which would bugger up the inquiry and leave him free for his next hit.'

'His *next* hit? How do you know there's going to be another one?'

Fulton drew down a lungful of smoke. 'I don't,' he said, then hesitated, debating whether he could now trust his former colleague enough to fill him in on the latest developments regarding Abbey. He was spared that difficult decision, however, by the sudden screech of an alarm, which tore through the building with the force of an erupting cyclone. It was the ultimate conversation stopper and both men immediately recognized it for what it was. Someone had hit the panic alarm in the custody suite downstairs.

CHAPTER 20

THE CORRIDOR LEADING to the custody suite was in darkness and nothing happened when Gilham skidded to a halt to fumble for the light switch. The scream of the panic alarm was so loud that it was actually on the pain level now, even drowning Fulton's cursing as he clapped a hand over one ear.

'Someone nicked both the bulbs, guv,' a shadowy figure yelled from the end of the corridor, briefly masking the ghostly light streaming out of an open doorway.

Fulton was surprised to see it was Dick Prentice and pushed past Gilham to join the DS in the doorway. 'Can't you turn that bloody noise off?' he shouted.

'Already sorted,' Prentice shouted back and just as he said that, an unseen hand obliged, the alarm abruptly dying in a choking hiccup.

There was a pool of blood on the floor of the small office on the other side of the doorway and two uniformed police officers were bending over a prostrate figure in one corner. The iron gate leading to the cells stood wide open and the metal ring normally attached to the custody sergeant's belt now dangled from the big black key in the lock.

Fulton didn't need Chapter and verse from anyone as to what had happened. The fact that the panic alarm had sounded, the gate to the cells was open and the figure lying on the floor wore the chevrons of a sergeant on his epaulettes told its own story and even as he headed for the iron gate, he felt a knife-twist in his gut that had nothing at all to do with his physical condition.

McGuigan was in Cell 2 and he had died in a welter of his own blood, his throat bearing the familiar vicious signature of the so-called Slicer and his body lying on its back, half in, half out of the integral toilet cubicle. Fulton stared at the sightless eyes and the glistening muscular tissue now creeping from the rent in his throat and made a tight grimace. 'Poor bastard!' he said.

Gilham slumped back against the door frame with his eyes half-closed. 'And slaughtered in our own nick,' he added. 'The press will tear us to pieces over this. I've only just persuaded Dee Honeywell to authorize extended detention—'

'Never mind the press or friggin' Honeywell,' Fulton cut in, studying the dimly lit passageway leading to the remaining cells. 'I'm more interested in where our killer went. Check each of the other cells thoroughly.'

Then he was striding back along the passageway, leaving Gilham smarting like a castigated schoolboy and staring after him in a cold fury.

The injured sergeant was no longer in the custody office when Fulton lumbered back through the iron gateway, but the place was far from empty. At least half a dozen uniformed officers – several of them missing ties, indicating that they had probably been on meal break when the alarm had activated – were milling about the room, one actually standing on the edge of the pool of blood the sergeant had left behind.

'Get out of here – all of you!' Fulton yelled. 'This is a flaming crime scene and you prats have already trampled over half of it.'

As the uniforms began to melt, DS Prentice pushed through them towards him. 'Ambulance en route, guv,' he said, automatically reporting to him, despite the fact that he was on suspension and should not have been there in the first place. 'I've also told control to get hold of SOCO plus the Home Office pathologist – oh yeah, and Superintendent Honeywell has been advised and is making her way.'

Fulton's mouth tightened at mention of Dee Honeywell. 'Oh joy,' he muttered under his breath, then glared at the departing uniforms. 'Who's on the front desk?'

One of the bobbies turned back towards him. 'I am, sir – PC Sharp.'

'Who else?'

'Just me, sir. Civvy station duty officers only work until midnight here. Has to be one of us after that.'

Fulton raised his eyes to the ceiling. 'Ye gods! So whoever did this had a clear exit to the street afterwards? Now that really *is* brilliant!'

Sharp shook his head. 'I responded the moment the alarm went off, sir. No one passed me in the corridor and it's the only way out of the nick. Rear door is security locked at night.'

Fulton snorted. 'So what? The killer was either on his toes well before the alarm sounded or he found somewhere to hide until you were out of the way – like in one of the damned interview rooms next door, for instance.'

'Well, I – I suppose that *is* possible, sir.'

'Possible? It's not just possible, man, it's obviously what bloody well happened!'

Then, presenting his back to him, he turned to Prentice again. 'Did you sound the alarm?' he snapped.

'No, guv, I'd only just got back from the Derringer job at the hospital when it went off,' the DS replied. 'Must have been DI Morrison.'

'Morrison? He was here?'

'Coming out of the cell when I arrived. He sent me to call for an ambulance for the skipper. I made the call, then you and Mr Gilham turned up.'

'And where is Mr Morrison now?'

Prentice gave a soft chuckle in spite of the situation. 'Probably in the bog, guv. He looked a bit pale when he passed me in the corridor afterwards and he weren't hanging about neither.'

'The bog? I can't see him being upset by a bit of gore – the man's an ex-marine.'

'Claimed it was something to do with an injection he'd just had.'

Fulton scowled, remembering what Gilham had said about the DI's accident. 'Well, get him Tannoyed. I want him down here pronto. Also, get hold of a couple of uniforms to secure the scene.'

'Right away, guv.'

'What about the custody sergeant?'

Prentice half-turned on his way to the door. 'Huw Davies?'

'If you say so. Where has he disappeared to?'

'Couple of the lads took him to the doctor's room to await the ambulance.'

'You mean, they moved a head-injury case?'

Prentice said nothing and Fulton shook his head in resignation. 'Bloody woodentops,' he murmured and headed for the door.

Sergeant Davies was lying on the examination couch, a couple of pillows under his head and a hastily applied bandage round his forehead which seemed to be getting redder by the second. A balding thickset constable was sitting on a chair beside the couch. He stood up smartly when Fulton burst in.

'How is he?' Fulton snapped.

Before the constable could reply the sergeant's eyelids fluttered open and he gave a weak smile. 'Bit of a headache, sir,' he said in the soft lilting tones of the Welsh valleys.

Fulton nodded. 'Did you see who did this to you?'

Davies automatically shook his head, then released a sharp cry, one hand darting to the bandage, his eyes tightly closed in pain. Fulton waited for him to recover.

'Heard a knock on the custody office door, sir. Unlocked it, but corridor was in darkness so couldn't see a thing. Then *wham*! Something hit me.'

He swallowed with difficulty, a haunted expression surfacing in his blue eyes. 'Get to my prisoner, did he, sir?' he asked.

Fulton waited while the station Tannoy blasted Ben Morrison's name three times, then nodded. 'You could say that,' he said, 'but it wasn't your fault.'

The Welshman's mouth tightened. 'Maybe had something to do with that damned note, sir?'

Fulton stiffened. 'Note? What note?'

Davies took a deep breath, wincing again in pain. 'McGuigan wanted the SIO. Something about new information. Wouldn't say what it was though. He – he asked for pen and paper and jotted something down, which he insisted on sealing in an envelope. PC Brooks, my gaoler was going off sick, so I got him to drop the envelope on the SIO's desk for when Mr Gilham came in.'

Fulton resisted the urge to strangle an injured man.

'Should have called up Mr Gilham straight away, shouldn't I, sir?' Davies said, reading the censure in his eyes.

Fulton grunted. 'Might have been better, skipper, but don't worry about it. You weren't to know.'

'Weren't to know what?' Gilham queried at his elbow.

Fulton steered him firmly to one side as a pair of uniformed paramedics appeared through the doorway. 'Skipper says McGuigan had some new information for us,' he replied, studying the other's face for a reaction. 'Apparently a note was left on your desk.'

'*My* desk? But there was nothing on my desk.'

There was a cynical gleam in Fulton's eyes. 'So you say – just a stolen mobile, right?'

The dig was not lost on Gilham. 'What are you getting at?'

'Forget it. How were the cells?'

Gilham looked confused by the sudden change of direction. 'The – the cells were clear,' he replied. 'Seems McGuigan was our only guest tonight.'

'Nice and convenient for his killer then?'

The other released his breath in an exasperated hiss. 'Jack, what is all this rubbish about a note? I've just said there was nothing on my desk.'

'OK, so there was no note. Someone must have lifted it then. Maybe we should ask Ben Morrison about that too.'

Gilham's mouth tightened. 'Jack, can I have a word?'

'If you must.' Fulton followed him out into the corridor and into one of the adjacent interview rooms, where he leaned against the wall, knowing exactly what was coming. 'Well?'

Gilham lowered his voice, but his tone was nevertheless very brittle. 'I'm fed up with all these snide comments of yours, Jack,' he said, 'and I don't know what you think you are doing here anyway. You have no right to be interrogating anyone or bellowing out orders. That's *my* job. I'm SIO now. You're on suspension and you shouldn't even be in the nick.'

Fulton lit a cigarette. 'Finished?' he said, his tone pure acid. 'Good, because I want to make something perfectly clear to you. Until I'm absolutely sure you're kosher, I intend following this business through to the bitter end – suspension or no suspension. So we can either work together and share information or against each other and foul up a major police inquiry better than any killer could ever hope for. It's your choice.'

Gilham had difficulty keeping his voice down. 'You just don't get it, do you?' he hissed. 'It's not a question of choice. You've been ruled out of the inquiry and have no option but to stay out.'

Fulton gave a thin smile. 'Is that so?' he replied. 'Well, the killer seems to have ruled me in again and, as far as I'm concerned, he has the final say – *whoever* he might be.'

'Meaning what exactly?'

'Meaning whoever he might be – and that includes everyone in this nick.'

'But you can't *still* think of me as a suspect, surely?'

'Let's just say I've not yet entirely dismissed the possibility that you are involved somehow.'

'Oh come on, Jack. After what I told you upstairs, you know damned well I couldn't have killed Lyall – and I was actually with you in the SIO's office when McGuigan got sliced.'

Fulton remained unmoved. 'The jury is still out on Lyall,' he growled, 'and as far as McGuigan is concerned, who can say exactly when Sergeant Davies was clobbered or McGuigan had his throat cut? Minutes can count a lot, as you well know, and you could easily have done the job yourself, then retreated upstairs, leaving the next visitor to custody to sound the alarm.'

'Which just happened to be Ben Morrison, didn't it? For heaven's sake, Jack, use what little of that atrophied brain you have left. Doesn't it strike you as a bit odd that Morrison should be the one to stumble on it all – especially in view of his behaviour earlier tonight? I mean, why was he in custody in the first place? When I confronted him on the top floor earlier, he said he was going home.'

'Maybe he was and then the alarm went off.'

'But that was nearly an hour later. What was he doing all that time – reading the note Huw Davies says he put on my desk? OK, so maybe he's a slow reader, but come on!'

'All very suspicious, I grant you, but if Ben *is* our man, I can't see him luring you to the nick for the phone call from me, then being stupid enough to be there when you arrived.'

'Could be he cut it too fine after planting the evidence in the drawer?'

'And could be he didn't put it there in first place?' a voice snapped from the doorway behind him.

Ben Morrison's face was ashen, his ever restless eyes still for once and locked on to Gilham with obvious hostility.

Fulton raised an eyebrow and took another pull on his cigarette. 'You shouldn't be listening at keyholes, Ben,' he commented.

The DI slipped a new strip of chewing-gum into his mouth with a bandaged hand. 'Wouldn't need to if I could trust me own guv'nor,' he said.

Gilham was plainly embarrassed at being caught out, but that didn't stop him hitting back hard. 'Trust *me*?' he ranted, jerking round to face him. 'You've got a flaming nerve. You're the one who's got the explaining to do, not me. You go missing half the night, turn up later in the incident room with some cock and bull story about being scratched by a cat, then just happen to be the first one on the scene of McGuigan's murder.'

Morrison snorted his contempt. 'Do me a favour! If I was the friggin' killer, would I hit the bloody panic alarm?'

'Maybe you heard someone coming and wanted to make things look good.'

'That's crap and you know it.'

'Is it? Then why disappear so rapidly afterwards? To wash McGuigan's blood off your hands in the bog?'

Morrison took a step towards him, neck muscles bulging and fists clenched by his sides. 'And how come *you* had Lyall's mobile in your desk drawer? Nick it from him after you slit his throat, did you?'

Gilham smirked in triumph. 'And how is it you knew it was there in the first place?'

'Drawer was half-open. Saw it inside, right?'

Fulton straightened up off the wall and raised both hands in censure. 'Listen to the pair of you,' he growled. 'You're behaving like a couple of five-year-olds.'

But Gilham was still not finished. 'OK, so ask him what he did with the note Huw Davies left on my desk. He obviously took it.'

Fulton raised an enquiring eyebrow. 'Valid question, Ben,' he said. 'Did you take it?'

Morrison hesitated, reddening appreciably, then nodded. 'Popped into nick on me way home from hospital to explain to Phil where I'd been. He weren't back from Derringer hit, so decided to wait.' He shrugged. 'Just happened to see sealed envelope on desk and had a dekko, that's all.'

'That's all?'

Morrison's face hardened. 'Been with this firm a long time, guv. Always been a leg man – doin' shit jobs while others got the bleedin' glory—'

'So you decided to grab some of that glory for yourself by getting the SP from McGuigan first, eh?'

There was almost an entreaty in Morrison's eyes as he glanced in his direction. 'Well, thought it would be good to make DCI before I retired. Saw this as me big chance.'

'What a load of rubbish!' Gilham exclaimed. 'How gullible do you think we are?' He stabbed an accusing finger in the DI's direction. 'After you left me on the top floor, you were gone around an hour before the alarm went off. Where'd you go? Midnight mass?'

Morrison took a deep breath, now completely on the defensive. 'Couldn't get me car started and came back in—'

Gilham's derisive chortle cut him off in mid-sentence. 'Oh come on, Ben. Can't you think of anything better than that?'

Fulton grunted, apparently no longer interested in Morrison's explanations and keen to move on. 'Where's the note, Ben?' he said.

The DI nodded again and reached in his jacket pocket to produce a crumpled piece of paper. 'Hung on to it,' he replied, slumping into an adjacent chair. 'Thought it might be useful evidence later.'

But Fulton was not listening. He was too busy smoothing out the A4 sheet on the nearby table to study the cramped writing.

LIED WHEN I SAID I DIDN'T SEE WHO DELIVERED ENVELOPE AFTER LYALL'S MURDER. CAUGHT SIGHT OF HIM AS HE SCARPERED. SAME GUY

PASSED ME IN CORRIDOR TODAY BEFORE THEY BANGED ME UP AGAIN AFTER INTERVIEW. NEED TO TALK TO YOU PDQ!

Gilham whistled. 'So our local hack was actually on to the killer.'

'Yeah,' Fulton growled. 'and a fat lot of good it did him.' He threw the other a quizzical glance. 'So why was he being interviewed again?'

Gilham shrugged. 'I believe his solicitor called in to see him.'

'So he would have been taken to one of the two interview rooms near the custody suite – maybe even this one?'

'More than likely. Custody record should say. What's your point?'

'My *point* is that whoever he saw in the corridor must have been there for a specific reason. The corridor itself is a dead end, so the killer must have been there on custody business and the last thing he would have expected was to come face to face with the one person who might have been able to identify him.'

Gilham's eyes flicked to his number two. 'Like Ben Morrison, you mean,' he sniped.

Morrison left his chair with an angry snarl, but Fulton moved more quickly and blocked his path. 'Just pack it in, the pair of you,' he rapped. 'Having a go at each other will achieve nothing. Now, where's the envelope the note was in, Ben?'

The DI hesitated, then, with a curt nod, abruptly fumbled in his pocket and produced a buff-coloured ball of paper. Fulton snatched it from him, smoothing it out on the table beside the note. 'Now that *is* interesting,' he murmured.

Morrison frowned. 'What is?'

Fulton grunted. 'Take a look,' he invited.

Morrison complied, partly obstructing Gilham as he pressed in closer to the table. The envelope was marked 'Confidential' and addressed to 'Det. Supt Fulton' in blue ballpoint pen.

'OK,' Gilham observed. 'McGuigan was obviously unaware of the fact that you were no longer SIO – so what?'

'Not that,' Fulton snapped. 'Look at the handwriting, man. The envelope may have been written in block capitals like the note, but it is pretty obvious, even to my untrained eye, that it's in an entirely different hand.'

Both his colleagues looked blank and he swore his exasperation. 'Oh, come on, the pair of you are supposed to be bloody detectives! This is obviously not McGuigan's original envelope. That one was torn open, so the killer had to replace it with another one and readdress it.'

There was a pregnant silence for a few moments and sensing the two pairs of eyes boring into him, Morrison gulped quickly and shook his head several times. 'Don't look at me – I had nothing to do with it. Note was in envelope when I found it.'

Fulton's eyes narrowed. 'You sure about that, Ben?' he said.

Morrison took another deep breath, a hunted look in his eyes. 'Look, guv, I just give you the note, didn't I? Hardly have done that if I was the flippin' killer, would I?'

Gilham shrugged. 'Who knows how a psycho's twisted brain works?' he retorted.

Fulton threw out a restraining arm as Morrison went for him again. 'Shut it, Phil,' he rapped. 'Don't forget, you're not above suspicion yourself.'

Gilham flushed. 'Neither are you,' he fired back, 'and you're carrying a lot more baggage than either of us.'

Fulton gave a bitter smile, too tired now even to get angry. 'You mean because I've got previous for battering my wife and her lover to death, is that it? Funny, I didn't realize there had already been a trial.'

Gilham swallowed hard, averting his gaze. 'Sorry, Jack,' he muttered, 'that just came out.'

The big man nodded, his expression contemptuous. ''Course it did, Phil,' he acknowledged. 'You're right though. I've got more against me than most, but as everyone at the nick is under suspicion until this swine is nailed, it leaves you with an arse of a problem, doesn't it?'

'I don't follow you?'

'Don't you?' Fulton pushed past him to the door. 'Well, think about it,' he said, turning briefly with one hand on the handle. 'Not only have you got to decide whom you can trust, but how you are going to convince the rest of the team that they can trust *you*!' He jerked the door wide. 'As for me, bed sounds like a pretty good idea.'

The prospect of soft sheets and a cool pillow was certainly foremost in Fulton's mind as he left the police station, but that indulgence had to be relegated to the back burner when he eventually got home, for there was a sliver of light probing the back lawn through a chink in his lounge blinds. He had an intruder in his bungalow!

CHAPTER 21

FULTON BURST THROUGH the lounge door like a runaway JCB, but a few steps into the room he stopped short, staring first at the table lamp, burning like a malevolent eye on the coffee table, and then at the gaunt hunched figure occupying the armchair beside it.

'*Mazel tov*, Jack,' Mickey Vansetti said, taking a sip from a glass of whisky.

Fulton stared at him in disbelief. 'You cheeky bastard!' he choked, starting towards him with both fists clenched. 'How the hell did *you* get in?'

The former gang boss smiled with the warmth of an open tomb. 'That catch on your French winders was just askin' to be slipped, my son,' he answered. 'You ought to get it fixed.'

Fulton took another step towards him, his voice trembling with anger. 'You break into my place and calmly sit down and drink my Scotch? I've a good mind to wring your scrawny neck.'

Vansetti threw up his other hand in a swift defensive gesture. 'Not a good idea, Jack,' he warned. 'Not if you wants to nail the Slicer. Anyway, what was I supposed to do with the bleedin' press out front? Wait till you was in an' knock you up? Look good, wouldn't it, local villain callin' to see his ol' mate, the suspended police super?'

The big man hesitated, one part of him itching to grab his uninvited visitor by the collar and hurl him out into the night and the other urging restraint until he had found out what he had to say.

Vansetti seemed to sense his dilemma and made the most of it. 'Fact is, Jack, I ain't been that straight with you.'

'Now there's a surprise.'

'Yeah, well that's why I'm here, ain't it – to make it right and give you the SP on a few things?'

'And why would you want to do that? Just in case I had a touch of the seconds and thought about turning you in?'

'Close. You catchin' me in the same room as that stiffed copper might take some explainin' if it got out. But there's more to it than that.'

Fulton produced his packet of cigarettes and leaned back against the doorframe as he lit up without offering Vansetti one. 'OK, so I'm listening. But it had better be good.'

Vansetti drained his glass and brazenly refilled it from the bottle beside the chair before slopping whisky into a second glass perched on the arm.

'Sit down an' have a drink, Jack,' he said, nodding towards the other glass. 'Standin' there, you looks like you got a pole stuck up your arse.'

'You'll get my boot up yours if you don't get on with it.'

Vansetti stared into his own glass for a moment or two, as if seeking inspiration from the amber-coloured spirit. 'My ol' man's in Derryman 'Ospice, Jack,' he said at last, looking up. 'Took him there yesterday. Big C. They say he's only got a few days at most.'

Fulton grunted, remembering from his early days on the crime squad what a vicious antagonist Carlo Vansetti had been. 'Forgive me if I don't cry,' he commented. 'So what has he got to do with this confessional of yours?'

It was Vansetti's turn to hesitate. 'I ain't no grass, Jack, but seein' as Carlo's on the way out, what I got to say can't hurt him no more.'

The mobster produced a part-smoked cigar from his top pocket and fumbled in his pockets for a second before nodding his thanks when Fulton tossed him his lighter. 'First off, about tonight. I weren't after that little shit, Derringer, 'cause he done me at the tables. That was a load of ol' fanny – even though he did use my club an' shag one of the croupiers. Truth is, Derringer had been puttin' the black on me ol' man and had squeezed him for a few thou before I sussed what was goin' on. So I sent Bruno to find him, get back what was owed and give him a bit of a slappin'.'

'Sounds like Bruno did a good job there. So what did Derringer have on your father in the first place, apart from thirty years of villainy?'

Vansetti grimaced as if he had found an unpleasant taste in his mouth. 'At the start, Carlo told me it were to do with a bit of business involvin' some nicked gear, but it turned out he were tellin' me a load of ol' porkies. When they shunted him into Derryman, he decided to come clean – shit scared he was goin' to end up with his throat cut like the others.'

Fulton stiffened. 'Like the others? And why would he think the killer was after him?'

Vansettti appraised him with a cold reptilian intensity. 'That's what I come here to tell you,' he replied. 'What do you really know about our Mr Justice Lyall?'

'What *should* I know?'

'You'd be surprised. There were quite a bit to ol' Herbie.'

'Herbie?'

'That's what they called him on the street when he weren't wearin' his wig. Bit of a bad boy were our Herbie.'

Scooping up the spare glass of whisky from the arm of Vansetti's chair, the policeman dropped on to the settee with an explosive thud, his stomach juices stirring in anticipation. 'How bad was bad, Mickey?' he encouraged.

Vansetti leaned towards him. 'Bad enough to enjoy a regular bit of S and M, I'll tell you that.'

'Sado-masochism? You're saying he was bent?'

'As the proverbial. Been at it for years, long before he got the silk an' then became a judge.'

'Dirty old sod.'

'Yeah, an' not only him – good ol' Reverend Cotter too.'

'Cotter?'

'Yeah, Mr 'Oliness hisself. They was in a syndicate, see – like minds an' all that – run by a high-class shrink, called Score.'

Fulton drew in his breath sharply. 'Julian Score?'

'That's the geezer. Had some kind of private clinic for junkies an' screwballs out in the sticks not that far from here.'

'You're talking about Drew House.'

'Right again. Score had this cellar, see, rigged up like some bleedin' torture chamber, and they used to meet there regular as clockwork for a bit of what was on offer.'

Fulton thought about what he had seen for himself in the mansion's church crypt and felt his skin crawl. 'And what *was* on offer?'

'Rent boys mostly, them as would do any trick asked for an' could be relied on to keep shtum afterwards if they was paid enough.'

'And Carlo told you all this?'

Vansetti slumped back in his chair, a bitter expression on his skeletal face. 'Come out with it last night just before I left him at the 'ospice,' he replied.

'So he was in this syndicate too, was he? Why doesn't that surprise me?'

'No, Jack, you got it all wrong. Carlo weren't part of the syndicate itself. He just supplied the rent boys for 'em. Saw the whole thing as a nice little earner an' he made quite a bit of dosh out of it too. But then there was an accident.'

'The fire?'

'You know about that then?'

Fulton gave him an old-fashioned look. 'I *do* read crime reports, Mickey,' he snapped, but didn't volunteer any further information, determined to keep the conversation on track. 'So, what happened?'

Vansetti shrugged. 'Dunno exactly, as I weren't there, but Carlo says Score an' a young lad got crisped.'

Fulton remembered studying the crime report on the LIO's computer and nodded. 'Edward Heath.'

Vansetti avoided his gaze. 'Yeah, that's him. Papers had him down as some local junkie, who'd broken into the place lookin' for dope, but that were just somethin' they was fed. Truth is, he were one of Carlo's rent boys hired to do the usual tricks for the syndicate an' Carlo thought that were all there were to it when he run him there like he'd done with all the others before.'

'But this time it was different, eh?' Fulton suggested, sensing Vansetti had a lot more to divulge, but was still reluctant to put it all into words.

The other nodded and studied the carpet through the smoke from his cigar. 'Yeah, see, Score an' the others was bored with the same ol' bondage thing, so they decided to up the ante without telling Carlo. When the kid was delivered, they pumped a load of LSD into him to try and liven him up. But he went off his head an' as they was cartin' him back to the house from the crypt, he broke free, got into the library an' started a fire. Score tried to stop him,' and he shrugged again, 'but you knows the rest.'

'And how come only Score's name got a mention in dispatches?'

Vansetti's face registered contempt. 'It were all sorted by one of your own, that's why.'

'Nick Halloran,' Fulton grated before he could stop himself.

Vansetti nodded again. 'After everyone had scarpered, Cotter suddenly remembered they'd left the crypt door open and went back to lock up. Halloran saw the light in the church an' caught him with his frock down. In a panic Cotter grassed up the rest of the syndicate.'

'Paving the way for Halloran to cut a deal in return for a nice little earner – with no one to dispute a "no questions asked detected arson" except an incinerated Edward Heath?'

'Somethin' like that, yeah. How Derringer found out Carlo were mixed up in it all, I ain't got the faintest, but he were well in with that slime-ball, Lenny Baker, who used to do a trick or two himself in the ol' days. I reckon maybe Lenny come across some stuff an' passed it on for a quick buck.'

'And how do *you* fit into all this?'

'I don't. Knew sweet FA about any of it until last night. The ol' feller unloaded the lot on me out the blue, like some bleedin' confessional.'

Fulton grunted. 'The Nazis expressed the same sort of ignorance at Nuremberg,' he said with a wry grimace.

There was a flicker of alarm in his visitor's dark eyes. 'On my life, Jack, I had no part in it all and I want to set the record straight right now.'

'You mean, before the facts come out anyway and you get nailed as an accessory to manslaughter, conspiracy and maybe even sexual perversion with a minor?'

The ageing villain swallowed several times. 'You're a hard man, Jack, but this is legit, I swear it. I done many things over the years – blaggin', bit of protection, runnin' knocking-shops and spielers – yeah, I'll admit to it all. I been a naughty boy an' I done porridge for it too, but I ain't no nonce an' that's the truth.'

'Maybe it is, but with your form and all the baggage you're carrying for Carlo, convincing a jury you're Mr Clean would be a pretty tough job.'

Vansetti threw up his hands in desperation, almost knocking over his whisky glass in the process. 'Strewth, Jack, all this happened fifteen years ago. You had me banged up in Wandsworth then on a double blaggin', remember?'

'OK, but why come to me with all this?'

'I need your help, that's why. Carlo's shit scared he's next on the killer's list. That's why I went to see Derringer at the 'ospital, to find out if he knew enough to finger the Slicer before it were too late.'

Fulton made a sour face. 'Yeah, well it may have escaped your notice, but I happen to be suspended. You need to speak to a proper copper. Try Acting Detective Superintendent Gilham.'

'Do me a favour, Jack! How can I trust Ol' Bill when this nutter is probably a bleedin' copper hisself? Anyway, with my previous, if I told them what I just told you they'd just bang me up.'

'Chance you'll have to take.'

'An' what happens to Carlo meantime, eh? Can you see your mates givin' someone like him police protection?'

'He doesn't need it. You've got your own thugs to do that.'

Vansetti scowled. 'Already tried. 'Ospice won't let Bruno anywhere near the place – even though I offered 'em a nice little bundle. Said it would upset the other patients.'

'So, what do you expect *me* to do?'

The dark eyes studied him fixedly. 'Nail the Slicer before he gets to my ol' man,' Vansetti said simply.

Fulton shrugged. 'What's the point? As you said yourself, Carlo will be dead in a few days anyway.'

The other looked genuinely staggered. 'I can't believe you just said that, Jack,' he gasped.

Fulton fidgeted uncomfortably. 'Yeah, well, I've got problems of my own, Mickey.'

'Find this nutter an' they'll all be sorted.'

'You reckon?' The policeman hauled himself to his feet, picked up the whisky bottle and poured himself another drink. 'Maybe it's time to retire anyway.'

Vansetti nodded. 'So you just goin' to give up, that it? Let this bastard butcher a few more people? Don't sound like the Jack Fulton I used to know.'

Fulton snorted. 'You don't give a damn how many more people are butchered, Mickey. You're only interested in your old man.'

Vansetti stood up and buttoned his coat with an air of finality. 'Maybe you're right, Jack,' he replied, turning for the door. 'But, as a copper, shouldn't you be interested in that as well?'

Fulton made no effort to stop him leaving and sat scowling into his whisky glass for a long time after the back door had slammed and his visitor's footsteps had receded along the gravel path outside. Being reminded of his moral obligations by someone with Mickey's track record was more than a bit rich, but he knew the mobster was right. Carlo Vansetti was as much entitled to the protection of the law as anyone else, regardless of what he had done in the past, and now that Fulton knew the old man was at risk, he was duty bound to do something about it. But what, that was the point? He had not been able to prevent the murder of any of the Slicer's victims so far, so what chance did he have where Carlo Vansetti was concerned? Then there was Abbey. He was still no nearer to finding her than when she had first been seized. Everything was a diabolical mess and after compromising himself by quitting the scene of Derringer's murder, enlisting the help of his former colleagues was out of the question.

He was still agonizing over it all, the whisky glass cradled in both hands, when his over-wound body clock finally took the initiative and shut down. As the whisky glass slipped from his nerveless fingers, spilling its contents into his lap, he pitched sideways on to the settee and left reality behind him. And while his depleted batteries slowly began to recharge, the figure in the hooded anorak slipped round the front of the bungalow from the back garden, under the very noses of the two reporters drinking coffee in the car parked outside, and thrust a padded envelope through the letterbox. It was just after four and much too early for the Royal Mail.

CHAPTER 22

FULTON WAS RUNNING A bath and about to get undressed when the doorbell rang and he levelled a curse at the ceiling. A good five hours' sleep might have gone some way towards helping his exhausted body to recharge its batteries, but it had done little to soften his bad humour. The battered settee he had been abusing for so many years could not have been a worse place to crash out on, especially in the contorted position in which he had ended up, and now even the chance of steaming away the pain eating its way through his locked back muscles had been denied him.

'This better be important,' he shouted, storming to the front door and wrenching it open.

'It's that all right,' Phil Gilham said, his expression grim as he pushed past him into the hallway.

Fulton's eyes narrowed and he nodded towards the lounge. 'In there,' he snapped, bending briefly to pick up the post from the mat. 'And you've got exactly ten minutes.'

'Have I indeed?' Gilham retorted, following him into the room and turning to face him again. 'Then answer me this, Jack, where the hell is Abbey Lee?'

Inwardly, Fulton jumped, but he was careful not to let his feelings show in his expression or tone of voice. 'Abbey?'

he repeated, avoiding the other's gaze and sifting through his post. 'How should *I* know where she is?'

Gilham's mouth tightened. 'Well, you've been using her flaming car, haven't you?' he said. 'I saw you drive it away from the nick when you left there this morning and it now seems to be parked in the lane behind your bungalow.'

Fulton threw him a swift glance. 'And what makes you think it's *her* car?' he prevaricated. 'There's more than one Honda four-by-four on the road.'

'Because it happens to have personalized number plates.'

'And how would you know that?'

Gilham hesitated. 'Who do you think the old university friend was I've been over the side with?'

Fulton gaped for a second, then shook his head in disbelief. 'Abbey Lee?' he exclaimed. 'You've been shagging *Abbey Lee*? You dirty little bugger!'

Gilham gave a dismissive snort. 'Only because you fancy her yourself, Jack – now, where is she? I've been round to her flat twice this morning, but the place is deserted.' He held up a single Yale key to emphasize the point. 'And her colleague, Ed Carrick, seems to think she has disappeared.'

Fulton tossed a bundle of junk mail on to the settee, keeping only the bulky envelope. 'I'm her keeper now then, am I?' he said, frowning when he saw that the envelope was addressed to him in bold block capitals, but bore no address or postmark.

'Well, how do you explain the car?'

The big man looked up quickly, suddenly angry at the apparent inference. 'She leant me the damned thing, OK? My Volvo would have attracted too much media heat every time I went out, so I started using hers.'

He crossed to a small bureau, produced a paper-knife from inside and went to work on the sticky tape sealing the envelope, relieved to have been provided with a convenient distraction.

But Gilham was not about to give up. 'So how is she getting around herself, if you've got her wheels?'

'How should I know? Because I borrowed her car doesn't make me her personal confidant.' Fulton glanced at him over his shoulder, a malicious gleam in his eyes. 'Maybe she's over the side with another DCI and is having an extra-long lie-in.'

'This is not funny, Jack.'

But the reproof was unnecessary, for Fulton was in no mood for laughing – even less so after seeing what he had just pulled out of the envelope. 'Mother of God!' he whispered, and stared at the grisly object in his hand with a kind of horrible trance-like fascination before suddenly recovering his senses and throwing it on to the flap of the bureau with a violent shudder as if it were a leper's bandage.

Gilham was by his side in a couple of strides. 'What is it, man?' he exclaimed, peering at the plastic bag lying on the square of green leather.

'What does it look like?' the big man gasped, the colour draining from his face as he grabbed at the mantelshelf over the fireplace to steady himself.

Frowning, Gilham reached past him and picked up the bag to study the contents more closely – only to drop it even more quickly than Fulton when he realized what it was he was holding. Made of transparent material and neatly sealed at the top with what looked like Sellotape, the bag was not unlike one of those used in supermarkets to hold grapes, but there were no grapes in it this time – only a severed human ear! 'Gordon Bennett!' he breathed. 'What kind of a sicko would send something like this through the post?'

Fulton gulped several times and pressed his chin into his throat as he belched repeatedly on the acid welling up from his stomach. 'The same kind of sicko who likes to cut off people's balls and slit their throats in front of a mirror,' he choked. 'And he has Abbey.'

'He has *what*?'

Fulton jerked a folded note from the envelope he was still holding and shook it open, scanning the unsigned message at the same time as Gilham. It was only very short, but the warning was unambiguous.

THOUGHT IT WAS TIME I SENT YOU A LITTLE SOMETHING FROM ABBEY, JACK. KEEP POKING YOUR NOSE AND I'LL SEND YOU A BIT MORE.

Gilham snatched the note from him and read it again, his own face also deathly white as he turned to face him. 'You *knew* he had her and you said *nothing*?' he shouted. 'You let him *mutilate* Abbey and told *no one*?'

Fulton's legs started to fold under him and he made the armchair just in time. 'Get me a drink,' he said hoarsely.

Gilham bent over him, his eyes blazing. 'A drink? You want a *drink*? You useless cretin! I'll see you in hell for this!'

Fulton's breathing became ragged and he clutched at the arm of the chair as a succession of fiery spasms ripped through his gut. 'Don't you think I'm already there?' he rasped, his mouth twisted into a savage grimace. 'Have been ever since he took her.'

Gilham hesitated, eyeing him narrowly for a second, then abruptly crossed to the cocktail cabinet and returned with a double whisky, thrusting the glass at him as if it were a closed fist. 'So what happens now?' he demanded. 'You just going to sit here and wait for this filthy psycho to deliver Abbey to us piece by piece or are you finally going to let me in on your little secret?'

Fulton stared at the floor over the rim of his glass. 'Haven't got any bloody secrets,' he muttered. 'Just nightmares.'

'Well you must know something.'

Fulton raised his head and glared at him. 'He snatched her from her car in the hospital car park last night when she took me to see Derringer,' he snarled, 'and that's it, OK?'

'You went to see Derringer last night? But that's when—'

'Yeah, I know. He was dead when I got there.'

'When you got there?' Gilham turned away from him, running his hand through his blond hair and staring at the ceiling in total exasperation. 'This gets worse and worse, Jack – quitting a murder scene, concealing a kidnapping, withholding evidence, taking and driving away a motor vehicle; is there any rule you haven't broken? And all the time you've been quizzing *me* as a murder suspect. It's beyond belief.'

Fulton downed the rest of his whisky and leaned forward in the chair to light a cigarette, his hands trembling so much that it took him three attempts to get his lighter going. 'History for now, Phil,' he retorted after a long pause, the combination of whisky and nicotine apparently restoring some of his former resilience. 'First priority is to find Abbey.'

Gilham jerked his vibrating mobile telephone from his pocket and studied the text message that had evidently just come through. 'Maybe we have already,' he snapped, heading for the door. 'That was control room. Woman's body's been found at a derelict asbestos factory just outside town. White, thirties, with long black hair – *and* she's minus an ear!'

The scenes-of-crime tent had seen better days, but it fitted neatly over the door of the Nissan hut and was effective in keeping the reporters at bay. They were forced to huddle together in a dispirited group just outside the encircling blue-and-white crime-scene tape: a dozen or so phantom-like figures, wrapped in the icy skeins of autumn mist.

Gilham arrived in the temporary parking area in a swirl of gravel. Fury had directed his right foot all the way, fury and bitter resentment towards the unwelcome passenger who was slumped in the seat beside him. He had used every means of persuasion he could think of to deter Fulton from forcing his way into the car, knowing full well that to turn up at a murder scene with a suspended superintendent in tow was likely to finish his own career for good. But Fulton had been at his most determined and short of calling up the cavalry to arrest his old boss, which would have raised more than a few questions about his own conduct, Gilham had been left with no alternative but to let his personal Jonah aboard. But he had made it plain to him that, as part of the deal, he was to remain in the car out of sight of the press and anyone else who might recognize him – not that there was much hope of him sticking to his side of the bargain.

The local DI, Jaspreet Sidhu, was a willowy thirty-something-year-old, who would have been attractive but for the hard cynical turn of her mouth, and she was waiting for them by her car. 'Guv,' she acknowledged, apparently recognizing Gilham immediately he got out of the car, but reserving a curious wary glance for Fulton as he clambered out after him. 'Corpse found around mid-morning by a couple of kids bunking off school. Took 'em a while to pluck up courage to ring the nick.'

She lifted the tent flap as the uniformed bobby manning the entrance quickly stepped aside. 'One of her ears was amputated,' she explained as she pulled on the pair of protective overalls and booties handed to her by a second uniformed constable inside the tent. She waited patiently while Fulton and Gilham did the same. 'Thought there might be a connection with your so-called Slicer.'

Fulton jammed the zip on his overalls and scowled when she stepped forward to help him. 'He cuts off balls, love, not ears,' he snapped, his agitation getting the better of him.

Her face froze, her resentment towards him tangible, perhaps because she guessed who he was. 'We thought it was worth a shot anyway, *sir*,' she replied, her tone brittle. 'Sorry if we've wasted your time.'

'Pathologist arrived?' Gilham put in, sensing the build up of hostility between the two of them.

'Yes, guv. Doc Carrick, twenty minutes ago.'

'So let's take a look, shall we?'

The familiar figure of Ed Carrick straightened when they entered the Nissan hut and he was shaking his head as they approached. 'Most peculiar,' he commented, 'most peculiar indeed.'

Fulton bent down to study the corpse and seconds later his sigh of relief was clearly audible. The woman was not Abbey Lee. 'Thank God,' he breathed without thinking.

Sidhu was obviously put out. 'Thanking God is hardly an appropriate sentiment under the circumstances, *sir*,' she said. 'The woman is dead.'

'Oh, she's dead all right, my dear,' Carrick put in before Fulton could respond. 'Been dead for about forty-eight hours, I would say.'

Sidhu bit on the 'my dear', but chose to keep her own counsel. 'And cause of death?'

Carrick shrugged. 'From my initial examination, I suspect that she died from a drug overdose and the track marks on her arms and thighs would suggest she was a heavy user, but only a post-mortem will be able to establish this for certain, of course. Quite why someone would want to cut off her ear though is most intriguing.'

Fulton was pretty sure he knew why, but he was not about to share his views with those present and instead turned to Sidhu with a curt, 'Do we know who the woman is?'

The DI met his gaze without flinching. 'Excuse me, sir,' she said, apparently now sure in her own mind as to his own identity, 'but should you be involved in this case at all in your present situation?'

Gilham winced, anticipating the other's reaction, but as Fulton's face hardened into familiar slab-like aggression and Carrick discreetly wandered away, the heat was taken out of the situation by a timely interruption.

'Bloody hell, what's *she* doing here?'

No one had heard the speaker approach, but his outburst at Gilham's elbow guaranteed him immediate attention. As all eyes focused on the scruffy-looking man with the spiky ginger hair staring down at the spot-lit corpse, Sidhu forced a frosty smile. 'George Jarvis,' she announced. 'Just joined us from the drug squad.'

But Fulton was not a bit interested in where he had come from. 'You know this woman?' he snapped.

Jarvis gave a short laugh. 'Should do. Name's Janice Long. She was heavily into speed-balling and one of my more productive snouts – when she wasn't spaced out, that is.'

'And when did you last see her?'

Jarvis stared at him. 'Yesterday, as a matter of fact – on a slab in Middle Moor Hospital mortuary.'

'*What*?'

'Yeah, she'd finally OD'd on bad coke. Always was a greedy bitch. Dumping her here must have been someone's idea of a joke.'

Gilham frowned. 'But how come no one missed her corpse? There are no signs of the usual surgical examination, so she can't have had her PM yet.'

Jarvis shook his head. 'PM was due for eleven hundred hours,' he said, 'but it was put back to fifteen-thirty, due to a break-in.' He gave a short laugh. 'Can you credit it? Some lowlife breaks into a mortuary – not a bank or a good-class drum, but a *mortuary* – and nicks a bloody corpse!'

Fulton grunted. 'With not a single member of staff being any the wiser?'

Jarvis frowned. 'But that's the other funny thing. They checked the fridges to make sure none of the stiffs had been interfered with and found they were all there, as recorded.'

'As recorded?' The colour literally drained from Fulton's face and he pulled Gilham roughly to one side, drawing astonished glances from Sidhu and Jarvis. 'Think, Phil,' he breathed, 'why is that the mortuary staff failed to notice that Janice Long's body was missing? Because it wasn't, that's why.'

Gilham looked confused and glanced past him at the corpse. 'You mean the dead woman is not Janice Long?'

But Fulton was in no mood to enlighten him. 'What time is it?' he rapped, suddenly realizing with a sense of frustration that he had left his watch behind.

Gilham stared at him. 'What's that got to do with anything?'

'The time, Phil? Never mind the crap, give me the bloody time!'

Gilham glanced at his own watch, unnerved by the intensity of his manner. 'Just – just after fourteen-thirty.'

Fulton swung for the door at a run. 'Come on, man,' he shouted over his shoulder. 'We may already be too late!'

Gilham cast a helpless glance in the direction of Sidhu and stumbled after him, catching up with him in the SOCO tent as he tore off his overalls. 'Too late? Too late for what?'

Fulton half-turned, almost falling over as he tried to shrug himself out of the clinging plastic. 'Should have sussed this out long ago,' he panted. 'Killer intimated as much when he rang me after kidnapping Abbey.'

Gilham paused in the act of pulling off his own overalls. 'The killer? For heaven's sake, Jack, what are you talking about?'

Fulton stared at him wildly as he tossed his overalls into a corner. 'Bastard gloated that Abbey should feel completely at home where he had put her,' he said. 'Abbey's a pathologist, isn't she? So where would she be most at home? In a soddin' mortuary, of course.'

Gilham felt his skin crawl. 'Good grief! You're saying our man substituted Abbey for Janice Long?' he whispered, cottoning on at last.

'I'd put money on it.'

'So you think she *is* dead then?'

Fulton's face had frozen into a bleak mask as he stumbled for the exit. 'No, Phil,' he threw back over his shoulder, I think she's alive – no doubt sedated, but very much alive – and if we don't get to the mortuary in time, she will be having Janice Long's PM!'

CHAPTER 23

THE YOUNG WOMAN lying face up on the examination table had been gutted like a slaughtered animal, that was the first thing Fulton saw when he burst through the double doors of the mortuary, and his shouted '*No!*' only succeeded in raising echoes off the tiled walls as the pathologist in his green overalls cast him a keen glance over the top of his wire-framed spectacles.

'Good afternoon, gentlemen?' the latter said, clearly irritated by the noisy intrusion. 'And what can I do for *you*?'

Fulton leaned back against the door, panting heavily after his run from the car and focusing his gaze on the ceiling to avoid looking at the corpse. 'Nothing now,' he replied harshly. 'It looks like she's beyond anyone's help.'

The pathologist glanced at the corpse, then back at Fulton, raising a curious eyebrow as he nodded to the attendant to begin the grisly process of sewing her up again. 'They usually are by the time they end up in here,' he observed, a tart edge to his voice. 'And you are who exactly?'

Gilham produced his warrant card, his hand noticeably shaking. 'Police,' he said, trying hard to control the quaver in his voice. 'We have reason to believe that—'

But he never finished the sentence, for Fulton chose that moment to lower his gaze and his sharp exclamation cut his colleague off in midstream. 'She's got dyed hair, Phil, dyed hair!'

Then the big man had pushed past him to the head of the slab, where he stood for a moment staring down at the face of the dead woman. 'It isn't Abbey,' he said, filled with relief for the second time that afternoon. 'It isn't Abbey.'

The pathologist leaned against the edge of the table and lit a cigarette. 'Do you mind telling me what this is all about?' he said, watching Fulton stride to the row of refrigerators and wrench one of the doors open.

For answer, Gilham stepped across to the foot of the slab and picked up the edge of the label tied to the woman's toe.

'Deborah Slatter,' the pathologist commented, his tone now so dry that his voice practically cracked. 'Cause of death: fatal asthma attack. Anything else you'd like to know?'

'Yes,' Fulton grated, slamming the door of the furthest refrigerator shut. 'You seem to be a stiff short.'

'Janice Long, you mean?'

'Exactly.'

The pathologist flicked the ash from his cigarette into the half-closed chest cavity of the corpse, watching with clinical indifference as the attendant continued to stitch up the rest. 'Over there,' he said inclining his head towards the far corner of the room. 'She's next. It seems someone dumped her out here instead of in the fridge. Most irregular.'

For the first time, Gilham noticed the trolley, bearing the bulky plastic body bag, which had been shunted unceremoniously into an alcove under the single frosted window, but Fulton was beside it and jerking the zip down before he was halfway across the room.

Abbey looked as if she were simply sleeping and although her pale body was very cold, it had a suppleness no corpse could ever retain. Fulton's gently probing fingers found a tiny flicker at the base of her throat which told him all he needed to know. 'She's alive anyway, thank God,' he announced with a sense of relief.

'Alive?' The pathologist dropped his cigarette in his rush to join them, pushing Fulton aside as he bent over the body to check for a pulse, then prise open one of her eyelids to peer into the immobile green pupil. 'She seems to be comatose.'

Fulton pulled the zip back over her breasts to preserve her modesty. 'Yeah, she was probably injected with some kind of anaesthetic and/or sedative, like GHB, before she was wheeled in here to replace Janice Long.'

The pathologist stared at him. 'You mean someone deliberately did this terrible thing?' he exclaimed. 'But what on earth for?'

'So she could enjoy a ringside seat at her own PM,' Gilham replied.

Fulton looked past him at the corpse on the slab and the ugly coarse stitches disfiguring the chest and abdomen like the drawstrings of some mediaeval doublet. 'Could have worked too,' he said grimly, 'if you'd decided to do Janice Long first. Now, don't you think you'd better call for an ambulance?'

Fulton felt stupid carrying the bouquet through the hospital corridors. It was the only one he had been able to find already made up in its patterned plastic wrapping paper and pink ribbons and he had bought it without really thinking about the mechanics of delivery.

He had assumed that by nine in the evening normal visiting hours would be over and he would be able to slip unobtrusively into the hospital, but that had been wishful thinking and lumbering through the place with the bouquet clasped awkwardly in one hand, he found the indulgent smiles of the passing nurses and departing visitors galling to the extreme. He couldn't wait to get to the private observation room where Abbey had been accommodated so that he could lose his embarrassing 'get well' gift once and for all, but he soon discovered that actually handing over the bouquet was not going to be that easy.

To be fair, the uniformed constable on guard duty outside the room did not seem at all interested in his bouquet and there was not even the suggestion of a smirk on the youngster's freckled well-scrubbed face when Fulton stepped out of the lift. This was one bobby who took his duties very seriously, however, and he stepped smartly in front of the big man the moment he turned towards the door. 'Sorry, sir,' he said with a firmness of tone that belied his years, 'I can't let anyone in without express authority.'

Fulton glared at him. 'Then you've got it, lad,' he snapped back. 'My name is Fulton, Detective Superintendent Jack Fulton, OK? I was the one who actually *found* the lady.'

The officer stuck to his guns. 'Perhaps I could see your ID, sir?' he said.

Fulton automatically went for the wallet in his back pocket, then froze, suddenly remembering with a renewed sense of frustration that his warrant card had been taken off him with his suspension, which meant he was totally stuffed. There was no way this eagle-eyed plod would be fooled by a Superintendents' Association membership card, which was the only ID he had on him.

'It's OK, Constable,' a familiar voice commented, 'I can vouch for Mr Fulton.'

Fulton swung round to see Detective Chief Superintendent Andy Stoller standing a few feet away, studying him analytically as he slipped his own warrant card back into his coat pocket. 'Hello, Jack,' he said. 'Flowers for the patient, is it?'

Fulton's stare was blatantly hostile. 'What are *you* doing here, Andy?'

He was rewarded with a tight smile. 'Same as you, I would think: visiting the sick.' Stoller indicated the door with a wave of an arm. 'Shall we go in together?'

Abbey looked like a ghost; her beautiful green eyes were closed and her face, framed by the mass of jet-black hair, was almost as white as the pillow her head was resting on. Fulton winced when he saw the number of tubes and wires that had been connected to her, but the electronic monitor seemed to be issuing a steady 'beep' and the oxygen mask covering the lower part of her nose and mouth trembled slightly in time with the faint rise and fall of her breasts, indicating that she was at least still in the land of the living.

'Doc reckons she should be all right after a few hours,' Stoller said, reading his mind, 'but she's been injected with some sort of coma-inducing drug. They're still trying to analyse the traces they found in her blood, but suspect that an overdose of gammahydroxybutrate may be partly responsible.'

'Liquid Ecstasy,' Fulton breathed. 'GHB – I thought as much.'

Stoller nodded. 'And almost certainly something else on top,' he said. 'Apparently she would have been fully aware of what was going on around her, but unable to move or speak.'

Fulton shuddered, thinking of the dismembered corpse at the mortuary. 'That's exactly what the bastard wanted,' he retorted. 'A PM carried out on her while she was alive. Thank God we found her in time.'

Stoller shook his head. 'According to the pathologist, Dr Kelly, there was no chance of that happening. He claims her vital signs would have been detected well before any PM had commenced.'

Fulton grunted. 'Then how come no one detected those vital signs when she turned up in the morgue? And how come this Dr Kelly didn't know who Abbey was? After all, she *is* one of his bloody colleagues.'

'Kelly wasn't a member of the resident team, Jack. He was borrowed from another area and was only asked to fill in at the mortuary for this week. It seems Abbey Lee's disappearance had resulted in a shortage of pathologists and the coroner was concerned that they were running behind schedule.'

There was a suspicious gleam in Fulton's eyes. 'You seem to know an awful lot about what's been happening in this neck of the woods.'

'My place to know things – especially now.'

'Why now?'

'Because I've been appointed Acting ACC operations, that's why, which means the buck stops with me.'

'ACC ops?' Fulton echoed. 'So where's Skellet gone?'

Stoller grimaced at his disrespect. '*Mr* Skellet seems to have had some sort of breakdown – probably due to overwork – and he's been signed off for an indefinite period.'

Fulton raised his eyebrows. 'Breakdown? You mean poor old Norman's lost his marbles?'

'Not quite how I would put it, but he is certainly ill. This inquiry seems to have affected him badly. Something must have snapped.'

Fulton whistled. 'Well now, there's a turn-up for the books. Good old Norman en route for the funny farm.'

Stoller scowled. 'Never mind, Mr Skellet, Jack,' he snapped, starting to lose patience. 'I want to know precisely what's been going on here. This inquiry has already produced more stiffs than a TV crime drama – including an AWOL police officer wasted in his hospital bed and a journalist slaughtered in our own bloody police cells. Now to cap it all, we have a Home Office pathologist kidnapped and stuck in a mortuary in place of a deceased junkie who just happens to turn up in a derelict asbestos factory, minus an ear!'

Fulton nodded sympathetically. 'All a bit confusing, I agree,' he said. 'But you'll just have to speak to Phil Gilham about things. After all, he *is* your new boy on the block.'

'I've already spoken to him – he's only just left here after visiting the patient – but I'm damned sure you can tell me a lot more.'

'Why should I know anything? I'm on suspension, remember?'

Stoller closed his eyes for a moment, as if counting to ten. 'Don't piss me about, Jack,' he said, a brittle edge to his tone. 'You've been running around like a loose cannon ever since your suspension. You know a damned sight more than anyone about what's been going on and you have a duty to tell me.'

Fulton turned for the door. 'Do I? Well, I'm sorry, Andy, but I can't help you.'

'Can't or won't?'

The big man half-turned. 'You're a chief superintendent – sorry, acting assistant chief constable – aren't you?' he said, pushing the bouquet into his arms. 'So I'm sure you can work that one out for yourself.' And he left the door wide open as he left.

The temperature in the car park seemed to have dropped by several degrees in the short time Fulton had been in the building, but he found the sharp freshness of the night air a welcome change after the stuffy atmosphere of the hospital. He stood for a moment in front of the glazed entrance porch, apparently trying to neutralize the nicotine in his lungs with deep breathing exercises.

Stoller was right, of course. If he was in possession of information, then he had both a legal and moral obligation to pass it on, but what he actually knew would be of little real value in catching the Slicer, besides which, now that Abbey was out of danger and under close police protection, a lot of the pressure on him had been lifted and with that came an increased reluctance to co-operate with an investigation team he firmly believed to have become dysfunctional and untrustworthy. What he expected to achieve on his own with no police back-up and no leads, he hadn't the faintest idea – especially as that vital snippet of information he had somehow picked up along the way, which had been bugging him ever since, remained buried in his subconscious, stubbornly defying every effort he made to retrieve it. Nevertheless, he was determined to keep chipping away regardless, in the hope that there would be a breakthrough of some sort before too long – but he was not holding his breath.

Losing his taste for oxygen, he lit another cigarette and headed for his car on the other side of the car park, unsure what his next move should be and thinking he might be able to decide that over a glass of whisky when he got home. But that luxury was to be denied him.

The white envelope had been left on the windscreen of Abbey's Honda, pinned behind one of the windscreen wipers, and his heart began to thud wildly again as he carefully extracted it. The envelope, which was not addressed, was unsealed with the flap tucked inside and it contained a single sheet of note paper. As usual, the message was short, but the chilling content made up for that.

CONGRATUALATIONS, JACK. KNEW YOU'D SUSS THINGS OUT IN THE END BUT IT BOUGHT ME SOME TIME FOR A BIT MORE SOCIAL CLEANSING. NEXT ONE WILL BE AN OLD REPROBATE NO ONE WILL MISS. HOPE YOU APPROVE. WE'LL GET TOGETHER AFTERWARDS FOR A PINT. GIVE MY LOVE TO ABBEY.

Fulton didn't need clarification as to who the old reprobate might be and he wrenched open the door of the four-by-four in a panic, ramming the key in the ignition even before he was fully in his seat. He had fallen for one of the oldest tricks in the book, he realized that now. Abbey had been nothing more than a diversion – an unwitting participant in the killer's sick game – and through his own preoccupation with her welfare, he had forgotten all about the last surviving member of the Drew House syndicate. Carlo Vansetti might have been in the final stages of terminal cancer, but if the Slicer had his way, his end would come, not in a painless morphine-induced coma, but with the slow agonizing slice of a cut-throat razor. As the big man sent the Honda careering off across the car park towards the service road, he knew in his gut that he hadn't a hope in hell of getting to the hospice in time, but he owed it to his guilt-ridden conscience to at least try.

CHAPTER 24

FULTON CAME UPON Derryman Hospice without warning when the lane he had been following ended abruptly before twin stone pillars surmounted by huge lions, rampant and ghostly white in his headlights. He braked beneath the jaws of the sculptured guardians, extinguished his headlights and slipped into second gear, half-expecting the beasts to leap on to the car from their crumbling stone pillars and tear their way through the metal to get to the soft flesh inside. That they didn't was no small surprise to him in his almost surreal state of mind. He pulled away again at a crawl, nosed through the open gateway and bumped off the driveway into some trees.

For a few moments he just sat there with his window down, listening to the ticking of the hot engine. He was taking one hell of a personal risk, he realized that only too well. Alone, unarmed and tracking a psychopathic killer in wooded grounds at night, he couldn't have been more vulnerable. He knew the rules – had spent enough time in his service telling his staff to comply with them (even if he himself often failed to practise what he preached) – but with the killer already en route, there had been no time for phone calls or rules. This was his shout. He had let Carlo Vansetti down, just as he had let Abbey down, and he had no choice but to deal with it.

Buttoning up his coat against the cold, he grabbed Abbey's torch from the front seat and climbed out of the car, carefully pushing the door shut behind him before picking his way through the trees towards the house. Wide lawns, silvered in the moonlight by a light frost, encompassed the turreted mansion and the grass crunched underfoot like fine shingle as he took a chance on being spotted by night-duty staff or a resident insomniac and headed for the ornate porch at the front of the building.

The main doors were locked from the inside; Fulton could hear the bolts rattling when he gently tested the large brass knobs that served as handles. So it was a case of looking for another way in, then – and he completed nearly a full circuit of the building before he found it.

The ground-floor transom window had apparently been forced open and not too expertly either. The killer? Probably, and he was no doubt in a hurry. Directing his torch inside, he saw the beam bounce off rows of book spines. The hospice library? Must be.

He ducked through the open window, swung a leg over the sill and felt thick carpet beneath his foot. Somewhere above his head a clock provided a discordant version of the Westminster chimes. Swinging his other leg over the sill, he dropped into the musty darkness of a long, galleried room with stuffed bookcases and a heavy panelled door at each end. Fortunately the nearest door proved to be unlocked and he was able to make his way without difficulty along the corridor that lay beyond – only to freeze in the archway giving access to the front foyer.

A rectangular workstation stood in a pool of light to one side of the main entrance doors, the swivel-chair behind it conspicuously empty, though a transistor radio on an adjacent filing cabinet played soft music. Obviously someone was around somewhere – a night nurse perhaps – but there was no sign of him or her, so it was likely that they were out and about on their rounds. Then he grimaced as another possibility occurred to him, prompting him to stride across the foyer and subject the area behind the desk to closer scrutiny.

But there was no body lying there, nor any dark pools glistening in the lamplight, and he breathed a sigh of relief. He had been presented with enough corpses during this hideous business to last him for the rest of his enforced retirement. He just hoped Carlo Vansetti would be as lucky as the hospice's night nurse seemed to have been – though that depended on his finding the former gang boss before the Slicer did, which would not be easy in a building this size.

His break came when he happened to glance at the computer monitor on the desk top. The night nurse had not shut the system down before leaving his or her station and the menu was clearly visible. He grabbed the mouse and quickly clicked on to 'Patient List'. There were some thirty names on the page that materialized on the screen, all in alphabetical order. He found Vansetti's immediately. 'Room Eighteen,' he breathed and headed across the foyer towards an illuminated 'Stairs' sign, well aware of the fact that if he had been able to locate Carlo Vansetti so easily, his quarry would have been able to do exactly the same thing.

A security light fizzed into life the moment he went through the doorway, revealing a wide stone staircase in front of him marching up into a darkness pierced by shafts of moonlight from a high window. To his left a narrower iron staircase dropped away into its own black pit. A notice on the wall provided a list of the room numbers on each level and he saw that Room Eighteen was located on the top floor. 'Just my luck,' he muttered as he started up the staircase, wondering whether the Slicer had thought much the same thing a short time before.

The security lights activated all the way to the top floor, spookily sensing his presence a fraction of a second before he got to them and shutting down again the moment he passed by. When he eventually reached the upper landing, however, the light was forced to remain on a lot longer while his nicotine weakened lungs did their best to catch up after the climb. As he stood there gasping for air and holding on to the banister rail for support, he was struck by the unnatural silence that prevailed.

There was not a sound to disturb the stillness of the night; no footsteps from a patrolling night nurse, no snoring from sleeping patients, not even the creak or groan of expanding or contracting timbers. It evoked a weird sense of isolation within him and, staring down the staircase into the hostile blackness that cowered before the pool of light in which he now stood, he felt vulnerable and exposed.

Not surprisingly, he was relieved when his breathing returned to near normal and he was able to move on again, but straight away he encountered a different sort of problem. For some reason, the light sensor system did not extend beyond the stairs and when he jerked the landing door open, he found himself confronted by an even deeper brooding darkness. Despite the aid of Abbey's torch, it took him a few seconds to find and operate the light switch and then it seemed like for ever before a row of strip lights flickered into life in uneasy succession along a wide yellow-painted corridor with white-panelled doors on both sides. A strong smell of antiseptic greeted him the moment he stepped through from the landing, but the corridor itself was deserted.

Room Eighteen was halfway along on the right. The door stood ajar, a glimmer of light showing through the crack, but not a sound was audible from inside. He took a deep breath and pushed the door open, expecting the worst. Instead, he found himself staring into a smart well-appointed bedroom with the resident patient apparently soundly asleep in his bed, just the top of his head showing above the sheets. He frowned, an innate sixth sense telling him that something was wrong, though he was unable to put his finger on it.

Stepping into the room, he wheeled quickly to check behind the door, half-anticipating an ambush, but there was no one there. Next, he crossed to the en suite bathroom, pushing the door open on one finger and peering inside. The room was empty. Still that strange, uneasy gut feeling, but why?

Leaving the en suite, he stood for a moment by the door, his gaze travelling slowly round the bedroom, trying to spot anything that did not look quite right. The transom window was open at the bottom, the curtains stirring slightly in the draught, but otherwise everything appeared neat and tidy – only the oxygen cylinder, standing on a trolley beside the bed and the chart on its clipboard at the end indicating that this was a sick room, rather than a suite in a good-class hotel.

He moved closer to the bed, studying the motionless shape beneath the sheets and wondering whether he should waken the old man to see if he was OK. Somehow it didn't seem right, but there again, Carlo Vansetti was the reason for his being at the hospice, so it was the logical thing to do.

Holding his breath, he bent over the bed to carefully peel back the sheets – then promptly recoiled with the shock. Carlo Vansetti was certainly the one lying in the bed, though it was not sleep that had claimed him, but something a lot more permanent. The pale skeletal features resembled those of some mummified pharaoh, with the lips drawn back over toothless gums in an obscene rictus grin. Death seemed to have amused him – probably because in the end, by succumbing to the cancer that had been eating away at him, he had cheated the Slicer of his prize.

Fulton's mobile rang as he pulled the sheet back over the corpse and he guessed who the caller was even before he jerked the phone from his pocket.

'Hello, Jack. Bit of a bummer this time, isn't it? Old bastard snuffed it before I could get to him.'

Fulton crossed to the window and peered out, hoping to spot where his caller could be hiding, but his gaze met only moonlit lawns and purple tinted shrubbery. 'Got yourself a new mobile then?' he commented, keen to keep the conversation going while he worked out his next move.

There was a chuckle, embodying all the warmth of a death rattle. 'Courtesy of the hospice team, Jack. Little night nurse on reception left it on her desk when she went walkabout. Very careless of her – oh, by the way, you'll find her in the laundry cupboard next door, recovering from a chloroform hangover.'

Fulton's involuntary sigh of relief was louder than he had intended and there was another chuckle. 'What's up, Jack? Did you think I'd stiffed her as well?'

'It wouldn't have surprised me.'

A loud sigh down the phone. 'As if I'd slice a nice little girl like that – especially after she'd let me have her mobile to enable me to keep in touch with my old mate, Jack.'

Fulton grunted. 'You're really getting off on all this, aren't you? You think you're some kind of celebrity.'

'Well, it's gratifying to know I have earned a place in crime history – become a somebody at last – though I must admit I would have preferred a better nickname than the one that was picked. At least the Yorkshire Ripper received the accolade of being linked to his celebrated predecessor, whereas in my case Sweeney Todd has not even had a mention.'

But Fulton was no longer listening, for the psychopath had unwittingly triggered a reaction in the policeman's weary brain that was little short of cataclysmic and he swayed drunkenly for a moment, his eyes widening and his whole being suddenly coming alive as understanding erupted from his subconscious with the force of a massive heroin fix. Sweeney Todd! But that was it; that was the missing link and it had been so obvious all along. Now he knew what had been bugging him all through the inquiry and as the last few bricks were swept from the wall that had been constructed between the conscious and subconscious parts of his reactivated brain, whirling strands of previously unconnected thought fused into one, providing a composite picture that was as unsavoury as it was illuminating.

'Forget about your place in history,' he said, a new confidence in his tone. 'Just think about the place that's been reserved for you with all the other nutters in Broadmoor.'

Another chuckle. 'Why? Feeling lucky, are we, Jack?

'Could be – now that I've finally sussed who you are.'

The killer seemed unperturbed. 'What if you have? It won't do you any good anyway. The last miscreant on my little list will have been chastised long before you have any idea who it might be.'

Fulton froze. 'The *last* miscreant?' he echoed and, caught off guard for a second, said a lot more than he intended. 'But all the members of the syndicate are now dead.'

A harder, more measured laugh. 'Aha, so you know more than I thought, *Mr* Superintendent. But never mind, you're still way off course and by the time you manage to extricate yourself from your current predicament my job will be done.'

The meaning behind his words suddenly became clear as, right on cue, a battery of blue beacons illuminated the night sky beyond the perimeter of the hospice grounds and, lurching to the window, Fulton was just in time to see a convoy of police cars sweep up the drive.

'Thought I'd give the old three-nines a ring on behalf of the night nurse, Jack,' the killer continued, 'just to let them know there was an intruder on the premises. Could take a while explaining to your old colleagues why you broke in – and why you chloroformed that nice young nurse and stuffed her in a cupboard.'

As the phone went dead, Fulton saw maybe a dozen uniformed figures springing from their vehicles to fan out round the front of the building and, seconds later, he heard the inevitable heavy pounding on the front doors of the hospice as flashlights grazed the upstairs windows, neatly capturing his silhouette. Once again he had been expertly fitted up by his antagonist and as he lumbered out into the corridor, snarling a succession of choice curses, the question uppermost in his mind was how the hell was he going to get out of this one?

CHAPTER 25

THE HOSPICE WAS already waking up, with doors banging and people shouting on the floors below, as Fulton lumbered from Carlo Vansetti's room and made for the illuminated fire escape sign at the end of the corridor. But his luck was out. The door was securely padlocked. So much for fire regulations and health and safety, he mused grimly as he turned on his heel and headed back towards the main staircase.

Anxious faces peered at him round a couple of the doors when he reached the second floor and he glimpsed a short, thickset woman in a white dressing-gown hurrying towards him from the far end of the corridor with the look of 'staff' imprinted on her. 'Just a minute,' her authoritative voice boomed after him as he went for the next flight. 'What the devil are *you* doing in here?' But he had no intention of stopping to explain and he reached the ground floor well before she began her descent. The corridor below was miraculously empty, but the assault on the front door by the police was continuing with a vengeance and he glimpsed flashlights probing the shrubbery outside as he slipped into the library, closing the door tightly behind him.

'Window open here, Sarge!' a voice shouted above the now muffled banging and he breathed another curse. 'Going to take a look.'

The next instant a powerful beam exploded in the gloom, just missing him as he slipped behind a convenient bookcase. The bobby stood there for a few seconds, sweeping the room with the flashlight before clambering inside, his heavy boots scraping on the sill in the process. Fulton tensed behind the bookcase, stepping quickly to one side when a floorboard cracked a little too close for comfort and taking refuge behind a stout wooden pillar a second before the flashlight illuminated the spot where he had been standing. Silence. Even the banging on the front door had stopped. Maybe 'Florence Nightingale' had let the police in after giving up chasing her intruder down the stairs.

'Where are you, Snell?' Another flashlight probed the library from the window and Fulton heard sudden movement directly in front of the pillar sheltering him.

'In here, Sarge. Thought I heard something.'

A loud snort. 'You're always hearing things. Get yourself round the front. Guv'nor wants to organize a proper search of the grounds.'

The flashlight traced an arc round the library one more time, then Fulton heard the unmistakable sounds of the policeman scrambling back over the windowsill. He was alone at last and he made the most of it.

There was no one outside the library window when he got to it and he was through and into the adjoining shrubbery without being challenged, pausing only briefly among a forest of rhododendron bushes to get his breath back and work out his next move.

Trying to reach Abbey's parked Honda was out of the question. By now that would have been secured by the police units and before long a dog team or teams would be on the scene to sniff him out. He had to get clear of the grounds before that happened or he was finished, but in brilliant moonlight it would not be easy. Fumbling for the torch he had taken from Abbey's car, he pushed his way through the shrubbery, trying to make as little noise as possible and taking a route that kept the lofty walls of the hospice immediately on his right.

He heard the faint barking of the dogs as he emerged from the shrubbery a few minutes later and felt his stomach jolt. Before him stretched another vast expanse of lawn, but it was dotted with copses and as far as he could see, it was clear of police patrols. Gritting his teeth, he broke cover and hauled himself across the open ground to the first clump of trees, where he was forced to pause to get his breath back. The barking of the dogs was louder now and he guessed their handlers had them on short leashes, probably heading for the front of the house to report their arrival to the officer in charge. Making a sudden decision, he went for the next clump of trees, but only reached it in the nick of time as a heavy thudding sound preceded the sinister shadow of a giant flying bug that suddenly skimmed across the moonlit lawn, to freeze into immobility just yards from the trees sheltering him. The force chopper. Talk about piling on the pressure.

It was tempting – almost a compulsive reaction – to try and focus on the helicopter as it hovered directly overhead, but he knew that would be fatal and instead he dropped into a crouched position in some scrub, waiting for the inevitable. It came a second later – a shaft of brilliant light that seemed to erupt from nowhere, lasering the trees and holding for a few frightening seconds before leaping away to traverse the open ground he had just crossed. Then the shadow was moving again, racing away across the grass towards the other side of the house. Glancing upward, he watched the flashing red navigation light disappear into the night. How the hell had they missed him? He knew the chopper was equipped with every conceivable electronic aid, including thermal imaging, so they should have picked him out easily. But he had no time to ponder the point and, risking all, he went for the last few yards of open ground until he was through a broken perimeter fence into the belt of woodland enclosing the grounds.

A few yards of ferns, tangled roots and wet dripping trees and he broke out on to a hard road surface. He was in a lane of some sort, chippings in the surface glittering like polished glass in the moonlight.

Which way, that was the point? He chose left, his feet crunching on loose gravel at the road edges – only to stumble back into the woods almost immediately when he glimpsed headlights approaching round a shallow bend ahead of him, accompanied by the throbbing note of a slow-running engine.

The police traffic car was lit up like a carnival float, the driver scanning the woodland bordering the lane with a powerful roof-mounted spotlight, which Fulton knew only too well would have no difficulty in penetrating the sparse autumn foliage to pick him out when it reached where he was hiding. And to add to his woes, as the car drew closer to his hiding-place, he became aware of the distinctive thud of approaching rotor blades, accompanied by the excited barking of several dogs. Jerking round to peer through the trees behind him, he saw the helicopter silhouetted against the face of the moon as it narrowly cleared the tall chimneys of the hospice and homed in on the belt of woodland in which he sheltered, quickly overtaking a ragged line of torches that bobbed across the wide expanse of open ground towards the lane.

He was trapped! The realization hit him with a numbing sense of finality, but as he straightened up to await the inevitability of discovery, there was a totally unexpected reprieve. For no apparent reason, the patrol car suddenly lurched to a stop just feet away from where he stood and almost at the same moment, the uniformed officer at the wheel threw open the door and leaped out. Leaving the headlights blazing and the engine running, he dashed into the trees with the panic of a man in acute physical distress. His groans of satisfaction as he relieved himself in the bracken brought a sympathetic smile to Fulton's tightly compressed lips, but he recognized an opportunity when he saw one and was behind the wheel of the car and pulling away in a shower of gravel even as his 'saviour' was shaking off the last few drops.

In fairness, the patrolman reacted pretty quickly and he obviously didn't wait to do up his trousers, for he was out in the road and futilely giving chase on foot before the car had gone more than a hundred yards. But the powerful 3.5 litre engine soon reduced him to a speck in the moonlight and Fulton noted with a feeling of relief that in addition to the radio fitted to the car, there was a mobile phone lying on the front passenger seat, which meant that, unless his dispossessed traffic man had a second mobile or a portable radio pack-set in his pocket, he was not in a position to report what had happened to anyone.

The test came when the helicopter thudded overhead, forcing Fulton to brake right down to avoid attracting attention. The traffic car was supposed to be looking for a fugitive – a difficult thing to do when travelling at fifty miles per hour – and he waited for the call he knew was bound to come.

He was not disappointed. 'Tango Two-five,' the car's built-in radio suddenly blasted, apparently on the open channel 'talk-through' facility. 'This is Hotel X-ray 19. What's the hurry? Do you have a sighting?'

Fulton made a grimace. The flying bug was now pacing him, the curiosity of the crew evidently aroused. He had to assume Tango Two-five *was* actually the call-sign of the car he was driving, which meant coming up with an answer straight away – silence would only create suspicion – but he prayed no one who knew the regular patrolman's voice was listening in and that the observer in the chopper failed to spot the bobby he had just left in the woods.

'From Tango Two-five,' he responded. 'Thought I saw something up ahead. False alarm. Just a fox.'

A pregnant pause and then, to his relief, a throaty laugh. 'Copied, Tango Two-five. Suggest you change your optician.'

The next instant the helicopter had banked sharply to the right and disappeared into the night sky, its flashing red navigation light soon becoming just an acne spot on the face of the moon.

Fulton took a deep breath. So far so good, he mused, but it would only be a matter of time before the bobby he had left in the woods got to a phone or attracted the attention of one of the search teams. Then that would be it, with the clearly marked and highly visible traffic car suddenly becoming a liability instead of an asset, drawing all the other police units to it like flies round a jampot and shouting its identity to the force helicopter through its radio call-sign, which, like the rest of the police fleet, was certain to be printed in giant black letters on the roof.

Almost as a reflex action, he hit the accelerator pedal hard and felt the powerful vehicle respond instantly, leaping away into the night with a snarl of pure class, as if it actually sensed his urgency. He all but lost it on the next bend, chopping a sizeable chunk out of the nearside verge, but slackened only briefly when the lane then ended in a T-junction, before he swung hard left on to an empty dual carriageway with a squeal of tortured tyres.

A speed camera flashed as he passed it at over ninety miles an hour, but he hardly noticed. The demon on his shoulder held him possessed and his focus was far removed from the strictures of road traffic regulations, his thoughts concentrated instead on the daunting task he had set himself.

OK, so he now knew who the Slicer was – or at least he thought he did – but it was one thing knowing his identity and quite another proving it. He needed hard evidence, but there was no time for that. Search warrants, forensic analysis and the rest of the official trappings of the criminal justice system would only get in the way and make it all too late for the killer's next victim. The old-fashioned 'Ways & Means Act' (traditionally resorted to by bobbies seeking a practical, though not strictly legal solution) was the only realistic course open to him in the circumstances and he would worry about the consequences of that later. After all, he had enough criminal charges to look forward to already – murder, withholding evidence, breaking and entering, taking and driving away a police car and excess speed – which meant that whatever he did from now on was pretty academic anyway.

Yeah, but what if he was wrong about the identity of the killer and it was actually someone else, what then? His teeth clenched tightly for a second in an involuntary spasm. Well, in that case it would be the end of Plan A, wouldn't it? And the only problem he had then was that he didn't have a Plan B.

CHAPTER 26

THE MAN IN the red silk dressing-gown had been pacing his bedroom for the best part of two hours, throwing searching glances out of the window as he gradually emptied his half-bottle of brandy into the lead crystal glass he was gripping tighter than a baby grips a favourite toy. His cadaverous features were even more drawn than usual and his eyes had an unnaturally bright glint to them which suggested a heightened state of anxiety. In fact, he was right on the edge: stressed, exhausted, but most of all, very frightened – and he had every reason to be.

His Nemesis would come, of course – if not tonight, then tomorrow – and though he had prepared his security as well as he could, with all the doors and windows of the house locked or bolted and his pet Dobermann left to wander the half-acre garden at will, he had his doubts as to whether this would be enough. The creature they called the Slicer seemed to be able to kill with impunity and even a team of experienced detectives had failed to put a stop to the catalogue of atrocities that had already been committed.

But what else could he do to protect himself? Enlisting the help of the police was out of the question, for they would want to know why he considered himself to be at risk in the first place. That would mean revealing the guilty secret he had nursed for fifteen long years and destroying himself and everything he had worked for in the process.

Ironically, it had not occurred to him when the first two murders had been committed that he might later become a target himself. He had naturally assumed Lyall's death was something to do with his previous position as a crown court judge – a revenge killing by an ex-con maybe – and that Lenny Baker had probably been a key informant in the same case. Even with the murder of the Reverend Cotter, he had tried to convince himself that he was looking at nothing more than a coincidence. It was only when the link with Drew House had been established, that he was finally forced to face reality and scurry for cover.

Now his only hope was that he could stay out of harm's way until the Slicer was caught – with his departure for Malta in six hours on a last minute holiday his best chance of doing just that – but, as a gambling man, he knew that the odds in his favour were not great.

Emptying his glass, he set both it and the bottle on the bedside table and stretched out on the coverlet, the pillows banked against the headboard behind his head. In a few hours it would be light. Time enough to think about the sleep he so desperately needed once he was on the plane. For the present he would have to remain vigilant. The dog should warn him if he had any visitors, and anyway he was confident that his own sharp ears would pick up the sounds of anyone trying to force an entry. His hand closed on the bayonet lying beside the brandy bottle – a Second World War relic he had inherited from his deceased father years ago – and his mouth set into a hard uncompromising line. Were they to try it, he would certainly be ready for them – at least, that's what he told himself.

He was wearing the same determined expression as he drifted off to sleep and despite his sharp ears, he failed to pick up the soft 'crunch' of an expertly taped-up window breaking downstairs or, shortly afterwards, the squeak of a loose floorboard in the corridor outside his room.

The police helicopter located Tango Two-five exactly twelve minutes after the displaced traffic patrolman ran into one of the search teams and reported his car stolen. Fulton could not have felt more relieved that he had acted on gut instinct and ditched the car when he had, rather than driving what would have been a fatal extra half-mile to his objective. As it was, after abandoning the vehicle on a patch of waste ground in the middle of town, he had only just managed to lose himself in the labyrinth of adjacent streets when the familiar thud of rotor blades announced the chopper's arrival.

He had kept to the backstreets after that and, apart from one scare when he was forced to throw himself into a pile of rubbish to escape the powerful spotlight of the helicopter during a low-level sweep of the area, he had got to Saddler Street without any major problems. Once there, gaining access to the police station itself proved easier than he had anticipated. A transom window had been carelessly left open in the basement – the locker room, as it turned out – and a convenient external drainpipe enabled him to haul himself up on to the sill. The locker room was empty and in darkness, but a sheet of brilliant white light washed down the side of the building and flooded into the room like an advancing tide as he levered himself off the inside sill. He knew it was unlikely that the helicopter was directly targeting the police station – more likely that its probing beam was scanning streets much further away and had brushed the building in passing – but he couldn't take the chance and he remained crouched on the floor below the window for several minutes until the light was suddenly withdrawn and the helicopter's rotors faded.

The locker-room door made a cracking noise as he opened it, but there was no one around to hear; the corridor outside was empty. He glanced at his watch. It was just on two. There would only be a skeleton staff upstairs now anyway: the station duty officer, the team of communication operators sealed up in their control room and a replacement custody officer. The rest would be out on patrol – no doubt looking for him.

The station seemed dead and as usual was full of shadows. He made it to the first floor, which was unlit, then stopped abruptly in the darkness as a door closed somewhere along the corridor. He waited, listening intently. Soft footfalls sounded to his right, then another door opened with a groan and louder footsteps rang on what sounded like a bare stone surface (the back stairs?) as they faded away. He remained motionless until the walker had gone, then switched on his torch and moved off.

He found the office he was looking for – the words 'Administration' on the door – and carefully tried the handle. As he had expected, the door was locked, but it opened easily enough with the help of his Visa card, and he gave a critical shake of his head. He found it ironic that the very organization that liked to lecture the public on the importance of crime prevention failed to practise what it preached when it came down to fitting a modern thief-proof lock to the door of the office where, amongst other things, the police area's imprest account cash was kept. Still, the lapse served his purpose well enough now and he slipped inside and closed the door gently behind him.

The office was large, accommodating three separate workstations in the centre and a row of three-drawer filing cabinets along one wall. He guessed that, unlike the door, the cabinets would be securely locked because of their contents, and he shone the torch round the room, looking for the key cabinet that he knew would be there. When he located it he was astonished to find that someone had actually left the flap of the metal box wide open, with the keys still in the lock. It seemed that security at Saddler Street nick needed a very big kick up the backside.

The keys on the row of hooks inside were all neatly tagged. He selected the one labelled 'Area P/Fs' (personal files) and crossed the room to unlock the relevant metal cabinet. He eased out one of the long drawers on its runners with great care, knowing full well what a racket they could sometimes make if handled roughly.

The suspended files inside were neatly positioned and in alphabetical order, with senior officers grouped in one section, followed by supervisory ranks and then constables. This made his search a lot easier; within seconds of finding the file he was looking for and opening it up on top of the cabinet, he knew he had struck oil.

Like every other P/F in the force, the bundle of papers inside the familiar blue folder comprised confidential memos, letters and reports. Among these were the multi-paged annual appraisal reports, giving not only supervisory assessments and grades for each calendar year, but the officer's qualifications, achievements and personal details, including the information Fulton most wanted – his private address – which he quickly noted.

But there were other things in this particular personal file that were totally unexpected; things that made Fulton's heart once more beat twice as fast as he leafed through the documents, speed-reading as he went. 'Former military service in Royal Marines (commando unit) …' he murmured, his torch tracing a shaky path across the page. *The bastard knew how to kill, then*! 'Previously employed as charge nurse at Braxton psychiatric hospital.' *A charge nurse*? *So his killer had medical qualifications too. No wonder he knew how to use chloroform and drugs like GHB effectively. Probably had an illicit stock stashed away somewhere.*

And there was more, too. Thumbing through a clutch of papers near the back of the file, he came across something which really focused his mind. It was a three-year-old report notifying the headquarters personnel department of an impending medical operation. That in itself was not so startling, but it was the nature of the operation that gave Fulton a shock as he noted the contents: '… Specialist diagnosis – testicular cancer … No option but surgical removal … Necessity for several weeks' sick leave …'

Before returning the file to the drawer, the big man leaned on the cabinet for a few moments, digesting the information. Testicular cancer? Surgical removal? It was too much of a coincidence. There had to be a connection between his suspect's misfortune and the mutilations that had accompanied the murders of both Herbert Lyall and Andrew Cotter. Any lingering doubts he might have had as to whether he was going after the right man were now put to rest. It had to be him and all that remained now was to find the swine and nail him. To do that, though, he needed some wheels – and he knew exactly where to get them.

There was no one in the briefing room when he poked his head round the door and the place was in darkness, but his torch soon picked out the row of ignition keys on the cork board just inside, each with a metal tag attached carrying the vehicle's registration number. With a grim smile he remembered what Derringer had said to Phil Gilham about car keys being so easy to obtain. He made the mental observation that the station was a long time learning its lesson.

The high level of police activity still appeared to be ongoing when he climbed out through the open window, but the river of blue light pulsing among the buildings was much further away this time, and the helicopter's silhouette in the night sky had shrunk to the size of a child's toy as it hovered over the east side of the town. It reminded Fulton of some nocturnal bird of prey about to swoop on its unsuspecting victim.

The vehicle he was looking for turned out to be one of two marked area cars, parked alongside a couple of CID cars. He wasn't too happy about using such a highly visible vehicle, but he couldn't risk returning to the station to swop the keys for those of a plain CID car. He was behind the wheel and heading for the exit within seconds, feeling relieved that at least he had got away without detection.

Unbeknown to him, however, his departure had not gone completely unnoticed and he would have been more than a little concerned had he been aware of the other car pulling out of a corner parking bay moments after he had driven away. Significantly, the vehicle not only paused for a moment in the wake of the exhaust plume he had left floating in the entranceway, but then headed off in the same direction, maintaining a discreet distance behind him and hugging the nearside kerb with its lights extinguished. He would have been very interested indeed to see who was behind the wheel.

CHAPTER 27

RAFFERTY CLOSE WAS a cul-de-sac on the east side of town, adjoining a disused branch of the East Molten Canal and almost within spitting distance of the street where John Derringer had had his flat. Number 13 was at the end of a terrace of former Victorian workers' cottages, which could not have been more unsympathetically renovated if the developers had tried. Like its neighbours, it scowled over a tiny unkempt garden into a potholed street, which had once echoed to the clop of horses' hoofs, as the heavy drays had rumbled through the gates of the long since derelict Wimbles Wharf to meet the barges off-loading their cargos of black gold from the Midlands pits.

Fulton parked the police car behind a beaten up VW camper van, left half-on and half-off the pavement under a broken streetlamp, and sat there for a moment, studying the target premises along the inside wing of the other vehicle, wondering why someone with the sort of money his man must be earning would choose to live in a rathole like this. The place was in darkness, which was to be expected at – and he consulted the luminous dial of his watch – 2.45 in the morning. But if he was right, this particular resident would not be found buried under a mound of bedclothes; he would already be closing in on his next victim – if he was not there already – and Fulton just prayed that by adding burglary to his own growing list of offences, he would be able to discover the identity of that victim before another life was lost.

He took a deep breath, climbed out of the car into the frosty night and pushed the door to behind him. Then, keeping to the shadows, he followed the low walls of the neighbouring two houses along to the end – only to freeze into immobility beneath an overhanging tree when the thud of rotor blades announced the arrival of the police helicopter carrying out yet another low-level sweep of the area, with its powerful spotlight tracing a diagonal path across the street.

A couple of minutes later it was gone. He slipped through the open gateway of Number 13 and mounted the three stone steps to the front door. He was quite certain that the doorbell would only ring in an empty house, but he pressed it all the same, just to make sure. Nothing stirred and he grunted his satisfaction. On returning to the small patch of garden, he discovered a sideway between the house and the corrugated iron fence of Wimbles Wharf and investigated further.

The rear garden was as unkempt as the front, though slightly bigger, and through gaps in the rear fence he caught the gleam of the moonlight on the turgid water of the canal. The back door gave access to what many years ago would have been called a scullery and his elbow soon took out one of the small panes of glass to enable him to reach the key left in the lock.

His torch picked out a Belfast sink and a pile of washing in a plastic basket on the draining board as he made his way through an internal door to the kitchen. He almost trod on a black cat, which shot out of a litter tray by his feet and disappeared through the back door with a blood-curdling cry that made the hairs stand up on the back of his neck. *Good or bad luck?*

A poky dining room and sitting room opened off the hallway that lay beyond, but they contained nothing of interest, save shabby furniture and photographs of military vehicles and helicopters in various locations around the world.

The stairs creaked like arthritic joints as he headed for the upper floor and he felt a bit like the private detective in the cult horror film, *Psycho*, when he reached the landing, half-expecting a nightmare figure to suddenly rush out of one of the adjacent rooms wielding a long-bladed knife.

To his relief no such apparition appeared, but he felt a definite sense of unease as he strode towards a half-open door, unable to shake off the feeling that he was not alone. He checked a sparsely furnished bedroom, finding little of interest there, and was about to move back out on to the landing when he stiffened to what sounded like stealthy movement in the hallway below. He strained his ears to listen, but the sound was not repeated and a few moments later the returning helicopter put paid to any chance he had of hearing anything.

With the room temporarily caught in the beam of the chopper's spotlight as it raked the street, he instinctively flattened himself against the wall as much as his bulk would allow and waited. Eventually the beam passed on – jerked away as if on a length of elastic. In the darkness, he strained his ears again and this time he heard a series of familiar creaking sounds. His face hardened. Someone was coming up the stairs.

Shuffling sounds on the landing. Fulton held himself in check, resisting the urge to charge out of the bedroom to confront whoever had followed him into the house. But instinct urged caution and he waited, heart pounding and fists clenched tightly by his sides.

A light blossomed in the gloom and he edged closer to the door, inwardly cursing when his knee caught a projecting handle on a chest of drawers, shaking the glass ornaments on top and producing a tinkling sound.

'Jack, you in there?'

Fulton jumped. The last thing he expected was to hear his name called, but the familiar voice drew him out of his hiding-place. Phil Gilham's flashlight blazed in his eyes and he jerked the other's hand away irritably. 'What the hell are *you* doing here?' he snarled.

'Following you,' Gilham retorted, his tone cold and hostile.

Fulton snorted. 'I thought you'd be dealing with the intruder at Derryman Hospice.'

'I would be if I hadn't seen you borrowing an area car from the nick as I was about to drive out of the car park.'

Fulton pushed past him and flashed his torch around a second bedroom. 'So how come you weren't already tucked up with the missus tonight?' he said without any real interest. 'Lover's tiff?'

Gilham took a deep breath, stepping quickly to one side as the big man came back out of the room. 'Worse than that. Helen and I had a massive row. She'd stumbled on one of Abbey's old letters in my study and when I got back from seeing Abbey at the hospital, she went totally ballistic.'

'Serves you right.'

'Yeah, well, I spent the rest of the evening at my local and when they closed, I decided to head for the nick and kip in the office rather than return home for round two.'

Fulton nodded. 'Brave of you,' he said, rattling the handle of another door. 'Damned thing's locked,' he muttered.

Gilham watched him bunch his shoulder and, realizing what was in his mind, quickly grabbed his arm. 'Jack, I can't be privy to something like this.'

The big man shook himself free. 'Then piss off!' he retorted and, slamming his shoulder into the thin panelling, whooped his satisfaction as the lock burst open and the door flew back against the wall with a splintering crash.

Gilham groaned. 'For heaven's sake, Jack, what do you think you're doing? You've already got half the force out looking for you as it is?'

Fulton gave a short laugh. 'Yeah, I seem to have become quite the celebrity, don't I?' he said, brushing against the shattered door as he flashed his torch around the room.

Gilham followed him with obvious reluctance, throwing nervous glances over his shoulder towards the blacked-out staircase. 'Jack, you're right out of order. I mean, whose house is this anyway – and what the devil are you looking for?'

Fulton's sharp intake of breath was like the 'phut' of a bullet discharged from a silenced pistol. 'Why don't you see for yourself?' he said grimly as he threw caution aside and switched on the main light.

Blinking in the harsh, unshaded glare, Gilham found himself in a cramped study, maybe seven feet square, furnished with a corner desk and a couple of drawer units. A laptop computer occupied the centre of the desk, connected to an adjacent printer, and both were switched on, with the computer displaying the photograph of a ruined mansion as a screen-saver.

Gilham stared at the photograph for several seconds, then emitted a low whistle. 'Gordon Bennett, that looks like Drew House.'

Fulton followed his gaze. 'It *is* Drew House,' he said. 'And the rest of what we have here speaks for itself.'

It was not difficult to see what he meant by that either. The left-hand wall was occupied by bookshelves and what looked suspiciously like a hospital drugs cabinet, with rows of small bottles visible through the glass door. Part of the right-hand wall directly above the desk was covered by what appeared to be a map of the Maddington police area, peppered with coloured markers. Beside it, a large cork board carried photographs of several buildings, each one shot from a number of different angles, with the most distinctive being that of St Peter's church where the Reverend Cotter had been preaching the night he died. Even more interesting was the whiteboard on the outer wall beside the window and the passport-size photographs that had been arranged in a vertical line down one side, with blocks of neat handwritten notes alongside each picture.

'Well I'll be damned,' Gilham gasped. 'This place is set up like a mini version of one of our own incident rooms.'

Fulton had pounced on a thick buff-coloured folder lying beside the computer. He didn't look up as he leafed through the pages. 'That's *exactly* what it is,' he said. 'An incident room. Only, the intelligence that's been gathered here was designed to *facilitate* murder rather than investigate it.'

Gilham squeezed past him for a closer look at the whiteboard, curiosity overruling his initial objections to the illegal search operation. Peering at the top photograph, he whistled again. 'That's a picture of Judge Lyall,' he exclaimed. 'And there's the Reverend Cotter's too.' He broke off, half-turning towards Fulton. 'But there's another old boy here and I certainly don't recognize him.'

'If it's photo number three, it's probably Carlo Vansetti.'

'Vansetti? What, the gangster you introduced me to at Derringer's flat?'

Fulton gave an impatient shake of his head. 'His father,' he corrected, continuing to flick through the folder.

'So how—'

Fulton closed the folder and held it up in front of him. 'Never mind that now,' he cut in. 'I've found the missing crime file on Drew House, which is what really matters. The bastard had it all the time and I can see why he didn't want anyone else to see it.'

But Gilham did not even look at the folder. His gaze had returned to the whiteboard and was now riveted on the last photograph. 'Jack,' he said and his voice was suddenly cracked and shaky. 'You'll never believe whose picture is up here with the others?'

Fulton dropped the folder back on to the desk, his eyes stony. 'Assistant Chief Constable Norman Skellet, no doubt,' he said, more as a statement than a question.

Gilham gaped. 'How on earth did you know that?' he exclaimed. 'You haven't even looked at the whiteboard.'

'It's in the crime file. Seems he was DCI when Drew House was torched and he and Halloran were the first officers on the scene.'

'But if he was an IO on the Drew House job and his picture is up here with the rest, that means—'

'He must be the Slicer's next victim,' the big man finished.

Gilham lunged for the telephone on the corner of the desk. 'Hell's bells!' he choked, 'then we need to get some units over to Skellet's place pdq.'

But Fulton was already through the study door, heading for the stairs. Gilham dropped the telephone receiver with a loud curse to stumble after him, tugging at the mobile caught up in the lining of his coat pocket with one hand as he directed his own flashlight into the yawning shaft of the staircase with the other.

'Jack, don't be a damned fool,' he shouted. 'You can't do this thing on your own.'

Conscious of a sudden familiar and increasing clatter above the house and a blaze of white light sweeping across the glazed top panel of the front door as he reached the hall, Fulton struggled furiously with the door catch. 'Thanks for the advice, Phil,' he snarled. 'But this is strictly personal.'

The next moment he was hammering down the steps into the path of the helicopter's spotlight.

'But you haven't even said who we're we looking for?' Gilham shouted after him. '*Or* whose place this is?'

Fulton threw a savage glance at the clattering monster hovering overhead and jerked the door of the area car wide. 'You mean you really don't know?' he yelled back. 'Think about it, Phil – there's only one person it could be!'

Then he had spun the car round in a tyre-screeching turn and, after mounting the pavement, careered out of Rafferty Close through a sea of pulsing blue light as a convoy of police cars swinging into the cul-de-sac was forced to swerve out of his way. By the time the mêlée of vehicles had sorted itself out, he was several miles away, hurtling through the leafy outskirts of town, and praying with every ounce of his being that the hunch he had chosen to follow would prove to be right.

CHAPTER 28

THE BIG PSEUDO-Georgian house sat squarely in around half an acre of neat lawns and mixed laurel and rhododendron groves that screamed landscaping from every glossy moonlit leaf. The place was ablaze with light when Phil Gilham swung in through the open gateway at the head of the police convoy, and he spotted the Dobermann pinscher dog lying motionless beside the ornate stone fountain as he jumped out of his car. He approached the animal with caution, well aware of the breed's nasty reputation, but a cursory examination was enough to confirm that the animal was dead. There was froth around its gaping jaws that suggested some kind of virulent poison, and a bloody wound was visible in its side.

'Someone wasn't much of a dog-lover then?' the uniformed inspector commented at his elbow as he straightened up.

'Well, the brute didn't top itself, that's for sure,' Gilham retorted, his tone terse and strained as he added: 'You'd better have your crews check the grounds.' He threw an irritable glance at the police helicopter now hovering noisily overhead. 'And get that dratted chopper doing something useful, will you?'

The front door of the house stood wide open and there were ominous dark spots on the step, with a wet smear on the inside edge of the doorframe itself that looked suspiciously like part of a bloodstained handprint. Gilham was conscious of his heartbeat quickening as he stepped into the hallway and his narrowed gaze followed a trail of dark spots either leading to or from the foot of the staircase.

'Hello?' he called automatically, wondering why he was bothering with such a pointless formality in the first place. 'Anyone about?'

Outside, car doors slammed and loud voices joined with the clatter of the helicopter to drown any response he might have received, but he didn't try again, sensing that there was no one there to answer him anyway.

He saw more blood spots on the stairs and further smears on the banister rail as he headed for the next floor. The trail finally led him across the landing to a luxuriously appointed bedroom.

'Broken window round the side of the house,' the inspector said, joining him again. He bent down to study a wicked-looking bayonet lying on the carpet, resisting the temptation to touch it. 'Something nasty happened in here all right.'

Gilham nodded. A table-lamp had been knocked over on its pedestal beside the double bed and telltale red spots dotted the badly rumpled coverlet and one pillow. 'Someone certainly sprang a leak,' he agreed, 'but whoever owned the bayonet, it doesn't look as though that was the culprit.'

The inspector shook his head. 'Blade seems to be completely clean,' he confirmed. 'Could be the dog had the intruder before he managed to get into the house.'

'Gilham frowned. 'Let's hope that was it, but then how was he able to poison the brute afterwards?' He sniffed loudly. 'And what's that awful stink?'

His junior colleague also sniffed the air. 'Smells like antiseptic, sir.'

'Chloroform,' Gilham exclaimed, wheeling on him, his eyes gleaming. 'Quick, where's Jack Fulton?'

The uniformed man seemed taken aback. 'Mr Fulton, sir? I haven't seen him.'

'But he must have been on his way here. He knew Mr Skellet was to be the killer's next target.'

The inspector thought a second. 'Well, I know he left Rafferty Close pretty rapid – nearly caused a multiple as we drove in – but that's all, and the chopper's since radioed in to say he shot off in the opposite direction to us.'

Gilham's expression was incredulous. 'He did *what*? Then why the devil didn't someone go after him? He's still a damned fugitive, isn't he?'

The inspector shrugged a little uncertainly. 'I suppose so, sir, but when you called in from Rafferty Close to say Mr Skellet was at risk, control instructed all units to head here as a priority – including Hotel X-ray 19 – so any pursuit would have been abandoned.'

Gilham seemed to sag under an invisible weight. 'Gordon Bennett,' he breathed. 'So it's all down to Jack now, is it – wherever he's off to? I just hope he knows what he's doing.'

Fulton left the area car in a lay-by and headed up the long driveway of Drew House on foot, keeping close to the adjacent shrubbery and directing anxious glances at the moon which, though clearly visible, was beginning to lose some of its brilliance with the approach of first light. He fully anticipated the police helicopter's reappearance overhead at any second and was surprised that it wasn't actually there already. But the flying bug did not materialize and after a few minutes it dawned on him that the chopper had either lost track of him, which was pretty unlikely, or had actually abandoned its initial pursuit – maybe to provide aerial back-up for the troops en route to Norman Skellet's house instead. Whatever the reason, however, the absence of Hotel X-ray 19 could not have been more welcome as far as he was concerned. The last thing he needed was his quarry to be alerted by the clatter of rotor blades before he could find him.

He was convinced that Drew House – or more specifically, the church at Drew House – *was* where the Slicer would be heading to carry out his final bloody execution. The fact that those sinister ruins had now become an active police crime scene would be no deterrent to him either. The murderous psychopath had already shown himself to be an arrogant risk-taker and, as the church crypt and what had taken place there all those years ago was central to the pursuit of his bloody vendetta, it was logical to assume that he would seek to end his killing spree in the place where it had all started.

But logical or not, the big man knew his hypothesis relied heavily on what really amounted to nothing more than a hunch. As he slipped down the side of the sprawling carcass that had once been Drew House, he was unable to shake off a growing sense of unease, with the little doubting voice in his brain starting to dissect that hypothesis and ask some challenging questions that he preferred not to think about. What if his hunch was actually false and his own arrogance had led him to entirely the wrong conclusion? What if the killer was nowhere near Drew House, but miles away on the other side of the police area? What if, even as he wasted his time searching an empty ruin, Norman Skellet was being forced to stare into a mirror somewhere else and watch his throat being cut?

'What if, what if, what if?' he snarled, trying hard to ignore the negative whispers in his brain and concentrate instead on the task in hand – and it was then that he caught the glitter of moonlight on glass and knew, with a sense of relief, that his gut instinct had not played him false after all.

The old black Transit van had been reversed into a break among the trees a few yards ahead of him. It was so far in that he might have passed it by altogether had the headlamp glass not given the vehicle away. Taking a closer look, he found the back doors had been left half-open and a familiar strong, sickly smell hit him as soon as he stuck his head inside. The van contained little of interest, except a pile of blankets in one corner, but the chloroform smell was enough of a giveaway on its own and there were dark smears, like blood, on the outside of one door. He returned to the front of the vehicle and placed his hand against the radiator grille. He found it was still warm, suggesting the vehicle had only recently arrived. He felt a new sense of optimism. Maybe there was still time. He paused only long enough to immobilize the Transit by removing the rotor arm from the distributor, which he slipped it into his pocket and returned to the track, following a thin trickle of moonlight towards the back of the house.

Then the ruined church was there, directly in front of him, cold and hostile. He studied the place for a few moments, looking for any sign of movement, listening for the slightest sound, but there was nothing; just a heavy threatening stillness as if the building itself were holding its breath in some sort of gleeful anticipation. He made straight for the front porch, his feet kicking up clods of earth from the derelict kitchen garden as he cut a diagonal path through the overgrown plot and his eyes narrowed when he reached the double doors. The blue-and-white 'Police Crime Scene. Do Not Cross' tape, which had been strung across the entrance, had been ripped from the corner posts to which it had been fixed. Moving into the shadows of the porch, his torch picked out dark spots on the flagstones, which glistened like droplets of melted wax in the light. He remembered the smears on the Ford Transit's door and grimaced. Someone had been injured, that was for sure, but the question was who?

Gently easing one of the double doors open, he was immediately greeted by the flutter of wings in the gloom beyond, but otherwise there was not a sound. He switched on his torch, masking the beam with one cupped hand, and negotiated his way through the dismembered pews towards the north-east corner, where the stairs to the crypt were. He heard the muffled cry before he had gone more than a few feet and stopped dead, dispensing with caution by removing his cupped hand from his torch and directing the full beam into the blackness in front of him.

Something erupted from a niche in the stonework to his left and skimmed over his head, stirring his thinning hair – another bat, just like before – but he saw nothing else and was about to direct his torch elsewhere when he heard another cry, apparently coming from the far end of the church. He moved forward again, picking his way round fallen debris and trying to avoid walking into anything likely to cause injury, conscious all the time of an uncomfortable prickling sensation at the base of his neck as if he were being watched from somewhere in the gloom close by. Twice he actually turned to direct his torch back down the nave, convinced he had detected stealthy movement among the pews, but he saw nothing and in the end he put it all down to the mischievous action of a newly arisen wind, which seemed determined to restore the ruins to life and awaken the ghosts that had slept there for centuries.

Reaching the north-east corner, he was surprised to find that the hole in the bricked-up archway leading to the crypt had been sealed with a steel plate – no doubt by the SOCO team in an effort to preserve the scene – and closer inspection revealed that the plate was still intact, secured to the wall with businesslike bolts. The discovery certainly threw him, for it meant that no one could possibly have visited the crypt since the thing had been fitted. So where the hell had his quarry disappeared to?

His answer was not long in coming. The high-pitched scream seemed to issue from directly above his head, cutting through the suffocating gloom with the surgical precision of a laser and sending the bats into a panic-stricken frenzy as his torch flashed wildly among them in the ruins of the vaulted roof. The sound lasted for no more than a couple of seconds before it was abruptly cut off, but that was long enough to tell him exactly what he wanted to know. The tower! The bastard was up in the tower.

There had once been a padlock on the half-open tower door, but it now lay on the floor with the buckled remains of the hasp. The notice on the wall beside it was faded, but still legible:

DANGER. KEEP OUT. TOWER STRUCTURE AND BELL MOUNTINGS UNSAFE

Fulton bared his teeth in a fierce grimace as he jerked the door wide. Obviously health-and-safety issues did not feature prominently in the killer's mind at the present time – and neither did they in *his*.

The stone staircase that started up the shoulder-width gullet inside the doorway curled away sharply to his left, disappearing behind the curve of the wall, and his torch picked out what looked like more blood spots on the lower steps. The steps themselves were chipped at the edge and worn away into hollows in the centre from centuries of heavy use, and there was no handrail or guide-rope in evidence. He decided that the easiest method of tackling the steep climb was to revert to his childhood days and lean on each rising step with both hands, then grope for the next as he went up in a semi-crouched position. He switched off his torch and pushed it through the belt of his trousers, his straining eyes making as much use as they could of the weakened moonlight stealing in through the long narrow windows.

The feel of the cold stone beneath his palms and the taste of the damp mortar at the back of his throat evoked poignant memories of another time and place when, as a boy, he had climbed similar steps in his father's own church in exactly the same way. Then his mission had been to help with the ringing of the eight huge bells secured to their equally massive A-frame high up in the bell chamber, his legs shaking with trepidation at the thought of having to mount the wooden box waiting for him in the bell-ringing room above, where he would have to grip the thick rough rope under the glare of the fanatical bell captain, Harry Duncan.

Now, all these years later, his legs were shaking once again, but this time it was due to fatigue rather than trepidation as he was forced to draw on every ounce of energy he possessed to haul his ponderous bulk up what seemed like a never-ending spiral, while his heart threatened to explode under the strain and his lungs teetered on the edge of collapse. He should never have attempted such a climb in his poor physical condition, he knew that only too well. But what he lacked in natural stamina, he made up for in sheer dogged determination and that, coupled with the hatred that burned deep into his soul, drove him on regardless of the consequences.

As he climbed, the wind seemed to home in on him, buffeting the tower with increasing force, its moaning breath setting up unnerving vibrations that rippled through the ancient structure like mini seismic aftershocks, threatening to bring the whole lot down on top of him. Then, forty steps up – he could not help himself counting them one by one – the first glimmer of artificial light showed; a watery stain in the gloom that touched his fingers with a timid curiosity before strengthening appreciably as he rounded the curve of the wall. Now he was able to see the outline of a small wooden door on his right (the bell-ringing room?) past which the steps marched on, heading for the top of the tower and almost certainly the bell chamber itself.

At the same moment, as he stood there gasping on the residues of oxygen still left in his depleted lungs, he heard a muffled whimpering, like that of a child in distress. Gently pushing the door open, he peered round the edge into a small vaulted room, graced with long narrow windows. Strands of moonlight filtered through the shattered panes and, at floor level, strategically placed paraffin lamps which smothered the damp smell of the tower with a powerful sickly-sweet odour of their own, provided more substantial illumination.

The room was unfurnished, except for a couple of wooden chairs and several square boxes of varying heights, which he immediately recognized as similar to those he had been forced to stand on as a child when ringing the bells. To his surprise, the wooden spider, the hooks of which would normally have secured the bell ropes at ceiling level for reasons of safety, had been released and lowered on its pulley so that the noosed ends of the ropes now hung free, casting sinister shadows across the walls, like those of some early eighteenth-century scaffold rigged for a mass hanging.

Twenty feet up the wooden ceiling itself and part of the bell chamber floor above it had been stripped away from the massive supporting beams, with the lengths of timber and what he assumed to be soundproofing material piled up against the wall to his left, indicating that the renovation programme referred to in the write-up he had seen on the LIO's computer a few days before had been very much in full swing before being halted by the legal wrangling over ownership of the building.

More significantly, the moonlight filtering through the slatted windows of the bell-ringing chamber revealed that at least two of the bells were still *in situ* – and that surprised him a whole lot more, even though the note on the tower door had already suggested as much. As far as he knew, it was the usual practice for bells to be removed to a safe place when a church was decommissioned, as those enormous crafted domes could be worth a small fortune – particularly the huge tenors, often weighing in excess of a ton – so someone seemed to have slipped up badly here.

A much more serious slip-up was evident, however. Though one of the bells appeared to be right side up – its mouth gaping at him through the gap and its uvula-like clapper clearly visible – another (a big tenor bell, Fulton thought) had been left in the upside-down position, with its mouth pointing upwards. This amounted to a dangerous and irresponsible lapse on someone's part now that the bell ropes were so accessible, and he couldn't help wondering whether the stay restricting the bell's movement was still intact. He visualized with a shiver what was likely to happen if it had been removed or was broken and the rope was given a determined pull, for this would allow the bell to achieve a full revolution – with disastrous consequences for the person holding on to a ton of Whitechapel cast iron turning over on itself.

Then he saw the thin figure of Norman Skellet and realized in a flash that that was precisely the killer's intention. The elderly ACC was in his dressing-gown and pyjamas, his hands secured in some way (probably cuffed) behind his back as he sat on a high three-legged stool with the noose of the tenor bell rope round his neck. A hard pull on the rope was all that was required to wrench him off the stool and up towards the gaping bell chamber, as if on the end of the recoiling rubber band of a macabre bungee jump, initiating a hanging in reverse and snapping his neck like a piece of crisp celery.

Fulton felt sick as he pushed through the doorway, but he immediately froze when a second figure, crouched behind Skellet, straightened up, something glinting in his right hand.

'Jack,' the killer greeted him softly. 'How nice of you to join us.'

Fulton stared at him for a moment, his eyes drawn with a sort of horrible fascination to the cut-throat razor he was holding. Although the figure was still largely buried in shadow, Fulton did not need to see his face to know his identity. 'Hello, George,' he said at last. 'It's all over now, you know that, don't you?'

George Oates stepped directly into the light, perspiration glistening on his domed forehead, blood dripping from the bandage wrapped round the hand holding the razor. 'On the contrary, Jack,' he replied, 'the party has just started.'

CHAPTER 29

NORMAN SKELLET COULD honestly claim never to have been frightened by anything – mainly because he had never been put in any frightening positions to start with. A few short years at university, then selection for the police service under the graduate entry scheme and speedy ascent through the ranks to chief-officer status, had ensured that the only scary moments he had had to face were in his disputes with his dominant wife, Eunice, who had finally walked out on him after ten years of matrimonial disharmony.

But all good things tend to come to an end eventually and Assistant Chief Constable Norman Skellet BA was frightened now – terrified, in fact – and his whole body shook fitfully as his bladder continued to empty sporadically on the floor at his feet. Even the gag held in place across his thin lips with sticky tape failed to suppress the whimpering of this former high-powered flier whose atomic escalator had suddenly collapsed beneath him.

Fulton felt no real sympathy for his boss – which was hardly surprising after the way the head of force operations had treated him in the last few days – but, however despicable Skellet was, he did not deserve the fate that had been reserved for him and the big man determined to do his utmost to try to save that scrawny neck, whether he wanted to or not.

Oates was ahead of him, however, and even as he tensed his huge frame, the moon-faced LIO brought the hand holding the razor to a point just below Skellet's chin. 'Steady, Jack,' he warned. 'You don't want me to slip now, do you?'

Only a few feet separated them, but Fulton recognized the futility of trying to get to Skellet before the blade managed to slice through his windpipe. He relaxed his taut muscles after just a moment's hesitation.

'So what put you on to me in the end?' Oates continued, his tone surprisingly conversational despite the circumstances. 'I must admit, I'm curious.'

A cautionary voice in Fulton's head cut in on his chaotic thoughts.

Take it easy. Play him along while you figure out what to do.

'I suddenly remembered something you said,' he replied at length, clearing his throat.

Oates straightened. 'Something *I* said?'

Fulton slipped a hand into his pocket, pausing when the other stiffened suspiciously. 'Cigarette?' he queried as blandly as he could manage. On receiving a curt assenting nod, he produced his packet of filter-tips and lighter, hoping Oates hadn't noticed his trembling fingers.

'Straight after Lenny Baker was stiffed, you suggested we were dealing with a serial killer,' he continued, 'but how would you have known that unless you were the killer himself? We hadn't announced a link between Baker's death and that of Judge Lyall, and the full SP on the snout's murder had not been given out anyway – not even to the control room. As for Cotter, he was not even in the picture then.'

The big man leaned a shoulder against a supporting wooden pillar, lighting up and taking a long greedy pull on the cigarette (hell, he'd needed that). 'But what really put you in the frame as far as I was concerned was your comment about the killer's MO being "in the Sweeney Todd tradition". At that time, no one, except the killer, knew enough about the crimes to be able to make that sort of analogy.'

Oates grinned. 'Oops!'

'And going on to claim you'd never heard of Drew House – even finding difficulty in spelling the name properly – was just plain stupid. You must have known the service record in your P/F would show you had been the local ABO for Little Culham on the night of the fire, which meant that Drew House would have been on your patch?'

Oates raised both arms, with the razor blade still extended in his right hand, and made a show of a slow clap. 'So, it's clever old Jack after all then, is it?' he sneered. 'Took you long enough to pull everything together though, didn't it?'

Almost too casually, the psychopath reached up to grip the bell rope sally above his head with his free hand. 'And I've still won the final round,' he added.

Fulton swallowed hard, dropping the half-smoked cigarette on to the floor and quickly coming off the wooden pillar, his eyes locked on to the rope with an anxious intensity.

Steady! Say something – anything to distract him.

'Maybe,' he agreed, his voice strangely constricted, 'but it won't do you much good unless you get some medical help pretty soon. You're bleeding like a fractured drainpipe.'

Oates glanced at his injured hand, which still appeared to be dripping, and drew a muffled choking cry from Skellet when he gave a sharp tug on the rope. '*His* bloody Dobermann,' he explained with feeling. 'Thought I had totalled the thing, but that was a big mistake. Still, I enjoyed finishing it off.'

Fulton's eyes flicked desperately round the room, looking for something – anything – that would give him an edge. But there was nothing.

He eyed the noose round Skellet's neck and grimaced. 'Don't you think you've got enough blood on your hands already, without his as well?' he rasped.

Oates grinned again. 'No blood this time, Jack – quite clean really – and old Norman here deserves a proper send-off after what he did. That's why I decided on a different sort of exit from the others.'

'Perverting the course of justice in exchange for a hefty bribe is hardly a hanging offence.'

Oates was unable to conceal the admiration in his voice. 'Very good, Jack,' he said. 'You're certainly on the ball tonight.'

'It wasn't that difficult to work out, George,' he retorted. 'With Halloran as the SIO, there had to be corruption involved somewhere and I was able to put the rest of the bits together when I screwed your house.'

'Ah, you found the crime file then?'

'Yeah, and it put you right at the scene of the Drew House fire with Skellet and Halloran. Surprised you live in that dive in Rafferty Close after the bung you must have received, though.'

Oates affected an exaggerated sigh. 'Blame the old gee-gees for that, Jack. Blew most of my cut paying off bad debts incurred at Cheltenham and Ascot. Still, the deal for me was not just about money; it was also my ticket to CID, all courtesy of good old *Corkscrew*—'

'Which you later cocked up by falling asleep on the job,' Fulton sniped, then changed tack when he saw Oates's expression harden.

Careful, man. Don't wind him up!

'So what made you suddenly decide to turn on the others, then? Conscience catch up with you, did it?'

'No, Jack, testicular cancer did. Second hit. Matter of weeks left, I'm told.'

As with Skellet, Fulton was fresh out of sympathy. 'So that's why you mutilated Lyall and Cotter,' he said, more as a statement than a question.

There was an unholy light in Oates's eyes now, a backlit madness which made Fulton's flesh creep. 'The whole lot of them needed to be punished and publicly humiliated for what they'd done,' he rasped. 'Score and Halloran had already got their just deserts, so it was time the others were called to account. After all, why should they escape retribution? Be allowed to carry on with their nice comfortable lives as if nothing had happened, while I've just an early grave to look forward to?'

But Fulton only half-heard him, his eyes flicking involuntarily towards the roof as he detected the unmistakable thud of approaching rotor blades.

Damn it, the cavalry! The last thing he needed was for the force helicopter to zoom in with all the panache of Top Gun *and spook razor boy before he could get to him.*

'Go to church, as a child, did you, Jack?' Oates queried, giving another light pull on the bell rope and eliciting a further predictable choking cry from Skellet.

The question was sudden and unexpected and with his mind already focused on the approach of the helicopter, Fulton was thrown for a couple of seconds. 'What if I did?' he replied.

'Do any bell-ringing, did you?'

What the hell was he on about now? Surely he had to be aware of the helicopter closing in?

'Some.'

Oates sighed. 'Me too. Happy days, weren't they? Innocent, uncomplicated.' He peered up towards the ceiling, as if searching for something. 'Not like today, eh?'

The sound of the helicopter was unmistakable now and the thud of its rotor blades had been joined by the faint wail of sirens.

Damn the idiots! Whatever had happened to the so-called silent approach?

Oates cocked an ear in the direction of the sounds and his grin returned with a vengeance. It was obvious that in some perverse way he was enjoying the brinkmanship of the situation, especially the frustration it engendered in Fulton. 'You see, I got to thinking,' he said, 'that deep down, old Norman here might like to try his hand at a bit of campanology.' He chuckled. 'After all, going by the look of him, it must be ages since anyone rang *his* bell. That's why I thought I might ring it for him.'

The rope tensed slightly as Oates's left hand almost imperceptibly adjusted its grip on the sally. The movement was not lost on Fulton.

He's going for it, man, move!

The voice in his brain galvanized him into immediate action, but even as his toes dug into the soles of his scuffed suede shoes, Oates sprang on to one of the wooden boxes behind Skellet, his right hand still clutching the open razor and joining his left on the sally as he hauled on the bell rope with all his strength.

The thunderous roar of the helicopter, now hovering directly overhead, was accompanied by the erratic clanging of the heavy tenor bell. Fulton glimpsed an ethereal shape, writhing and twisting like some grotesque string-puppet as it sprang upward in front of him through the sudden blinding whiteout created by the chopper's powerful spotlight lancing through one of the windows.

Something struck him a sickening blow on the side of the head, bringing him down on to one knee, and a wet stickiness (blood?) began dribbling down his forehead into one eye. Though dazed and bewildered from the blow, some inbuilt sense of self-preservation kicked in and he managed to throw himself to one side, into the protection of the doorway, as a hail of debris rained down from the bell chamber and Norman Skellet's body, somehow parting company with the rope, was deposited on the floor just feet away.

At the same moment a choking scream came from somewhere in the midst of it all. Fulton wiped a sleeve across his clouded eye, and as his good eye tried desperately to adjust to the glare, his myopic gaze was instinctively drawn upwards. Like a vision from a nightmare, a huge domed shape had torn itself free of the bell chamber's massive A-frame and, with a tortured shrieking of twisted severed metal, was tumbling downwards through a tangle of displaced beams, which snapped like matchsticks in its path.

Oates did not stand a chance and his upraised arms were a futile defence against the ton of Whitechapel cast iron which bore down on him. The next instant the thing seemed to swallow him whole, smashing through the rotten floorboards of the bell-ringing room with the explosive impact of a depth charge, missing Skellet's prostrate body by a fraction, and carrying the psychopath before it – to spread his mangled remains over the unyielding stone flags at the foot of the tower.

For several seconds after the tenor bell's destructive plunge Fulton did not move. Instead, he sat there as if in a trance, staring through the glittering specks whirling like the grains of a mini sandstorm in the Cyclopean eye of the helicopter's spotlight. His gaze remained fixed, unseeing, on the gaping hole where the floor had once been, and on Norman Skellet lying beside it, miraculously still alive and jerking fitfully in a series of grotesque spasms as he desperately sucked in lungfuls of the stale polluted air he had been denied.

Then came the sound of heavy boots hammering on the stone steps of the tower and the intense red spot from the infra-red sights of a police Heckler-Koch sub-machinegun fastened on his right cheek, as a hoarse voice shouted: 'Armed police. Don't move!' That sharp menacing command prompted mental re-engagement with reality and the sudden realization that the nightmare was over. After the worst week of butchery he had encountered in his service – which had seen his own life torn apart and his career reduced to tatters – someone of a much higher authority than the English justice system had decided to ring the final bell!

AFTER THE FACT

THE PHONE CALL summoning Fulton to the chief constable's office came as he was wading through a pile of month-old newspaper cuttings covering the Slicer case, borrowed from the incident room. The chief's secretary was icily non-committal as to what the 'old man' wanted to see him about. 'Tomorrow morning at ten-thirty then, Mr Fulton,' she repeated and put the phone down.

Fulton stood there for several minutes, staring out of the lounge window and turning things over in his mind. He was relieved to see just two of his neighbours standing gossiping in the street by his gate, instead of the droves of press reporters and photographers who had besieged his home for so long.

He had already been officially told that he was off the hook for the murder of Janet and her boyfriend, Doyle, after Oates's DNA had been found on the abandoned pickaxe handle used to batter them both to death, and that had to be the best news he had received for many days. As a bonus, formal court proceedings for all his other misdemeanours had also been ruled out as 'not in the public interest' by an unusually conciliatory CPS, in consultation with the Independent Police Complaints Commission, and, incredibly, no disciplinary action was to be taken against him either. Someone at the top, it seemed, was doing their level best to ensure that the Slicer case was completely buried with the remains of George Oates, and he could certainly appreciate why.

The dramatic and gruesome end to the Slicer's bloody vendetta had resulted in a media feeding frenzy, fuelled by a leak suggesting a police corruption scandal involving Norman Skellet, and although the head of force operations had been packed off to the police convalescent home – ostensibly to recuperate from a broken leg and a dislocated vertebra – Fulton suspected that this was just a diversionary tactic, designed to remove him from public scrutiny for a while in the hope that the news media would tire of the whole issue and go after another more productive story.

The blaze of publicity that would have resulted from a crown court prosecution or internal disciplinary action against the 'old school' SIO the press had hailed as the hero of the hour was the last thing the chief constable needed. Without a doubt strings had been pulled and favours called in to ensure that it did not happen. But Fulton fully appreciated that this did not mean his transgressions had been forgiven, and whilst he was relieved to know that he would at least hold on to his job and rank until his retirement, he knew only too well that the force had other ways of showing its displeasure. He felt sure that the imperious summons to the 'big house' meant the end of his CID career and an enforced move to some dead-end position, like manager of the headquarters control room – with all the humiliation that that would entail.

The chief constable, Harry James, was not wearing a smile when Fulton was shown into the plush inner sanctum the following morning. He was surprised to see Andy Stoller, now resplendent in the uniform of an assistant chief constable, sitting in one corner, a cup of tea or coffee balanced on one knee, and the force personnel manager, Jennifer Strong, sitting in the other. His spirits sank even further. This was a hatchet job if ever he saw one.

'Good morning, Mr Fulton,' the chief snapped, motioning him to the chair in front of his desk. 'I thought it was about time you and I had a chat.'

Fulton sat down unsteadily, feeling much like the little boy confronted by the parliamentary inquisitors in W F Yeats's famous painting, *And When Did You Last See Your Father*?

The chief sat back in his own padded chair, his gaze fastened intently on Fulton's perspiring face. 'I have to tell you that I have today promoted Mr Stoller here Assistant Chief Constable, Operations,' he announced. 'Mr Skellet has been – ah – persuaded to take early retirement on health grounds which will take effect when he finishes his convalescence.'

'Should have been sent down,' Fulton grated, unable to help himself.

The chief frowned. 'I don't want to hear talk like that,' he admonished. 'Mr Skellet has been through a very traumatic time and only escaped death by the narrowest of margins. I gather Oates still had his razor clutched in his hand when he was found and Scenes of Crime believe that he must have inadvertently cut through the bell rope as he was pulling on it.'

'Lucky old Skellet,' Fulton muttered with heavy sarcasm.

Stoller's interruption was as sharp as it was unexpected. 'Shut it, Jack,' he snapped.

James threw his new ACC a swift, irritable glance, then stared at Fulton again with even greater intensity. 'Mr Skellet has been fully investigated,' he said softly, 'and he strenuously denies any wrongdoing. There are *no* witnesses to say otherwise and *no* documentary evidence to support the allegations made in the report you submitted. Therefore the matter is now closed.'

Fulton felt the anger rise in him, despite his precarious position. 'You mean "buried", don't you, sir?' he said and out of the corner of his eye he saw Stoller visibly wince.

James leaned forward, his eyes like gimlets. 'I mean "closed", Superintendent, and that is that – got it?'

Fulton had no option but to capitulate. 'Yes, sir,' he replied, but his truculent expression did not alter.

James continued to study him critically for a moment, as if trying to will him into submission. 'Good. Now, you should also know that I have promoted Detective Chief Inspector Gilham to Detective Superintendent, Northern Crime Area.'

Futon felt the room sway slightly. So that was it: his worst fears confirmed and the end of his CID career. 'Yes, sir.'

James gave a grim smile. 'And where do you think that leaves you?'

'In the shit, sir.'

The chief nodded slowly as if in agreement, then abruptly leaned forward again, staring at him almost balefully. 'You are a pain in the bloody backside, Jack,' he rasped. 'Always have been and always will be; awkward, stuck in the past, bloody minded and totally disrespectful. In fact, you are your own worst enemy!'

'Yes, sir.'

James sighed and straightened up. 'But unfortunately you are a damned good detective – and just the man I need to head the new force serious crime squad.'

Fulton stiffened in his chair and gaped, for once lost for words.

'A position,' the chief continued, 'that carries with it the rank of detective chief superintendent incidentally. So congratulations – and bugger off!'

Fulton was on cloud nine as he drove home, still hardly able to credit what he had just been told. Twice he nearly ran into the back of vehicles waiting at traffic lights and a speed camera flashed at him as he passed it at around forty-two miles an hour in a thirty limit.

He was still in a surreal light-headed mood when he eventually got home, but he came down to earth when he not only saw Abbey's Honda parked outside his bungalow, but the lady herself actually standing inside his open front door.

'Hi there, Chief Superintendent,' she called, waving a bottle in her hand as he lumbered up the path. 'I thought I'd pop by to help you celebrate.'

He stared at her in blank amazement. 'How the hell did you find that out?' he gasped.

She moved aside as he strode into the hallway. 'Aha,' she replied with an extravagant wink, 'news travels fast in these here parts, you know.'

He stared around him almost wildly. 'And how did you get in here?'

She followed him through to the lounge. 'Met a man coming out as I arrived.'

'A man?'

She nodded towards the coffee table and a bottle of champagne standing there on a silver tray. 'He left that for you.'

Fulton snatched up the small envelope leaning against the bottle and tore it open, his face hardening as he read the message on the card inside.

SAID YOU SHOULD GET THE LOCK ON THEM FRENCH WINDERS FIXED, JACK. CONGRATULATIONS, CHIEF SUPERINTENDENT AND HAVE THIS ONE ON ME!

MICKEY VANSETTI

'The cheeky bastard,' Fulton breathed, then turned when he heard the clink of glasses.

'I think the champers would be a lot better than my wine?' Abbey said with a grin. 'Do you want to open it or shall I?'

Fulton's face still registered bewilderment as he stared at her. 'I thought you'd be celebrating with Phil?' he said.

She picked up the bottle and began to remove the wire from the cork. 'Phil and I have broken up, Jack,' she replied. 'I told him it wouldn't work and he's now back with Helen.'

'What, just like that?'

'Just like that.' She carefully twisted the cork, held it, then removed it with a slight popping sound, but the